DEADLY SECRECY

Andrew Scott

Twa Corbies Publishing

Also by Andrew Scott

Novels

Tumulus

Estuary Blue

The Mushroom Club

The Big J

Non-fiction Books

Alexander Trocchi: The Making of the Monster

Bonnie Dundee: John Graham of Claverhouse

Britain's Secret War (with Iain Macleay)

Modern Dundee: Life in the City since WWII

The Invisible Insurrection of a million minds: A Trocchi Reader

Discovering Dundee: The Story of a City

The Wee Book of Dundee

Dundee's Literary Lives Vols 1&2

The Letters of John Graham of Claverhouse, Viscount Dundee

Poetry

Dancing Underwater

Further information can be obtained from

www.andrewmurrayscott.scot

First published in 2019 by **Twa Corbies Publishing**

Copyright ©Andrew Scott, 2019

Twa Corbies Publishing:
twacorbiespublishing@gmail.com

British Library Cataloguing-in-Publication Data
A catalogue record for this book is available on
Request from the British Library.

Acknowledgements

Some events in this book were suggested by
Britain's Secret War: Tartan Terrorism and the Anglo-American State,
Andrew Murray Scott and Iain Macleay,
Mainstream, 1990.

ISBN: 978 0 9933840 2 8

DEADLY SECRECY

Andrew Scott

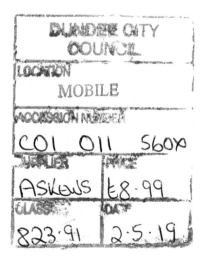

He knew every twist and tortuous turn of that remote narrow road. Even in the dark, even with the lights off. No other traffic at night - and only a faint risk of deer straying onto the road. He'd switched the lights off because he didn't need them. The moon silvered the bends far below and he could even pick out, on the hillsides, the flicker of quartz or moonbeam on running water. He was running for his life and knew it even though the sounds of pursuit were now less obvious. They were behind him but their lights had dropped away a mile or so after the Glenfinnan viaduct: that was nearly ten minutes ago. He was driving too fast, crammed in over the steering wheel, side window down, listening for engine noise other than his own. With one hand hauling the Volvo estate's wheel round at the bends, two fingers of the other propping his cigarette, his thoughts were jumping and tumbling. Sweat was thick under his chins and around his neck. His shirt collar strangling him and the steering wheel cutting into his gut. But all he could think about was getting away and getting some sleep. He was dead tired and the stink of soot was all over his clothes. It'd been nearly thirty hours since he'd slept because of the fire at his house – he'd been lucky not to suffocate – and after that, sleep had proved impossible. Then he'd started north and run into this trouble. He was dead tired.

But now he was on home turf – almost within sight of the glistening eastern-most edge of that vast deep inlet of the Atlantic known as Loch Ailort. He could almost smell above the bracken, salt water, the sea breeze. Arisaig village was five or six miles ahead, nearly all downhill, and then he'd be safe. He switched the lights on but kept the beams dipped, tried to relax. Nearly home. He was less than twenty minutes from his holiday house at Morroch Point.

His left hand fumbled on the passenger seat among the carton of packets of Gold Flake for the briefcase flap, found

1

it, pressed the brass stud and retrieved the revolver inside. His leather brogue stamping heavily on the clutch, he jerked the gear stick down to two, turned into the next sharp corner, engine complaining discordantly and brought the gun up close to his face to check that the safety was on. He had always thought of himself as a soldier. There had always been a war to fight. Although he was well-past the age of retirement, this last campaign, in his homeland, had been his greatest fight and had brought him his greatest triumphs – or almost. He had within him the glory of incipient greatness, all he had to do was survive this night and things would take their course and he would be a national hero, safe finally from all harm, bathed in the spotlight of public renown. As the headlights flickered weakly around the trees and bends of the South Morar peninsular his thoughts momentarily drifted to other battles. The Indian Ocean, chasing Japanese aircraft carriers, his days in Palestine, military intelligence - a fragment of a song was trickling around inside his tired brain. *What was it?* He hauled the steering wheel sharply to the left, the Volvo's engine protesting on the steep climb up towards the railway embankment. Gunned the accelerator at the top, trying to hum the tune even with a cigarette between his teeth, dislodging a stump of ash, some of which blew into his face. It was an old Gaelic hymn, keening sad, a nostalgic refrain insistent on three slow dree-ing notes, like bagpipes. He passed under the railway line and swerved out toward the trees as the road gathered pace and levelled out. Scotland… he felt his heart swell. For Scotland's sake… he must survive. It was vitally important…

The headlights flashed suddenly – or some other bright lights - as if they had reflected off something shiny, a tiny pinprick of light, just in front of the trees – surely not another vehicle? He flexed, peering ahead, anticipating a bump but the car was already leaving the road and flying… flying… out over the hillside, tumbling once, twice, bounding forward, spinning round, making hard crunching contact with rock and heather, a vision of the moon on a deep black loch and sudden forlorn recall of all that he loved, his memory fogged and slipping away. Empty fingers clutching at the cold night air, he went upside down, flopped, fell and crashed back into his seat as his breath went away in one final, unwilling, gasp of astonishment.

1

William James Morton was widely regarded as a competent investigative journalist by broadsheet and tabloid reporters in Scotland who knew his work.

'Willie Morton?' one would frown in The Vaults or a nearby Edinburgh howff, 'sharp, that one, good at following up leads – bastard!' Then the other would shake his head sagely and give the ultimate accolade. 'Aye, he's *nae bad*.' Then they would both agree further: 'Shame about his marriage. He needs to get a life.'

That also was true. For Morton's ex was Sally Hemple, shock-haired celebrity columnist for two Canary Wharf tabloids. Award-winner, TV game show panelist. Her incisive exposés of Hollywood gossip, her scoops on the big stars' lipo-suctions, their breast-augmentation denials and sneaky hair extensions, her world exclusives on the on-off-on-again remarriage of Tom and Nicole was the stuff millions were addicted to. Morton hated all that of course, even on a smaller scale, when Sally was a twenty-something writing frothy features for the *Daily Record*; surveys of erotic handbags and tip-offs about sexy new bras from Michelle Mone. *Then* Morton was a feature writer for the *Edinburgh Evening Post*, trying to get himself a name for tackling serious issues. Sally made twice the money he did. Now, she was slumming it in Kensal Rise on a hundred k a year, while some years he didn't earn enough to pay tax. As a freelance he'd had to tackle anything that came his way but found that investigations were what he was best at. Corruption in the Scottish Premier League transfer market, fraudulent use of housing subsidies, black market in videos, loan sharking in the schemes, a married MSP's affair with a senior civil servant (he thanked God for the arrival of the Scottish Parliament in

1999). He'd covered a lot of ground, earning respect and some enemies too. His divorce had forced him to get up early in the mornings, obtain commissions and seek out work. In the decade since he'd stopped playing rugby for his school FPs club he'd never settled to a fitness regime and consequently had gained a little weight. Luckily, being tall, it didn't show too much. He generally favoured tight jeans and covered his puffy middle with a zip-up leather jacket and shirts worn out over the waistband.

He hated shopping. Supermarkets, like the giant Lolo Store at the Gyle, were a drag, a necessary evil. Morton pushed his trolley slowly through aisles crowded with zombie-shoppers who seemed to enjoy it, to be addicted to it. He picked out a desultory tin here and there. He had no method because it took time to think of, to organise; and that was wasted time. Better just to blunder through it. He did it by habit, intuition. If manufacturers changed the colours or design of their packaging, he was lost and didn't buy it, whatever 'it' was. Baked beans, chilli beans, tinned tomatoes, pasta, rice, minced beef. He could live on various combinations of those for a week. Onions, courgettes, red, yellow and green peppers, garlic, coffee. That was about it. And bread, although he tried to cut out carbohydrates. Frozen chicken breasts, sweet corn. Enough! Out of here! That was the message throbbing through his brain. Most of the shoppers were women and/or elderly. He wondered if their men-folk were watching sport (one-word euphemism for *the fitba*). Slow-moving obstacles of indeterminate gender and age blocked his path to the checkouts. He resisted his desire to ram them mid-ships with his trolley. The queues were backing-up. The muzak – some kind of rap – piling on the stress – was battering his ears insistently with its moronic refrain.

But the checkout girl smiled at him directly and for a split-second, he was confused, wondering if it was a come-on and nervously patted his blond hair which he wore quite long over his ears. Of course it wasn't and the girl, who had a nose-stud and a lip-ring, was already swiping his purchases. He needed to get a life. A customer on the next till, he noticed, was buying six 4-packs of tins of baked beans. He felt inadequate. He had only two tins.

'Sorry,' he mumbled.

The checkout girl glanced up at him and smiled indulgently.

Morton tapped his forehead. 'Forgot milk. Back in a mo.' Ignoring the dark looks of those behind him in the queue, he sprinted to the fridges and snatched a 3-litre semi-skimmed container. The girl was waiting patiently. The queue behind was unforgiving.

'It's alright,' she said reassuringly. 'Take your time.' It seemed she liked to live dangerously.

Morton thought about her as he pushed the trolley with his bags to the car park. She was plain but he found himself lusting after her. Even tiny contacts like that could set him off. He wondered if he was starting a mid-life crisis? Some *other* mid-life crisis. Just lonely probably, he decided. The boot was under the bonnet, at the front, the car being an expensive second-hand, reconditioned Argentine-built white Volkswagen Beetle. An eccentric vehicle for an investigative reporter, he often felt, since it was the sort of car one would remember. Not exactly unobtrusive. One of Sally's whims, it had fallen to him after the split. He wouldn't part with it now. His Blackberry was ringing. Blast! He had to put his shopping down on the tarmac and fumble for the phone in his jacket. He could see that it was Hugh of the *Scottish Standard*.

'Hugh? Something must be up if you're not at the fitba.' He knew the editor was a fervent Hearts man. Football held

6

no interest for Morton but he was aware of its overwhelming importance to many. And knew for some it was even more crucial than that. He waited.

'Willie?' Hugh Leadbetter's voice gruffed – it was a voice that had always seemed, to Morton, to emanate from his bushy beard. 'Just checking that you're aware of the McBain thing that's just come out on the radio.'

'McBain?' Morton's mind was blank. He stared in at the till lines, shoppers, baskets, trolleys, the reflections of parked cars.

'Dead, so he is. Kicked the bucket. Found dead in his car on a hillside in Wester Ross.'

'Jeezo!'

'Police statement says they're not looking for anyone else in connection with it, of course. They would say that. Willie? Still there?'

Morton stared at his collapsing grocery bag below the car boot. 'This is... ehm... McBain, SNP candidate, a good few years back... lawyer too? What was his, first, um? Hamish... Arthur?'

'Angus.'

Morton smiled back at a nice-looking lady about his own age who smiled at him in passing. Was this his lucky day? 'Ah! *Angus* McBain. I met him a couple of times back in the day. A good while ago.'

'Thought that, Willie. Anyway, see if you can work up something and bung it in. We'll hunt up a piccy. Mind, it's to be with the subs before 10pm.'

'Okay. Thanks.'

Getting into the car gave him a sense of reassuring familiarity. When you got into a car you were going somewhere, had some purpose. Even if you were just going home to your computer and phone. The weekly shopping trip was almost the only time he could get to use the car. He loved the loose puttering of the engine, the basic dashboard, the comforting shape, its functionality. It gave him a connection to an earlier, more straightforward world. It was a car. No central locking, no CD player, no airbags, no power steering, but it had never failed to start first-time on a cold morning, was cheap to run, looked good. It was typical of Morton to get sentimental over a car that dated back to the Second World War. There was something defiant about it, anti-macho. It was like giving two fingers to the male obsessions with size, speed, technical innovation, newness and rpm. Morton felt sure it was female. He needed to get a life. Fact.

Sixty seven miles due west of Edinburgh, hillside mud loosened by heavy rain was starting to trickle between boulders on either side of the precarious track on the south flank of Ben Lomond, making footing even more difficult. You had to lean into the wet blasts with your Gore-Tex shell firmly zipped and velcroed into place around your fleece and over-trousers. It meant your view of the track ahead was severely limited.

Suddenly out of the louring mist four men are jumping down the track, four tough men competing and jeering each other as they race down the hill. You hear them intermittently through the sodden gusts of wind. They don't seem to be impeded at all by the treacherous terrain, nor, when they finally come close enough to see, do they seem to be in appropriate hill-gear. They're wearing army olive green camouflage shirts unbuttoned, two with red berets and two in black caps, all with heavy military rucksacks. With a couple of jokey comments in the passing they're away down the hill. There's snow lying above 1,000 feet and these guys look like they've been to the top, two and a half thousand feet higher up and yet it's only early afternoon. They must have bivouacked somewhere on the hill and spent the night. Tough – or mad?

The four were making quick work of the remaining distance between themselves and ex-Regimental Sergeant Major Norrie McIlwaine's BMW parked at the Rowardennnan Hotel on the east shore of the loch.

'Come on, ye auld lags,' McIlwaine jeered as they sprinted the last few hundred yards of bare hillside into the tree line. 'Last one down is on the bell and mine's a Balvenie 50!' Rain dripped off the tape of his red beret and down his craggy face in a continuous torrent. It was a well-worn in-joke, a nip of the 50 year old Balvenie reputedly being £750, except in Happy Hour when it could be as little as £749.50.

'I'll sort you out, boy!' Former Para Andrew Pasfield, eyes and nose just visible under the peak of his cap, pushed himself into a full sprint to catch up. 'And I'll be checking your… bloody pack…' he muttered under his breath, 'just in case… you've been dumping weight.'

'Cut the cackle, lads, let's just get down off this hill!' their leader shouted.

The path through the trees was treacherous. Exposed roots of trees, uneven stretches where mud was slick and slippery, narrow chasms between rocks faces or fallen trees. The light was fading with the winter afternoon. The men jogged in silence now, disciplined, each anticipating that first taste of cold beer in the hotel. Then at last the path began to widen out, the trees seemed less tightly packed and tiny lights could be seen which they knew was the car park at Rowardennan on the shore.

'Nearly there, guys,' McIlwaine grunted. Less than fifteen minutes, maybe just ten. Already reaching for his toggles to ease the straps of his pack. The others were jogging in a tight file along the tarmac past several parked cars, the loch on

9

their right behind a low stone dyke, a few distant lights on the far shore. They jogged in rhythm along the narrow, tree lined road towards the lights of the hotel, their boots clattering faster along on the tarmac of the last few hundred yards as if they were in competition.

'Told you I'd beat you!' McIlwaine smirked as they swung their heavy packs off their shoulders by a small stone dyke and began to unload. Each pack had five bricks in it.

'Ah, give it a rest, will ye?' Maitland said, tossing his bricks down the bank. He was the youngest and the only one of the four still serving in the regular army.

'Aye, let's get that bloody beer!'

'We made it. You're on the bell, chum!'

The heat of the Poacher's Bar walloped them as the men stepped over the smooth flagstone floor. The bar was hot and damp-smelling, nearly empty, just two couples nursing gin and tonics and a couple of hairy motor bikers. Nobody gave them more than a glance.

McIlwaine dumped his sodden kit on the heap next to the sturdy corner table from where the loch could be seen through raindrops beyond the electric candlelight on a stone windowsill.

'This'll do,' he said, wiping sweat from his forehead with paper napkins. 'I'm getting these damn buits aff right now.'

One of the party was collecting a tray of drinks. He laid it on the table and they sat down where they could, amid piles of sodden kit and muddy boots. 'Right, get fell in, chaps,' he instructed. He raised his pint of lager to the light. 'I'm bloody-well ready for this!'

'Queen and country!'

'Cheers!'

There was silence as each man drank, savouring that special sense of reward that comes after extreme physical and mental exertion. Of the four, three were old friends, having served as mercenaries in civil wars on the African continent and were now variously employed. The skin of their arms were shiny with sweat, each man's teeshirt dark green and steaming in the heat.

The fourth, Jason Maitland, currently serving with the Highlanders was on a week's home leave from his regiment. 'Magic!' he exclaimed, wiping his mouth on his sleeve. 'Bloody great pint!'

'Aye, tastes better when you've sweated a bit,' Pasfield observed, running a hand through his drenched hair. 'For another? My round.' His chair scraped on the stone floor.

'Aye, Daniel, man, we can still kick ass,' McIlwaine smiled ruefully. 'Just like back in Nygonga.'

'Well,' Maitland conceded, 'you old boys weren't quite as slow as I might have expected, given that you're not in regular training.'

'Awa!' McIlwaine jeered. 'Wha wis first aff the hill, eh? No you, ye wee... peelie wallie...'

'Anyway,' Daniel McGinley said, smoothing his thick moustache, 'I am at the gym regular. It's a condition of service with my lot.'

'And what lot is that, precisely?' McIlwaine grinned. 'Ye've no exactly said.'

'Well, it's not the SAS,' Daniel admitted cagily. 'Not old Premier Security either...'

'Here,' Pasfield said bringing a new tray of drinks, 'a toast. Premier Security... and the Nygonga Freedom Fighters of 96.'

'The good old days!'

'Cheers!'

'Aye, Jason, man,' McIlwaine grinned, 'you should have seen us back then – we didnae half kick ass - as the Yanks say.'

'You'd have been in school like, Jason, eh? When we was fighting the real shooting wars?'

Maitland strongly objected to this. 'And what was bloody Basra, then, eh? A stroll in the park?'

'Aye, laddie, almost,' said Daniel McGinley. 'Compared to what we went through.' He grinned and broke into a kindly chuckle. 'See boy... ach, you've to remember us three were in the regs before we ever joined up with Premier, so we ken the difference. You lot had it bloody easy.'

2

After putting the shopping away, Morton Googled. There was very little about Angus McBain. He was pre-digital. His life and political career existed in dozens of yellowing newspaper cuttings no-one had yet thought about scanning into a digital archive. But he didn't have time to waste in a public library so he phoned Bill Devine, a fellow freelance, who mostly worked for *The Scotsman* and the *Daily Mail*. There was no answer at his home number but he answered his mobile. Just about to tee-off at the fourth, he said.

'Yeah. Heard about it, Willie. PA put out a news par. I'll have a looksee: later though, I'm off till Tuesday. It can wait, I think. You doing a wee piece? If you find anything, I'd be interested, but I'm told the nearest relative is happy McBain shot himself, so where's your beef?'

Happy? Morton winced. 'Shot? McBain was *shot*…. Hugh told me the police statement only says he was "found in his car on a hillside." No mention of a gun.'

'Well. It's what I was told. Pretty much sounds like he… well - suicide.'

'Where did you hear about the gun?'

There was a pause long enough to make Willie frown. He could tell his friend had become a little reluctant. 'Well, Willie, look, I mean… you get the same briefings I do, I presume…'

'Briefings?'

'You know? Tame polis… someone you can phone. Well, I can't… Look, obviously, Willie, you can do a piece; dig up background details, a bit of context… but you have to admit he wasn't exactly, well, prominent in the ranks… not anymore at least.'

'Well that's true. That is true. Bill – I didn't know you had a tame polis. Don't suppose you'd be willing to go halfers?'

Devine chuckled. 'What do *you* think? Anyway, look, I'm one up here, so. '

Morton phoned Alison McBride at Lothian & Borders Police media office who gave him the number for her media colleague Dave Talbot at the Northern Constabulary in Inverness. Talbot was out of office so Morton left a message. Morton had never spoken to him before and idly thought about Inverness. He vaguely knew that the Police station was near the castle by the river Ness. Nice place, Inverness, a city now. Talbot phoned him back a few minutes later.

'Hello?'

Morton told him who he was and what he wanted.

'Oh, yes, we have a statement. It's pretty brief. I'll fax it to you.'

'Fine. And does it include details of the cause of death…'

'Well, he was found in his car on a hillside at Loch Dubh and we know the time of death and so on.'

'I mean, details about the gun?'

'*Gun*? Where did you hear that?'

Morton knew to wait. The pause became embarrassing. He still waited.

Talbot was first to crack: 'Look, I don't know you, Morton or where you heard that. There's a statement and I'll fax it to you. That's all there is, for now.'

And he rang off. A few minutes later, Morton's fax delivered a page onto the beige carpet. Two paragraphs. No cause of death. Found in his car, taken to hospital at Raigmore Hospital, Inverness, and pronounced dead there. It had McBain's home address in Glasgow and his age. He was 81. That was a shock. *81*?

Morton remembered McBain had been one of the objectors to a proposed nuclear waste dump in the Knoydart

14

peninsula and knew he had a cheaply printed transcript of the Public Inquiry. His workroom was the smaller of the two bedrooms in his flat and most of his papers were still inside the cardboard boxes in which they had been brought to the flat four years ago when his marriage had finally ended. It took him half an hour to retrieve *Don't Poison Our Peninsula*. It wasn't a transcript, merely a summary of the objectors' case. McBain was on every page. The flimsy booklet was riddled with his witty interjections. At one point, Morton read, he had threatened a nuclear industry scientist with an interim interdict and earned a headline in the national press. Then he threatened the UK Environment Minister with a Parliamentary Question and managed to get the information he required. Morton vaguely remembered the media coverage of the Inquiry. It had been big news, but it was fifteen years ago, 1992, a lifetime in political terms. McBain had been quite effective, given that he hadn't been an elected politician; not an MP and there weren't any MSPs then in those pre-Scottish Parliament days. Yet he had skilfully exploited contradictions and divisions between one government department and the next. And even now, with devolution in place, Energy policy was firmly under the control of London.

But there was humour too. Morton read that he had enlivened proceedings when the Inquiry had had to be moved out of the local village hall to allow an operatic group to rehearse their Christmas show. The editor of the booklet (perhaps that was even McBain himself?) had printed the stream of operatic jokes that McBain had turned against the nuclear industry's experts. He turned to the final few pages for a conclusion. Oh. And they had *won*! Of course they had. And the eventual judgment of the Inquiry against the waste site had been a big blow to the nuclear industry. The UK Energy Minister was unable even now to develop a long-term nuclear waste policy. All they could do now was keep the nuclear waste piling up in deep holes in the ground at the point of manufacture. How they must have hated McBain! And McBain was dead. Morton kept coming back to that fact. It was all in the past, true. Fifteen years ago, but a fact nevertheless. Could that be the basis of the story, he asked himself? No. Way too premature. The line he'd use would be... he placed his fingers over the keyboard and began to type: 'McBain: Police Statement Vague on Death Cause – Rumours of Gun Shot.' In the first para, he typed: "it is claimed, by a source who refuses to be identified, that Angus McBain was killed by a bullet." Then he composed a concise backgrounder on his career in the SNP, the fact that he fell out of favour, his irritant ability to annoy the UK Government, plus two paragraphs reminding readers of his success at the Knoydart Public Inquiry. His fingers flayed the keyboard and he had 450 words. He checked it quickly. Okay. Emailed it to the subs and copied to Hugh. That'd do for now. He suspected there was a lot more to come.

He phoned Sean Kermally, Chief Comms for the SNP at Holyrood. Like all senior Comms people in the party he was absurdly young and keen and available on his mobile 24/7. A whole generation of Kermallys seemed to have appeared alongside the rise of the SNP to power as a minority administration at Holyrood.

'Sean?'

'Hello Willie. What's eating you? No, let me guess,' he chuckled dryly, 'you, um, you read that presser I emailed you earlier with the First Minister's comment on the forthcoming whisky exports deal with India? No? Then, maybe the email I sent out about regional employment stats? Up 0.2% right across the board. No? Not that either?'

'Sean...'

'Okay,' he chuckled. 'I ken it's McBain, isn't it? Well, I haven't done anything on him yet. The news has only just come out. And he wasn't… well, really on our radar anymore.'

'Not a member of Donald's fan club?'

'Ha! You said that, Willie. I couldn't comment.'

'Look, Sean. I think they knew each other. What's the chances of a chat with Donald on it?'

'Phhooo! Willie, well… goodness… really? *McBain*? Is this really… well, listen, I'll put it to him, but you know how busy he is. It's highly unlikely. But if he doesn't or can't – I'll email you out a line from someone. We will need to comment officially. You do know he was rather elderly… a veteran no less.'

Willie made himself a coffee and stood looking out of his second floor bay window at the street lights coming on. He could see his own white face and wavy hair reflected and the white roof of his car further along towards the junction of Merchiston Grove and Shandon Street and see lights in the even-number sandstone tenements of Shandon Place opposite. He looked to see if there was anything interesting going on. Na. Nothing. No surprises. It was mainly retired couples in that block as far as he knew. He closed his blinds. It was Dalry really, almost Merchiston but certainly not Gorgie, a quiet, decent area, within walking distance of Tynecastle, although he had never been, and Murrayfield – he'd been there once and Scotland lost - to England. He'd been brought up in the Merchiston area and attended George Watson's where rugby was *de rigueur* for all male pupils. Girls played rugby now too. He wondered what he thought about it. Good, probably. Equality and all that. He missed the camaraderie of the rugby, being in the team, the boozing and banter.

His Blackberry went off. Sean Kermally. 'Hullo, Willie,' he said, cheerily. 'To my surprise, the First Minister will do an interview with you.'

'Really? That's great.'

'Yes, well. He said he's keen to know what happened and if he can help shed light... Anyway he has a window tomorrow.'

'Sunday? Well, okay...'

There was nothing on TV so he waited for the Scottish news at Ten O'clock but there was no mention of McBain, so he went to bed.

He was up early. A dull but dry day he noticed as he opened his curtains and blinds. Standing at the breakfast bar with a slice of wholemeal toast and cup of black Earl Grey tea he scanned the *Scottish Standard on Sunday* the paperboy had delivered through the letterbox. His piece was in, quite prominently, on Page 5. Looked okay. They'd headed it: 'Was Veteran Nat Shot? Mystery Over SNP Man's Death.' He'd have to see what the other papers had done but he was probably ahead of the game in having put some context, backstory, on it. He thought about McBain as he showered. What *was* the story? Why would an 81 year old man kill himself? And how did he come to have a gun anyway? If the gun was his, and if not, whose was it? He buttoned up a clean white cotton shirt, pulled on black jeans and a pair of trusty ox-blood brogues. He clipped on his imitation Rolex Oyster, which he'd bought ten years before in Barcelona. Unlike most fakes it actually worked and kept good time until the battery started to run down. He zipped his brown leather anorak, flipping the collar up and locked his front door behind him. Descending the dusty stone stairs in the dim close, he pulled the white outer door to lock behind him. Except for the weekly shopping trip to the Gyle, he rarely used the car. Parking was generally difficult, if not impossible. and anyway walking was helping him to stay relatively slim. The shoes rapped confidently on the pavement as he turned onto Slateford Road, heading into Princes Street. Never skimp on footwear, get the best quality leather shoes you can afford, was one thing he remembered his father telling him. It was a good twenty minute walk, ideal Sunday morning exercise.

Located in Charlotte Square in the New Town, Bute House, the official residence of Scotland's First Minister sits in a magnificent Adam Terrace dating from 1791. He had been there several times before. He went up the dozen or so steps and found that he was expected. The 50-something receptionist, a blonde of film-star gorgeousness with a husky voice in the lower register, ushered him to a deep burgundy sofa so low-slung that Morton was almost sitting on the floor. He chose to sit facing away from the reception desk, too distracting otherwise, and fiddled with his mobile phone. On the dainty tables nearby were a dozen thumbed issues of the *Scots Magazine* and a few copies of the nationalist broadsheet, *Scots Independent.*

When he felt the receptionist's soft breath on his neck, he climbed red-carpeted stairs, winding around a gigantic cheese plant, to an airy first floor ante-chamber office where, sitting complacently behind a modern, glass-topped desk, Donald Stevenson, Scotland's First Minister awaited him. He was on his own, Morton noticed, no spindoctors or flacks. That was typical, Morton felt. No-one else present to dilute the Stevenson charm offensive. This was a man who walked to the Parliament and even sometimes took a bus. Scotland had a political elite small enough that most knew each other by first names.

'Hello again, Willie,' Stevenson smiled cautiously, half-standing to shake Morton's hand. 'You wouldn't normally get me here on a Sunday, but I've to catch up after taking the day off yesterday.'

'Day off?' Morton smiled facetiously. 'Go anywhere nice?'

For a moment, Stevenson was about to answer, and then realised Morton wasn't being serious. He compressed his lips disapprovingly. 'I can anticipate that you're here to ask me if Angus McBain was assassinated by agents of the British State?' The former accountant's eyes were momentarily humorous behind thick lenses amid the puffy white unhealthy-looking adipose of his face. The suit he was wearing looked over-used, off-the-peg of course. He was the sort who didn't bother overly about his personal appearance or about trying to create an impression. That was probably why, Morton considered, he had won the leadership, back in 2005, despite making no obvious effort to build up a faction. The other leadership candidates, Salmond, Sturgeon and Roseanna Cunningham were charismatic and had considerable personal followings but to everyone's surprise, Stevenson had emerged from National Conference as leader, as if the delegates had panicked on the brink of power and backed the safe pair of hands choice. His obvious lack of personal ambition, his canny trustworthiness seemed to have mesmerized or bored them into submission.

Morton frowned. 'Is that your personal opinion?'

Stevenson's thin-lipped mouth framed an apologetic 'Actually, no.' He smirked. 'Not at all. Would you like a cup of coffee?'

There was an intermission while coffee was poured.

'So you believe it *was* suicide?'

Stevenson carefully placed his cup and saucer in the exact centre of his clean blotter. 'As Sean would have mentioned, this is an off-the-record interview though I'm not averse to being quoted in your story, if necessary. Though you will obviously have to clear anything you want to use from me with Sean. If that's okay? Well, now - suicide is what Iain McBain apparently thinks and I don't see how I could disagree with him. He should know his own brother.' He looked stolidly into the teacup and hesitated for some moments, then frowned more deeply and said: 'I did read your piece in the *Standard* and that *Sunday Mail* story about whether a gun was involved in cause of death...'

'Ah!' Morton said. 'So you're confirming...'

Stevenson sighed. 'I'm not in a position to do that, Willie. Of course not. I simply don't know if there was a gun involved. There seems little point in speculating...'

'But of course, you're going to...?'

'Mis-ter Morton!'

Morton sipped his coffee. He could tell from the slightly gleeful look on Stevenson's face that the First Minister, as rumoured, liked a good gossip. 'Well, someone must know something,' Stevenson admitted, 'but I'm only the First Minister!'

'Ha!' Morton dutifully laughed.

'It might be the cause of death was a gun shot, or it could be a car accident or maybe he had a heart attack while driving?'

Morton said: 'My information – about the gun – comes from within the police.'

Stevenson sat back and made a pyramid with his fingertips. 'Well. I'll have to take what you say on trust. Certainly, some of the circumstances seem mystifying if reported accurately. For example, when Angus was examined in Raigmore Hospital he was still alive, but his injuries were too extensive for recovery. I do know that Iain McBain was asked for, and gave, approval for the life-support machine to be switched off. A painful decision for him to take. Certainly, Angus had... problems,' Stevenson abruptly concluded.

'You mean alcoholism?'

'Oh, partly that, and... I believe that he had suffered from depression for years. I had also heard and this might only be rumour, that he had been convicted for a second time on a drink-driving charge, in which case, if true, he might be in danger of losing his driving licence. However, as I'm sure you're aware,' he added smugly, 'Angus had not been successful in getting elected onto the Executive Committee of the party for many years and in fact seemed to have moved away somewhat from our methods if not our aims.'

Morton looked up. 'He had joined… Vanguard?'

Stevenson looked uncomfortable. Morton was aware that some sections of the party viewed Stevenson as little better than a collaborator with The Beast of Westminster because of his lack of support for the idea of an independence referendum. His cup rattled slightly in its saucer as he raised it. 'I really don't want to talk ill of the dead but I understand he had some sympathy with those puerile and miniscule organisations - if one can call them organisations.' He compressed his narrow lips so that many lines gathered on his forehead above the lush eyebrows. 'But I suggest, really, that you consult with Iain McBain in the first instance for more detailed information.' He relaxed back in his seat and stretched and rearranged his gangly legs. Then he smiled and spoke in a lighter tone. 'It is quite a remarkable coincidence you know, Mr. Morton, that Angus should meet his demise – however it happened - on 6th April. A date well-known in Scots history as the anniversary of Scottish Independence.'

Delighting in the baffled expression on Morton's face, he continued, 'the anniversary of the signing of the Declaration of Arbroath in 1320.'

'Yes, of course,' Morton interrupted quickly. 'But what a coincidence!'

'A declaration guaranteeing the sovereignty of the Scottish nation, Mr. Morton', Stevenson reproved mildly. 'Not the sovereignty of the King, or of Parliament, neither Westminster nor even Holyrood, you understand - but of the nation - the people, the actual populace, what football commentators would call the *punters*.'

He removed his spectacles abruptly and held them up to natural light. The face, bereft of its glass defences, looked owlishly white, as if greatly lacking in sleep. 'A date of whose significance Angus would have been more than aware, I suggest.'

Morton had a fleeting image of the bespectacled former accountant in terrorist guise. Stevenson the Liberator, smoking Armalite held aloft. It was such an unlikely scenario that he began to smile.

Stevenson must have detected it for his voice became a fraction colder. 'And now, I'm afraid I must terminate our little chat since I have a lunch meeting shortly...'

Morton had a sudden brainwave. 'One more question, Mr. Stevenson. I believe that the gun itself is *missing*.'

The politician frowned. 'Gun? If there was a gun... I'm sure we'll hear all about it in due course...' He stood up and walked round the desk. 'Please do take my advice and consult Iain McBain and of course our Press Office before you rush into print. These are delicate matters,' he said and then the voice softened. 'I knew Iain years ago, you know, and he was always extremely approachable. You'll also find he bears a great resemblance to poor Angus, although of course, there was a considerable age difference. Angus was around sixteen years older.'

Morton was ushered grandly back down the stairs into the airy, sunlit vestibule, into the presence of that magnificent cheese plant which swarmed up the tinted glass from its white earthenware planter.

3

Almost a week of inhabiting a damp and crumbling flat in Dennistoun had given Daniel McGinley a seedy feeling. His nostrils seemed to be permanently filled with irritating plaster dust. And the clothes he'd had to wear, baseball caps and slouchy jeans – secondhand of course – and the necessity of not shaving every day just to keep in character – had irked him. The one good thing - frequent visits to pubs - had been spoiled almost completely by the company of neds, jaikies and bampots. The job had been second nature to him because in another life he could have been living it for real. Mostly he had been hanging around the Garngad and the Old Hundred in the London Road, waiting for something to happen. Most of the faces were Irish-involvement only and were being tracked from across the Irish Channel. Some were gunrunning on a very small scale but most were just talking about it, blowhards and fantasists, Celtic supporters with daft songs in their heads and silver phoenixes on chains around their necks. That wasn't his brief. He was watching for the other type, far fewer; the Scottish Republicans, the ones trying to import IRA-type activity into Scotland for Scottish motives. Dissatisfied with the devolution settlement and the seemingly-permanent parking of full Independence aims by Donald Stevenson, his quarry were fewer, much more specific and on a considerably lower scale of aptitude. It was almost certain that they had no guns, no semtex or explosive of any kind but there had been continuing and highly-irritating letter-bomb activity, including one sent to the Executive Director of AtomTech. His brief was to sit tight and let the action come to him. The members of the Vanguard movement had been carefully observed over a period of months and of about forty hangers-on only two gave grounds for further investigation. One of these was Desmond O'Leary, a Glasgow man who talked as if he knew everything that was going on. It could be a double bluff – acting daft to conceal a capable operator. The only way to find out was to baby-sit him, get close enough to smell him, day in, day out. McGinley had been seconded to that task, set-up as Daniel McGee in a grotty council flat. Unemployed, small-time dope dealer (allegedly), former supporter but never a member of Vanguard – that was his cover story.

So Daniel sat and sat under the high wooden beams of the Old Hundred in the mid-afternoon gloom of the back bar, covertly watching the front door. He'd been there on his own for an hour cradling a pint of Guinness and sucking on narrow roll-ups cupped in his hand. His sleeves were rolled up to reveal the saltire tattoo on his forearm, which he'd had done on leave from the Black Watch on his first tour at the age of 19. He'd let his hair grow long and he was wearing an old-fashioned zipped leather jerkin and faded jeans purchased from Sadie's at the Barras. It'd been ten minutes since the target had come in and begun hovering at the bar, joking with the barman. Daniel was calculating whether he could wave him over – or would that look suspicious? He had to dumb down his instincts, do everything slowly. But luck was about to get on his side.

'Danny?'

He glanced up. Len Reynolds, a man he'd spoken to once or twice, was returning from the toilet and had spotted him. 'Len, didnae see ye, there.'

'Danny in't it?'

'Aye, Danny McGee,' he mumbled, as if ashamed of it.

'Mind if I tak the weight aff.'

'Be ma guest.'

'I'll fetch my pint and join you.' Daniel felt this was lucky. Sitting with someone like Len Reynolds would soon lead to useful introductions and boost his credibility. Let them do the talking. Less chance of giving yourself away too. Despite being Scottish himself, he'd found the local "Weegie" accent difficult to perfect.

'What ur ye uptae the day?' Reynolds asked, carefully placing his pint on a beermat.

'Ah, no much,' Daniel admitted. 'Thinkin o getting a wee line on...'

After a few minutes of banal chat, Daniel nodded over at the bar. 'That's Desmond O'Leary, no?'

Reynolds didn't even glance round. 'How dae you ken him?'

'Dinna, but. Somebody said... think I spoke to him once. At a meeting...'

'Ah!'

'Whit of it?' Daniel chose to play it as if he thought he was being disbelieved.

Reynolds sniffed and leaned forward. 'A meetin ye said, Danny? Ye were at a meeting. Whit kind a meetin wid that be?

'Whit d'ye wannae ken fur? Whit's it to you, like?'

'Been in the poky, eh?'

Daniel pretended to bristle. 'I'm no wantin tae talk about that.'

'Awright. Same again?'

'Guinness,' Daniel agreed with a shrug of his shoulders. He rolled a thin cigarette – a Barlinnie Special - and watched out of the corner of his eye, and noticed, right enough, Reynolds say something to O'Leary at the bar and move away. It could just have been "Howsitgaun?" but he had the feeling it was something more significant. Sit tight and they'd come to him. Just a wee flick of the dry fly and the lunker trout would rise.

4

Giving the Volkswagen Beetle a good hour and half's run west across the central belt on the M8, Morton easily found Crosshill Gardens. The apartment, in a block of six in a quiet cul-de-sac in a good area of Glasgow, backed onto a park guarded by ancient oaks. An Estate Agents' sign fastened to a window on the top floor was the giveaway that told Morton which flat was McBain's. Like vultures, they never wasted time. The stairs were neatly carpeted, aspidistras standing proud in brass pots on polished tables on the landings and there was a smell of polish. The windows had stained-glass lower sections. Victorian tiling on the walls. Kneeling, he tried to look through McBain's letterbox and gained an impression of cold dusty emptiness. Press card at the ready, he knocked on the door opposite. An elderly lady with shoulder-length white hair appeared. There were streaks of a tired gold and faded brown among the ashen locks, but her cheeks were pink. She wore no make-up or lipstick.

'Mrs Donald?' he asked. He could see the husband hovering behind her, a genial-looking chap in Pringle cardigan and leather slippers.

Morton was shown into the fussy, old-fashioned living room that overlooked, through foliage of red geraniums, a line of gently swaying trees in the park. He was ushered to a wooden-armed settee, partially covered with two red tartan blankets. China wally dugs sat obediently on the mantelpiece while three pottery ducks flew in panic up the rose-patterned wallpaper. The smell of polish. They fussed over him and Mrs. Donald went to make a pot of tea. When they had all settled down, he began to question them. Retired Church Missionaries, the Donalds had seen a lot of their neighbour.

27

'We were the last ones to see him alive,' Mr. Donald said, 'according to that young man who came round yesterday.'

Morton looked up. 'Young man? Who was that?'

Mr. Donald chaffed his hands together repetitively as he leaned forwards. 'I'm afraid I can't remember his name, Mr. Morton - he said Angus had been like a father to him. He came round yesterday. The day after the police.'

'The police checked the flat?'

'Yes, the day we saw the sad news about Angus in the *Sunday Post*. They were here for the whole day, coming and going. They took away quite a few boxes of Angus's things.'

'The flat's empty now?'

'Well, his brother and two other men came and took some things away too. No one has come up to look at it since. It's in quite a mess because of the fire.'

'*Fire?*' Morton almost fell off the edge of the settee.

Mr. Donald squinted at him. 'Oh, did you not know? On Angus's last night here, there was a fire. The fire brigade was called. Angus was a very lucky man. He nearly died.'

And he's dead now, Morton thought. He flipped out his black notebook. 'Could you tell me more about it? How did it happen? Was it deliberate?'

Mr. Donald hastened to reassure him. 'Oh, nothing like that. It was an accident. He had been out for the evening – Thursday - and we heard him come back quite late. He fell asleep and, you know, he had a nasty habit of smoking in bed. Apparently, a cigarette set fire to the bedclothes and he woke up about 7am to find his blankets smoking and the bedroom full of smoke. He jumped out of bed and snatched up all of his blankets and dumped them in the bath and turned on the tap.'

'Did you hear all of this?'

'He told us all about it the next day. That would be Friday. The first my wife and I knew of it was when the fire brigade arrived a little later.'

Mrs. Donald interrupted him. 'Yes, dear, apparently, his bath - it was a new bathroom suite which he had just had installed - was acrylic and wouldn't you know, it burst into flames, filling the bathroom with smoke. Luckily, two young men going to work, walking through the park, saw the flames and one ran off to phone the fire brigade and the other ran upstairs and broke in the door. He found poor Angus unconscious on the floor. That was when somebody knocked on our door and we got up.'

'And was he alright?'

'He was in shock and he had inhaled a lot of smoke...' Mr. Donald told him, 'otherwise okay.'

'But he was just so filthy with soot, you know, Mr. Morton,' his wife added, 'absolutely refused to go into hospital for a check-up.'

'More than anything,' said Mr. Donald, 'and I'm sure my wife would agree, he was embarrassed about his carelessness and the danger he'd put everyone else in the block to. He wouldn't even have a bath in our flat although he did wash his face and hands. The water in his flat had been turned off you see, but he said he knew where he could get cleaned up.'

'Those were his exact words,' agreed Mrs. Donald, coiling her hair up into two long grey pigtails. '"I know where I can get cleaned up." We knew he meant his holiday home in the Highlands.' She pulled the two thick strands together and clasped them with a large brown plastic grip at the back of her neck.

'We were out for most of that day,' her husband continued, 'It was Good Friday - we had a church service and then went visiting friends - and when we returned we could see he was back. He looked depressed and he was quite grateful for a

29

bowl of soup we gave him and we had a chat about the incident. He was really sorry for all the trouble he had caused.'

'He said...' Mrs. Donald added, straining to recall... 'wasn't it...now what did he say... his business partner, yes, had visited him and he was going to go to his holiday home for the weekend.'

'We did hear him driving away at 6.30pm.'

'We were sure that was the time, remember dear, because Jill downstairs was just coming home and she's always back at the same time.'

'I see,' Morton said. 'But there was nothing suspicious about the fire? I mean, it was a pure accident?'

'Oh, no doubt at all.'

'Well, that was an amazing coincidence at the least. So what do you think happened to Angus?' Morton asked. 'You say he was depressed? Do you think he committed suicide?'

Mr. and Mrs. Donald shook their heads. 'I - we - can't imagine him doing anything like that,' Mr. Donald told him carefully. 'No, Bessie and I have talked a lot about it. We think he had inhaled a lot of acrylic smoke that must have had an effect on his driving. Maybe it caused him to veer off the road. But I can't believe that he would... shoot himself just because he was trapped and thought no one would come to his aid. It doesn't sound very convincing does it?'

'No, it doesn't,' Morton agreed.

Mrs. Donald looked plaintively at her furry slippers and red, swollen ankles. 'We really don't know what to think, Mr. Morton. We liked him. He was a nice man and a good neighbour... He loved his work and I was surprised to read that he was 81 years old. The same age as me. He didn't look it. I can't imagine why he'd want to be bothered with... work or politics at his age, but he lived for it, you know.'

'When we chatted in the evening on Good Friday,' Mr. Donald interjected, 'I said to him that the "Lord's been good to you," but he just hesitated and he didn't really answer. I think he was really angry with himself. But I was surprised to hear that he possessed a gun.'

The discreet brass plate of 'Angus McBain & Co, Solicitors and Notaries Public,' was mounted on the board in the entrance hall of a begrimed stone building in Bath Street, a mile or so away, amongst the plates of a shipping office, two accountants, a messenger-at-arms, and a football pools office. Morton squeezed himself through the cast-iron gates of the lift and pulled them across so that the lift clanked into operation. A brass needle on the dial swiveled violently past one and wobbled on two. Morton jerked the gates apart and stepped into the deeper gloom of the corridor. In the wood-panelled office of McBain & Co., an elderly receptionist wrapped in a greasy cardigan motioned him to a seat. It was Tuesday, early afternoon and business was… non-existent by the look of it.

Brian Dennison was not the personable man whom Morton had expected to meet. Morton had assumed he was the Donald's 'young man'. But he was nearly fifty, Morton judged, and unpleasant and abrupt. His face, neck and hands were the colour associated with freshly boiled lobster. He made it plain to Morton, before the door had closed behind them in the small chocolate-brown inner sanctum of his office, that he did not wish to discuss his late business partner's mysterious death. *Why the hell not?* There was something oblique about his manner that Morton found discouraging. His shirt buttons restricted the contours of his belly. A greyish white tee-shirt could be seen under his shirt and the narrow blue and green polyester tie had seen many better days. His pin-stripe jacket was shabby and crumpled. He smelled faintly of alcohol and even from his seat, the journalist had little trouble in locating the source; there was

31

no mystery about it; a bottle of a cheap whisky blend, cap already off, was in plain view, sitting upright inside the half-open drawer of Dennison's desk. It was plain that Dennison was not coping well with his promotion to sole partner.

'Look, I'm fed up with press speculation and busybodies nosing around,' he groused. 'Why cannae people accept Angus was depressed and just wanted to end it all? His brother accepts it. How can you no?'

Morton watched a bead of sweat between Dennison's eyebrows begin to run down the wide bridge of his nose. His eyes seemed yellow against the liverish purple of his face. He looked like a two-heart-attack-a-year-man.

Morton tried to soothe. 'I'm not saying I don't accept it, Mr. Dennison. I just want to get a bit nearer to the truth of what happened and why. For example, it's been suggested the business was in trouble - in debt...'

'It's been *suggested*...? By who?' Dennison's fist thumped the blotting pad on the desk, making the opened milk carton beside it jump. 'Who the hell has been spreading slanders like that?'

'But if it's true…?'

'It's no true, but I'm no going to talk about this any more. Time for you to leave, Mr. Morton.' He buzzed for the receptionist, who stood clasping and unclasping her hands as he went out into the hall and through the front door. As he walked down the stairs, Morton's nostrils were twitching and his suspicions were well and truly aroused. There was a story to be written. No doubt about it.

24 June 1996, Nygonga, SW Africa.

A heat-haze shimmered over the brown plains along the Topangjhi River, khaki, and thick as soup. Three or four crocodiles were waiting on the opposite banks, under the scant shade of acacia bush. Some distance away, bull elephants bellowed. The sun was at its zenith, the hour just past noon. It was nearly two hours since the shooting had stopped, which meant that the insurgents had either fled or moved position, which came to the same thing although he suspected the former. Sergeant Daniel McGinley adjusted the dirty cloth around the black metal frame of the powerful binoculars. Almost too hot to hold. He shifted his feet, seeking a more comfortable posture, without removing his eyes from the decaying rubber eyepieces. The heat-haze made everything seem myopic, dissolving into liquid. The landscape could only be glimpsed not studied continuously. At last, he let the binoculars fall back onto the front of his khaki tunic. Pointless. He lowered himself back to the ground and began to squirm vigorously backwards down the sand dune to his platoon. Halfway down, he stood up and jumped down in big strides back to the dusty roadway, landing with a jolt a few feet from the leading jeep. The African irregulars of the Nygonga Peoples Front stood up as he reached them and there were a few white-toothed smiles. McGinley often behaved like a *philosophe*, taking himself off in search of information or to get time to think.

'We'll move two kilometres further on, past the village,' he instructed Impopo the interpreter, who passed the word among the platoon. The two-dozen NPF men, although garbed in assorted pieces of various uniforms were good soldiers, well-armed and disciplined and this was due entirely to two month's hard training by McGinley and the other Premier staffers. They were his crack platoon, the picked best from the battalion of five hundred. They each knew personally the value of McGinley's leadership.

The soldiers piled into the three jeeps with a man standing up at the front manning the 9mm gun and keeping a wary eye on the bluffs. The convoy set off slowly, jolting and bumping on the narrow rutted road, sometimes almost wading in banks of sand. The sun was behind them now. McGinley pulled down the khaki peak of his forage cap as he minutely followed the contours of the crude, hand-drawn map.

Shortly the convoy stopped, pulled in behind some dunes for food. McGinley didn't feel hungry, took a mouthful or two of warm water from his canteen. Behind him the SW radio spluttered into life. Lieutenant Bhingoki, the radio operator, passed on the incoming message to the interpreter, who jumped up.

'Colonel Hakan reports insurgent activity coming this way!'

'Fine. We'll deal with them. Better they come to us.'

There was a commotion on the outskirts of the troop. He saw some of his men had captured a man. They brought him over, cowering and quivering in his ill-fitting combat jacket and patched denims, and McGinley could see that beneath the sweat and grime this was no battle-hardened veteran, it was just a boy.

'Name?' he demanded.

The Ethiopian corporal grinned. 'No speak… shit-scared.'

'He bad guy,' the other soldier grinned. 'Russian gun.' He held up a rusty AK-47. 'No bullets.' And he laughed. The others joined in. No bullets.

McGinley pondered what to do and all the while the prisoner whined and bleated in a most irritating way.

'Shut it!' he roared. Instinctively his fingers clutched the handle of the pistol. Almost before he knew what he was doing he had pistol-whipped the prisoner across the temple.

His men grinned at him. It was out of character of course. The heat… maybe? The radio-operator Bingoki checked in, mediated by Impopo. Insurgents now a mile away. They'd have to look lively and get off the trail. He visualised the terrain, the tracks and neighbouring villages and the river. It

34

was too close.... The prisoner's pleading suddenly intruded harshly across his line of thought. He raised the pistol and effectively put an end to the noise. The prisoner slumped.

Almost as an afterthought McGinley turned to the corporal who was grinning delightedly. 'Get a bloody trenching tool and cover him!'

There'd been a brief firefight that day but after the sunset had come and gone and everything was still, except for the persistent frogs and insect chorus, McGinley suddenly recalled the incident and felt the onset of guilt. What the hell had happened? He hadn't even thought about what he was doing. He had shot an unarmed man out of pure reflex. He had brought himself down to their level. This bloody war! He had three months of his contract still to serve. Suddenly, it couldn't come soon enough.

5

At the front desk of Strathclyde Police HQ in Pitt Street, Morton asked for Detective-Inspector Cornwell; whom he had never met. Perhaps usefully, he was told Cornwell was on leave. He insisted on seeing someone from CID and waited and he waited some more and was finally told that a Detective-Inspector Hugh McGregor would agree to speak to him. Morton waited a little more and then was given a temporary pass and ascended in the elevator to the fifth floor.

It didn't take him long to realise that McGregor, a lumbering plod with thick mutton-chop gingery sideburns in an unbuttoned double-breasted suit and sallow mustard tie, was a pompous windbag, who loved withholding information because of 'the regulations.'

'No,' he announced, 'McBain was not under surveillance by Strathclyde Police. Special Branch never reveal details but I can tell you, Mr. Morton, that McBain was not regarded as the brains behind any of these so-called tartan terror groups...'

'And about the fire?' Morton asked. 'Any ideas?'

'He had been drinking pretty heavily the night before, you understand,' the policeman said sonorously, stroking his heavy jowls. 'Aye, Mr McBain was a heavy drinker by habit, a hard drinking man. In fact, he had been drinking on the day of his death. A bottle of whisky - half-empty - was even found in the car.' He raised his impressive eyebrows significantly, squinting at Morton to see what effect this was having. 'Incident at the flat was a botched suicide attempt. Got drunk, started the fire you see - and then got cold feet. He probably decided it would cause risk to his neighbours. Aye, so he took himself off to the Highlands and tried to do himself in by driving fast off the road but he was still alive – he'd botched it - and so in the end he had to shoot himself.'

'Uh-huh, really? So what was his motive?' Morton asked, playing along with it.

The policeman had no doubts. 'Motives? By jings, that man had plenty of bloody motives – oh aye.' The chair creaked underneath him as he leaned forward and began to count off on the fleshy fingers of his left hand. 'One, he was depressed because of his mounting debts. Two, he was facing a court case on his second drink-driving offence. He was almost certainly going to lose his licence. Three, his relationship with Drysdale had broken up; you knew he was gay? And then the fire at the flat and his failure to do away with himself cleanly was the last straw. Did you know that he was a member of EXIT?'

Morton blinked. 'The euthanasia society?'

The policeman nodded sagely. 'Aye, that's them. Believe in suicide pacts and mercy killing you know. Had been a member for years. Told his brother, believe it or not, that if he ever faced life as a brain-damaged vegetable, he'd want to be allowed to die. That was why the life-support was switched off, see. His brother agreed because his brother knew about this wish.'

Morton was astonished at how neatly the policeman had wiped away any lingering doubts. His pencil was scribbling furiously. Then he remembered. 'Who is Drysdale by the way?' he asked.

The policeman was frowning. Morton knew right there he'd heard something he shouldn't and waited. *Drysdale*. The seconds ticked by. McGregor inhaled noisily as he tapped his little finger with the forefinger of his right hand - and changed the subject. 'Then of course, fourthly, McBain had been seeing a psychiatrist for years. Oh, yes.' After a few moments, his forefinger moved up to tap his temple significantly several times. He smiled and narrowed his eyes. 'Oh, I'm sorry Morton, I'm afraid; I should have said... no notes. And everything you've heard is of course strictly off the record.' He thrust out his hand. Morton was forced to tear the pages out and hand them over. He kept his irritation in check and as he was shown out, asked ironically. 'When is Cornwell back?'

The policeman was smiling in a superior manner and that further irritated Morton.

'Well, I'd like to speak to him.'

'Back on Monday. Yes. But, Morton, you know I think you'd do better to speak to the policeman in charge of the investigation at Fort William. Detective-Inspector Roy Wanless. Give him a call. Tell him you've spoken to me. He'll be able to set your mind at rest.'

Fuming at the plod's supercilious manner, Morton went back out and found his car. As he hastily jotted some notes, searching his memory for everything that McGregor had said, that last remark jarred. "Set your mind at rest". Why had the policeman assumed that he was seeking *reassurance*? Or that the police were able provide it?

When Morton got home he phoned the Berkshire number of the Hon. President of EXIT, the distinguished author, Sir Jasper Gombolds. He got straight through. The author was quietly spoken and Morton instinctively felt everything he would say would be truthful. Funny how you get that certainty with some people the first moment you hear them speak!

Gombolds listened patiently then informed Morton politely, in his cut-glass accent, that of thousands of members over several decades, not one single member to his knowledge had ever taken their own life with a firearm.

'That would be entirely contrary to our principles and beliefs,' Sir Jasper said. 'I can't, of course, confirm or deny whether this chap McBain was a member. If you say he was, then he was. But perhaps you should bear in mind that if someone is described as being a member, then, in the public perception it might be assumed the person's death *was* suicide. It might seem to establish, to the ignorant at least, some kind of motive. But that would be a matter for the police and the authorities.'

6

The sound of heavy rain in the car park wafted through the open window bringing with it a cool freshness. The meeting had been in progress for nearly three hours. McGinley's interest had waned as the room temperature had increased and several times he had caught himself on the verge of sleep. He wished he could go outside and walk around. The village of Risley was a mystery to him although he had been attending twice yearly meetings here since he had joined the organisation four years ago. Most of the regular business was done by telephone and email with occasional video-conferences. But the six-monthly face-to-face meetings would range back and forth, reviewing activity in each sector, in his case Scotland West. It was necessary for each member of the team to compile an extensive report but these merely formed the basis of discussion. McGinley was of the view that the entire business could have been done by emails. He detested bureaucracy and meetings, participated only minimally, allowing himself to drift off into other thoughts. The meeting's chair was Superintendent Jo Haines – his immediate superior - matronly, crisp and efficient with a dark tie and white shirt, man's suit, mass of permed curly dark hair on the back of her head that many had said was a wig. It wasn't – he knew for a fact, having once had occasion to grasp it. Her face powder was a little too thick. He could not imagine himself trying to shag her. There was one time when she'd spoken to him quite intensely at some social do or other – when he was new in the force. He couldn't get away from her. Others had been glancing over… You could read anything into that sort of thing, more likely she had simply seen him as a potential protégé, even though she was two years younger than he was. She had a firm grip on the ballocks of the organisation – no doubt about it.

'Operation Shamrock,' she announced, glancing down at the agenda. 'Roger…? Want to outline progress?'

The man sitting next to her at the far end of the table, Roger Thornton, was Haines' right-hand man, a behind-the-scenes cool operator. He wore dark suits and always looked unperturbed.

'Briefly, the targets, including Desmond O'Leary from Dennistoun, are not now regarded as any kind of active threat,' he told the meeting. 'Operation Shamrock has therefore been handed on to…. outwith our jurisdiction. They did ask me to pass on their thanks for a job well done.'

'Nice,' McGinley muttered.

Haines must have heard the comment for she looked directly at him.

'Sadly,' she said, 'onto the next item; the Unicorn file remains pending.'

Next to McGinley, Kevin Gray shifted in his seat.

'The Unicorn file?' a few voices asked.

'Scottish op,' Haines said. 'You have it listed in the Operations directory.'

'Yes, of course…' one of the English officers intruded… 'But the name…'

'A fabled beast that no-one really believes exists,' McGinley explained and laughed abruptly.

'Is that meant to be cryptic?' someone asked.

'A full briefing or case report would be inappropriate,' Haines said, 'as we just have to dot the I's and cross the t's. Isn't that correct, Daniel?'

'This Unicorn was the target?'

'It's done,' McGinley murmured.

41

'The Unicorn used to be the national emblem of Scotland,' Gray told the meeting helpfully.' He smirked. 'We thought that was appropriate.'

'National emblem? Along with Tunnocks teacakes!'

'Very amusing,' Haines interposed. 'The case is not quite closed?'

'No,' Daniel said and refused to elaborate further.

Haines tapped her pen on the desk. 'Complications – will it require further involvement?' But no one was listening, it being a peculiarly Scottish operation.

'The Scots have dozens of national emblems, kilts, whisky, hairy knees, thistles, porridge…' someone said helpfully.

'They are a very emblematic people…'

'Problematic too…'

'Careful,' McGinley frowned. 'These people include us,' he glanced at Gray and Ron Ramsay.' And under his breath, so that Gray would hear him, muttered: 'English git.'

'So you say.'

'I damned well do say, old boy!'

'Okay. The *next* item on the agenda,' said Haines with emphasis, is….'

So far, Willie Morton had amassed considerable background material and more conjecture on McBain's death and made smooth if unremarkable progress even if there was no actual news and the police were not giving any interviews or releasing any reports of their investigations. Morton was spending time phoning everyone he knew at Holyrood to try to get something more. Then the police finally put out a new statement admitting the cause of death was "gunshot wound" and the papers all ran with it, openly now speculating McBain had committed suicide.

With all the media chasing the story, Morton tried to think up a different approach. He had put in a request at St Andrew's House and the Solicitor General's office and expected it to go no further, but got an interview offer in an email. It was an unexpected coup. He had already interviewed the First Minister and now had an exclusive interview with Scotland's highest law lord, Nicolas Mortimer QC., the Lord Advocate. The benefits of working in a small nation. He gleefully phoned Hugh Leadbetter at the *Standard*.

'Right, Willie, well done! Fire over what you get and we'll use it asap,' Leadbetter told him on the phone. 'Double-paged spread. We'll use a stock image of Mortimer and we've found some more good pics of McBain. There'll be an artist's impression of the scene at Loch Dubh, crashed car and revolver etc, to whet the appetites of readers. We're looking at a minimum fifteen hundred words here. This could be – should be – definitive so far.'

And all Morton could think about was the kudos and the £450 extra he'd earn for the piece. He had no idea of the danger it would bring him or that he was going to put himself on someone's hit list.

Unicorn. Hadn't been his idea or his fault. Not entirely. Kevin Gray had given him only a part of the story. A strange assignment it'd been altogether. One minute he was Daniel McGee in the Old Hundred, the next he was being sped north up the A9 in a jeep for a briefing. A cock-up but no harm done. It had all been sorted out in the best traditions of the service. A veil had been drawn, an official clam-up. He was off the hook. Different story if there had been an FAI. They'd have had investigators crawling all over them like nits. Could still happen. McGinley caught himself wondering if he really cared but the ball was coming his way. He moved into space, intercepted it with his left boot, and with his right, toe-poked it to the man out on the wing.

'Nice one, McGinley,' someone on the touchline shouted, appreciatively.

He followed the attack forward and stood his ground to stop the counterattack but his lunging tackle missed its mark and he sprawled into the mud.

After that, he became almost a spectator in the game, barely getting a touch. He was glad when the final whistle blew. England South had walloped them 3-0 for a second successive year. He was knackered. Next time, he'd have an excuse ready. As they trooped to the pavilion, he reminded himself that participation in the game was not mandatory. Hardly anyone turned up except the idiots in the teams.

'Good game, eh Daniel?' Ron Hemphill enthused. 'Shame you got beat.'

'Mnn,' he acknowledged with the briefest of smiles.

'Going for a pint, man?'

'Of course. Or two.'

The showers at Risley were first class. Scalding hot water and gallons of it. McGinley felt his aches and pains dissolve. He towelled himself luxuriously and dressed in slacks and a crisp new white short-sleeved shirt. What he needed now was a pint of Guinness. He'd developed a taste for it during his fieldwork in Dennistoun.

On the slow walk to the pub down the quiet leafy lanes, walking slowly, he contemplated the Unicorn assignment, his incomplete file. An eccentric and dangerous target, a man who'd insisted on being a subversive at an age when others were tending their rose gardens. Driven by some political ideal. McGinley knew the attractions of idealism but had rarely been stirred by it. Flags were interchangeable, nations, independence – it was all ballocks. Britishness and Scottishness – strange how some people made so much of the difference. Of course things were presently in a sort of limbo; sort-of Scottishness with a good bit of Britishness still around. Everybody was a bit of both to varying degrees, but few were entirely one or the other. Half of the lads he had known in the Black Watch had been nats either overtly or by some unconscious inclination: a damn sight keener on the saltire than the union jack. And bagpipes, well, pibrochs could make him feel dewy-eyed on occasion but he associated them with his service in the British army. He'd looked into separation – of course it was *possible* but why? He preferred to take a pragmatic approach. The halfway-house of devolution with the nats in charge quite unable to move the country on to Independence. With a wry smile he recalled the knowing winking that went on when they participated in those summer full-scale tactical exercises. Terrorist scenarios; tartan terrorists invade the island of Skye, or seize an oil platform – devise a strategy to retake control. Always some behind-the-hand grinning and no shortage of volunteers to play the insurgents, the rebels.

The Four Bells was brightly lit up at the end of the lane. Hanging baskets of surfinias festooned the entrance. Through small panes of glass in the inner door he could see Kevin Gray and Ron Hemphill lording it in the lounge.

'Name your poison,' he offered, in the doorway.

He stood at the bar and not for the first time, as he waited to be served, he thought of the possibility of pulling the plug, getting out early. He'd been on active service since his late teens. Maybe get a nice wee cottage somewhere, probably up north, take up fly-fishing or buy a pub – or look up some old girlfriends – settle down. It wasn't too late. He felt a wry smile break out. 'Better snap out of it, old boy, or they'll think you're going soft in your old age,' he murmured to his reflection in the mirror.

Morton was putting in the hours on his laptop. Sean Kermally had emailed him to say that the SNP had agreed, following media interest, to commission an internal report on McBain's death. To find out if there was "any cause for concern." That was something he could use in a follow-up piece, although everyone else would have it too. He gleaned an interesting snippet from an anti-nuclear group's website that, in 1992, McBain had obtained a photocopy of a highly secret document from a Nuclear Energy Conference that was held in private under very strict security in Helsinki. The document was dynamite, definitely front-page material revealing British Nuclear plc had been allowed to secretly circumvent the public planning authorities. Nine out of ten proposed test-drilling sites were in Scotland and test drilling was to be conducted in secret *before* planning applications were submitted. The UK government had secretly agreed that 'in the national interest' planning applications could be submitted retrospectively and of course there was no Scottish parliament then in existence to consult with – or to get in the way. So with his Knoydart Inquiry success still making the news McBain was riding high, chief of the troublemakers, going head to head with the UK government. And no doubt giving them and the nuclear industry a real headache.

But then something went badly wrong. His press conference was pre-empted on the very morning that he planned to reveal the documents. The nuclear industry put out a statement through a media agency that the stolen document had emanated from a think-tank and was only a proposal by one freelance commentator entirely unconnected to any government agency. The documents had not even been discussed at the Helsinki Conference. So McBain was left to announce his great coup in an empty room and the story never appeared. No one ever got around to asking how the nuclear industry learned that McBain had the documents.

According to some, Morton learned, this was also when nasty slanders about McBain's private life first surfaced. He was a paedophile, he was an alcoholic, suffered from depression, even insanity. And at the next year's party conference McBain was dumped as the SNP nuclear spokesman, a bitter humiliation for him no doubt and his political career was effectively over. Did all this mean something? Were these events linked? There was something odd about it all, something unexplained and not just the mystery of how and why McBain had died. There was a link, a reason, a motive; something missing.

7

The wood-panelled waiting room smelled strongly of furniture polish and the tooled green leather armchairs shone in the light cast by brass lamp standards. The length of time one was kept waiting by an important person, Morton believed, was directly proportional to that person's conception of their self-importance. It was fully forty minutes since he had been ushered up the side stone steps by a uniformed janitor to this pleasant, varnished oak room. Here were no traffic sounds although the building was in the heart of Edinburgh. The heavy oak door was ajar and he could see black-robed figures passing in the corridor like ants bearing off corpses into the undergrowth.

Morton had travelled diligently in the pages of *Who's Who* and knew Nicolas Wilkie Mortimer to be a product of the Scottish upper class; born and raised in rural Morayshire and educated at Ampleforth and Baliol College, Oxford. A brief spell in a London legal practice then partnership in an undistinguished law firm in Edinburgh where he rapidly acquired a reputation as a man who never went without lunch. Mortimer's career improved when he won the parliamentary seat of West Banff in 1989 and was tipped for a Ministerial post. He lost the seat in 1997 and proved to be a bad loser, penning spiteful diatribes in the Scottish press against the new MP for West Banff and the SNP in general. But Mortimer was appointed by the Prime Minister to the post of Solicitor General for Scotland - a consolation prize - and, on the elevation of the Lord Advocate two years later to greater things (senior legal position in England), had assumed the highest legal office in Scotland. And when the SNP had taken over, they simply kept him on, a major surprise. He was a success, well-liked and popular even with ultra-nats. To all intents and purposes he had gone native.

There was a timid knock on the door and the deferential janitor looked in. 'Begging pardon, Mr. Morton, his Honour will see you now.'

The janitor led him to an impressively large oak double-door and stood aside respectfully, opening one wing of the door for Morton to enter a large, well-lit, well-appointed room. Antique furniture, heavy velvet drapes, enormous gilt-framed paintings of Highland scenes, even a coal-effect gas-jet fire in an iron grate beneath a splendid mahogany mantelpiece. And here too, Morton could smell furniture polish.

Nicolas Mortimer QC, wearing a black robe over a grey double-breasted suit and blue silk tie, fairly bounded around the glass-topped desk, with an agility which seemed to belie his paunchiness. The Lord Advocate was more affable that Morton had expected. He fairly beamed. His handshake was enthusiastic. Morton felt as if a large, friendly bulldog was overwhelming him, except Mortimer was shiny, pink and smelt strongly of expensive cologne. His peruke lay discarded and faintly yellow on top of a pile of legal volumes.

'Sit down, Morton. Mind if I call you William?'

Caught off guard, Morton mumbled a rather gruff and ungraceful assent.

'Can't abide the stuffy formality that's supposed to go with all this.' Mortimer indicated, with a sweep of his pink paw, the entire contents of the room. 'Like a drink?'

Morton's eyebrows must have risen a little too sharply because Mortimer's smile waned a little.

'You journalists... coffee I meant,' he explained, marsupial hands waving away the slight indiscretion. There was a silver tray of crystal decanters filled with golden whiskies but Mortimer vengefully jabbed a button on the side of his desk.

Sunlight was streaming into the warm room making a million brilliant points of contact and miniature rainbows struck from the decanters dazzled Morton. Beyond, he could see the khaki-green slopes of Arthur's Seat and the spring colours of trees in Holyrood Park.

Mortimer had seated himself behind his desk and elaborately composed the fingers of both hands into a pink pyramid. 'First of all, may I say...' he announced, flexing his stubby fingers, 'that I had assumed public interest in the McBain case was more or less at an end. Nevertheless, I can understand occasionally the press finds it necessary to review stories in the hope of digging up something fresh.'

Morton winced at the gruesome metaphor. 'I don't see this as something in the past,' he replied. 'It's not even a fortnight since McBain's death and there has been no public airing of the case. Legitimate public concern raised by the media remains unanswered.'

Mortimer beamed innocently like an overfed schoolboy. 'I must commend your dogged enthusiasm. But of course, William, unlike the United States, we don't go in for trial by the media in this country. Here we have a tried and tested - and if I may say, highly praised - legal system which acts to defend personal civil liberties. Angus McBain's death is not a matter for the gutter press.'

'I don't work for the gutter press, as you put it,' Morton snorted. 'And you must admit your tried and tested legal system has been unusually secretive and even perhaps paranoid over this case. I have been attempting for almost a week, to find out why no new statement was issued after the cause of death was known.'

The Lord Advocate's smile now seemed distinctly at odds with a new steely polite tone in his normally poised, careful voice. 'I will do no such thing, Mr. Morton,' he countered. 'While I accept you may be a journalist of more integrity than others, a number of persons clearly wish to use the tragic death of Angus McBain - a man for whom I had the utmost respect - for no other purpose than to attack the government and this office. Such persons certainly exist, whether you are one of them or not.'

The interview had reached a polite impasse and with considerable relief Morton heard the clattering arrival of a tea trolley, wheeled into the room from an antechamber. An elderly woman, oblivious to the entrenched silence, placed cups and saucers and a tray containing coffee pot, milk, cream and sugar on the glass-topped table and withdrew obsequiously.

Mortimer reached forward. 'Shall I be mother?'

It was a friendly gesture and the interview resumed, Morton intent on avoiding confrontation in order to secure answers to the questions, the Lord Advocate now more wary. Morton strove to put him at ease, to recapture the apparent friendliness of the initial few minutes.

'I note the Scottish National Party has remitted Rosemary Maclean MSP to produce an internal report on the McBain case. Will you be co-operating with her investigation?'

'I can say quite categorically I will, although the official files can be revealed to no-one except next-of-kin.' Mortimer smiled ruefully. 'Not even to elected members - of Holyrood or Westminster, but I will certainly be called to give evidence.'

'Would you be prepared to publish the papers?'

'We cannot. Besides, such a deal would be contrary to the expressed wishes of McBain's brother.' Mortimer's hands eloquently pleaded for his absolute decency. 'I would be put in an impossible position.'

'But surely you must respond to public pressure? We now have the formation of an Angus McBain Society to fight for a Fatal Accident Inquiry.'

'Cranks and extremists!' Mortimer expostulated. 'The McBain Society is full of political cranks and extremists, led, I understand, by a man expelled from the SNP for extremism, Malcolm Farquharson. I doubt whether he could be regarded as truly impartial. By contrast, I have had a discussion at some length with Donald Stevenson who has been highly supportive of my conduct on this case.'

Mortimer considered for a few moments and then continued, in less bombastic tone: 'nor have the relatives of McBain expressed any less than full satisfaction with my decision. Unless the relatives change their mind, I am not empowered under the legislation to hold an F.A.I. I need not tell you how hurtful and distressing lurid speculation in the press might be to McBain's relatives.'

Morton almost laughed. He felt his anger rising but kept calm. 'Speculation is only continuing in the absence of the facts though, isn't it, and because of the apparent secrecy surrounding the circumstances,' he said. 'If these could be made public, no doubt our fears could be allayed. For example, the public was led to believe for nearly a week McBain died in a car crash. But when it was publicly revealed to have been a gunshot death you did not issue a further statement.'

'On the contrary. I spoke to the press on the day the death certificate appeared.'

'But only because it *had* appeared. And you did not add anything to your original statement.'

'What did you expect me to do? The police inquiry was complete and all facts were known.'

'But were they?' Morton queried, 'your own statement on the case reveals McBain's death is still a mystery. You don't know what really happened at Loch Dubh. You are simply making a guess based on very flimsy evidence.'

'Of course - to some extent,' the Lord Advocate conceded. 'We merely have to decide whether the death was murder, suicide, accidental or undetermined. Rarely can we be completely sure. The forensic evidence led the police to conclude there were no grounds for criminal prosecution but neither could they agree it was an accident. The presumption by the experts therefore was suicide.'

Morton casually tossed his ace. 'A gun found thirty yards from the car when McBain was trapped in the driving seat?'

Mortimer's lips pressed tightly together. He nodded. 'Those circumstances might seem unusual. But the bullet in his head was from his own gun. The gun was not found immediately. It was certainly further away than expected if it had just fallen from his grasp. However, after extensive post-mortem examination the conclusion of the forensic experts was suicide and we must abide by that.'

'And had two shots been fired from the gun as has been suggested?'

'I believe so. But according to the experts, Morton, it is extremely common for suicide victims to "test-fire," as it were, the gun before shooting themselves. And, of course, 80% of handgun suicides are caused, as in this case, by shots to the temple and in 80% of such cases, the weapon is not found in the victim's hand.'

'But not usually thirty yards away...' Morton said, resorting to sarcasm. 'A senior policeman told me McBain had been drinking heavily on the night of the incident yet witnesses deny he smelt of alcohol when they found him.'

Mortimer shut his eyes momentarily and waggled his fingers in their pink basket. 'I am surprised to hear a senior policeman has discussed such crucial and confidential details of the case with you.'

'Did McBain have alcohol in his bloodstream?'

'He did not.'

53

'No? Well - why...?'

'I have no idea why it should be suggested he had been drinking. The post-mortem was quite clear. There was no alcohol. Of course, a whisky bottle was found in the car and this may have led to rumours he had been drinking. Such rumours have no foundation in fact.'

Mortimer stood up and adjusted his robe and began pacing in front of the window. His wish for the interview to be terminated was clearly apparent. He seemed to be struggling with his notoriously quick temper.

Morton sat as long as he dared but after a few moments, perhaps almost a minute of absolute silence, he stood up. 'But what were McBain's motives?'

The Lord Advocate turned away from the window and Morton fancied he heard a sigh. Perhaps the view of Edinburgh's early summer treescape and the stately architecture of Holyrood Palace beyond (if not the modernistic hotchpotch of the Parliament building itself) had modulated his temper for his voice was low and pleasantly modulated: 'I suspect if you have discussed the case with anyone at all, you have already discovered a number of very plausible motives. I am rather glad, Morton, that you are not involved in politics. You would be a very dangerous adversary.'

Morton felt a sudden chill despite the sunshine and the flames leaping in the fireplace. The sibilance of the word *adversary* lingered in the room.

'Very dangerous indeed,' Mortimer repeated. Then he beamed and bounded forward, offering his hand.

As they shook hands at the door, Mortimer said: 'Contrary to what you may think, I greatly respected Angus McBain as a fellow member of the legal profession and although I disagreed with him politically, I welcome the opportunity which his brother has given me to keep the details of his

private life from the hands of the scandal-mongers of the...'
he smiled ironically... but did not complete the sentence.

As often as he could manage it, Daniel McGinley would take
off for two or three days solo and try hard to disappear. He
would drive north into the mountains and park on a narrow
road somewhere then set off on foot along a route he had
planned. The idea was to push himself to the limits of his
fitness. Unencumbered by companions and the need to make
conversation, he could travel long distances at speed,
yomping along under his heavy pack. What he liked was to
get onto a ridge and just keep walking along it as far as
possible. The more desolate and isolated the terrain the better
he liked it. In fact, he often stepped off the track into trees or
behind large boulders if he saw people. Having to even say a
gruff 'Hello' in passing was an ordeal to him. He liked to
commune directly with nature. He could easily make thirty
miles in a day, rising soon after dawn in his bivouac, cooking
up some nutritious goo in his mess tin to go with a tin mug
of black coffee and a chunk of dried biscuit. Then he was off,
striding quickly, using the features of the terrain to keep
himself out of sight. And every minute of it he savoured - his
wilderness experience - and every minute of it reminded him
of his days as a mercenary in charge of guerrilla fighters in
the backcountry of Nygonga when he was being paid
handsomely to fight someone else's war. So these treks of his
were holiday, stress-relief and a reliving of history. He never
told anyone where he went, where he had been or where he
next planned to go. It was his time and it was an ideal
personal space in which to sort out his head. It was very
different to his hill walks with his old army buddies – which
were infrequent due to the difficulties of getting everybody

together. Easier just to go off and do it. And the habit had stuck.

McGinley was 45 and although as fit as he could be, was mournfully aware of creaks and twinges in his bones which struck him in the cold mornings just before the sun came up. He was contemptuous of it, despised it as weakness, and tried his best to ignore it.

Sometimes that was difficult. He felt the twinge in his lower spine almost as soon as he opened his eyes and grunted as he levered himself onto one elbow. He unzipped several inches of the front flap and felt the cold breeze on his face. A pale orange stain was expanding in the east over the dim grey landscape. He fumbled for the zip of his sleeping bag and pushed it down. The middle of nowhere. The cool air surrounded him like a pleasant massage. He sat up; his head bulging the polyester inner flap and the nylon outer of the tent then began to crawl out. The mossy ground was wet underfoot as he stood in his briefs urinating onto the heather. After ten minutes of vigorous exercising, he reached into the tent for his tee shirt and combats and then the small toilet bag hanging under the circular frame. The small stream trickled brightly just thirty feet from his bivouac and he splashed his face and the back of his neck, brushed his teeth. The sun was emerging over the Cuillin. It was going to be another glorious day. The strong smell of coffee bubbling on his camphor fuel stove was unbelievably wonderful. It was great to be alive and free of all duties and responsibilities. McGinley thought of these moments, these simple off-grid days in the wild as his blowhole moments, what kept him alive in a life of utter meaningless crap and boring duty rosters.

8

They were very alike; Angus and Elizabeth McBain, that was Morton's first thought when they turned up unexpectedly on his doorstep the next day. Angus McBain's nephew and niece, in their twenties, the brother older than his sister by four or five years, both dark, their hair thick and so shiny black it looked navy blue, their skins pellucid, pale, photogenic. Angus had a tidy moustache, which drooped at the corners towards a strong chin already bluish-dark a couple of hours since a shave. They were dressed smartly in dark suits, Elizabeth's skirt modestly knee-length.

Angus fingered his tweed tie and the buttoned-down lapels of his Oxford shirt with neatly manicured fingertips, and explained: 'After reading your newspaper story, we felt we had to come. We talked it over with some of our relatives first.'

'Better come in,' Morton said. An attractive pair, he decided irrelevantly as he watched them arrange themselves on the sofa in his living room.

Elizabeth turned to look at him, hair framing her oval face. 'And so we're here on their behalf as well as our own. We got your address from… the editor of the *Sunday Standard*. I hope that was alright?'

Morton felt himself being regarded by the blue-green eyes of Elizabeth McBain. His ears began to feel hot. 'Well – yes…'

'Our father,' she glanced back at her brother, 'is of the opinion that Uncle Angus committed suicide and will not discuss the matter with anyone, even us.'

Her brother took up the story. 'But some in the family, besides us, share our unease. There are… unexplained circumstances… which we simply cannot ignore.'

Morton nodded. 'But, um, your father is the nearest blood relation and it's up to him to say yes or no to an inquiry. Have you tried to talk to him?'

'We have tried,' Elizabeth said, 'but he refuses to discuss it. My father, Mr. Morton, is a very stubborn man - as was our uncle. He was the only one who was given official information. The rest of the family have neither been consulted nor informed. Our uncle is dead and all we know about it is what was in the papers.'

Morton noticed that her lips, apparently without lipstick, were moist and pink. 'But has your father not shown you the death certificate... or, the post-mortem report?'

Elizabeth flicked a dark strand of hair from her eyes. 'The death certificate was mentioned in the paper of course, but I don't think my father even has a copy of a postmortem report. You see, he was in Raigmore, at the hospital, when the life support system was switched off and... Being a doctor... maybe he didn't bother to ask for a copy. He certainly had some official-sounding phone calls a day or two after the accident.'

'We both feel that our father doesn't have an actual written copy of the PM report,' said Angus.

Morton frowned. 'He must have. It's a legal requirement.'

'Only if requested,' said Angus. 'Maybe father hasn't requested it?'

'Couldn't you request it - on his behalf?'

'That'd be highly dishonest!' Elizabeth said indignantly.

'Only an idea.'

Elizabeth coloured slightly. 'Actually, we did something a little sneaky ourselves. Apart from this visit to you which father is unaware of, we looked through his papers to see if we could find the PM report. We searched everywhere.'

'No sign?'

She shook her head. 'That's why we feel he may not have bothered to obtain a copy. He knew or thought he knew what was in it. It's like he just shut off after he came back from Inverness. He never spoke of it to anyone at the funeral. He wouldn't even look at the newspapers. In some way, he seems to have shouldered the blame... or something. He's bottling it all up inside. Cauterizing himself.'

'The point is,' said Angus firmly, 'as my sister has said, all we know is what we have read in the papers. For example, in your piece, we read that Angus's gun was found some distance from the car. Almost thirty yards, I believe...'

'And it *was* his gun?' Morton asked.

Angus and his sister looked at each other in consternation. 'We don't know,' said Angus. 'We really don't... but we have the feeling there *was* a gun in the family... that Uncle Angus had a gun, from his war days probably.'

'It's ridiculous, to say the least,' Morton said, 'that - what – more than two weeks after his death I still can't say for certain whose gun it was.'

'But many members of the family find the idea of uncle committing suicide impossible to believe,' Angus continued.

'Angus is right,' Elizabeth said quietly. 'We are all agreed that he would never have taken his own life. He would never have put the family through such grief. The family was really all he ever cared about, apart from his political causes of course.'

'I see.'

'What do you think yourself, Mr. Morton?' Angus asked him.

'I'm not sure.' It was true. Confronted by the evidence, or lack of it, Morton suddenly realised he did not know what he thought. He cleared his throat. 'Like you, I find the suicide theory a little unlikely.' He tried to concentrate and be professionally detached. 'Not that I knew your uncle well - or

59

even at all. Heard him speak publicly at conferences, but I'd only spoken to him twice, maybe three times, and then only for a few minutes. He impressed me with his... honesty,' he concluded tamely.

Since neither spoke, he tried again. 'I have other reasons to doubt the suicide theory. What you could call logistic reasons. You've already touched on one of them.'

'You are still looking into it, then?' Elizabeth asked.

'Um, sort-of. Some friends of your uncle have formed the Angus McBain Society to fight for a Fatal Accident Inquiry.'

'Oh! That wasn't in your article. Maybe we should get in touch with them?'

'Well, they've indicated they want to publish a booklet on the case and have suggested…' Morton blushed… 'that I could write it.'

'Are they reputable people?'

'They have a political axe to grind of course.' He moved to the door. 'I was just about to make coffee.'

As he busied himself in the kitchen, Elizabeth appeared in the doorway, a slender shape in the afternoon sunlight. He realised she was, very probably, the only woman who had been in his flat. The thought made him a little nervous. His ex-wife, Sally had never visited, having made a new life in London. Their six years together had been spent in a flat in Leith.

'I don't know father's reasons for standing in the way of an inquiry,' she said. 'I think possibly the lawyers, even the Lord Advocate were willing to hold one.'

'Maybe not,' Morton said, gently, placing mugs on a tray. 'The impression the Lord Advocate gives is that he would be willing, but he was quite open about using your father's decision to justify his not holding an inquiry. He was pretty smug about it too. He's a smart operator. Now he can hold

60

up his hands in innocence and claim credit for being sensitive to the feelings of the relatives.'

Morton poured boiling water into three mugs. 'What the Lord Advocate has done is very clever indeed. By not having an inquiry, the press and the political hacks have been denied direct answers to their questions, so the myths and rumours and slanders can proliferate and the truth be very effectively obscured. It's government by innuendo. I wouldn't be surprised if he's not churning out black propaganda behind the scenes. Another thing that's pretty weird is the silence within the SNP. I mean, they have the internal inquiry but it's private. You'd think there'd be all kinds of theories on the go. There isn't.'

'Are you a full-time journalist?' Elizabeth suddenly asked, examining the memos crudely scrawled on the calendar pinned beside the fridge-freezer.

'Yes, freelance.'

'We did get your phone-number from the paper but we found your address from the phone-book.' She smiled wanly at the chaos of dirty dishes in the sink. 'Just in case you were wondering.'

'Uh-huh. What do you do yourself, Elizabeth?'

'I'm at Cambridge studying Art History. And Angus is a final year law student at Glasgow.'

'Following in his uncle's footsteps,' Morton said, then checked himself and added, 'as a solicitor I mean, not...' he winced.

She frowned. 'I suppose. He sat his finals this week.'

They returned to the living room.

'What is your next move, then?' Angus asked him.

'Don't know really if I'm going to do much more. I need to get on with other things.'

Out of the corner of his eye, Morton noticed the surprise and disappointment in their faces. 'I have to make a living you see,' he said apologetically.

'Well, of course,' Elizabeth said. 'It is a great pity. We wanted to offer you our help. We're both on holiday and this is important to us. It's five weeks now since our uncle was taken from us and we want to find out what really happened.'

'Unfortunately, we couldn't afford to pay you to continue...' Angus began.

Morton was horrified. 'Oh, no... I wasn't... I couldn't... I'm honestly just as keen as you are to get at the truth,' he said. 'Okay, maybe I could stay with the story for another week or so... Anyway, I need to speak to a man called Drysdale who knew your uncle. Problem is - he's in jail at the moment. Don't suppose you've heard of him?'

'No. But we'll give you all the help we can,' Elizabeth enthused. 'By the way, someone contacted us with some information, which we think you'd better handle. A man called Stoddard. He's an HM Customs official in the Highlands but he's very wary about his name being used. His first name is Peter...' Elizabeth told him. 'As in the badges... you know, Blue Peter?'

'Ha! And what did he want to tell you?' Morton asked.

'He wouldn't say over the phone. He referred to your article. We thought it funny at the time that he didn't contact you himself. He asked us though if we were in contact with you.'

'Strange. And what did you say?'

'We told him we didn't know you. We suggested he contact you through the paper. Here's his number anyway.'

'I'll give him a ring,' Morton said, frowning. 'More coffee?'

Despite being pressed to make a further public statement, the Lord Advocate, Nicolas Mortimer QC., steadfastly refused to do so. Now, nearly six weeks after McBain's death came an announcement, designed to end speculation:

> *A full report has been received from the Procurator Fiscal about his investigation into the circumstances surrounding the death of Angus McBain of 6 Crosshill Gardens, Glasgow, on 7th April.*
>
> *This report has been considered by Crown Counsel who are satisfied that there are no circumstances to warrant criminal proceedings. The results of the Procurator Fiscal's full investigations have been disclosed to the next of kin and discussed with him.*
>
> *He has expressed himself satisfied with the extent of that investigation and has indicated that there is no wish on the part of the family for a public inquiry. No public inquiry under the Fatal Accidents and Sudden Deaths Inquiry (Scotland) Act 1976 has been instructed. That is the statement. There will be no amplification of this.*

Morton's Blackberry was ringing, he had had to run and retrieve it from the living room.

'Mr. Morton? Malcolm Farquharson here.'

Morton stood looking out of the window. Farquharson, the crofter? 'Um, right. You were a friend of Angus McBain?'

'Indeed. Mr. Morton. I was his oldest friend. In both senses.' He chuckled. 'I suppose that you have read the latest pronouncement from on high?'

Morton watched rain drilling onto Shandon Place. He heard tyres slicing into water and saw a few flurried umbrellas at the junction with Merchiston Grove. He relaxed on the arm of his leatherette sofa, lifting his stocking-ed feet onto the coffee table. He felt a cool breeze between his toes. 'Nothing new,' he said. 'Typical Mortimer bombast. "That is the statement. There will be no amplification of this..."'

'Done, if I may say, with a distinctly hollow sound. Well, Mr. Morton, I am phoning you in my new official capacity as Chairman of the Angus McBain Society. As if my old head did not already have enough hats to wear... Mr. Morton, concerning our investigatory booklet, have you given the matter any thought?'

Morton remembered an email on the subject that had come in to his inbox a few days before but that was from someone called Siobhan. 'Ah, I did get an email about that. Well... I'm not sure if I can come up with something new. And anyway, I can't associate myself with a political group.'

'But we are being very scrupulous to avoid being that... Very well, but perhaps you will think about it? On the matter of fees... we are not well off but could promise about one hundred pounds sterling with whatever else we could raise at a later date by fundraising and donations... And of course, you'd be free to publish, in part, elsewhere.'

Morton smiled. A hundred pounds probably sounded like a lot to the crofter. 'Let's wait and see what I can come up with,' he said. 'And if nothing, then we can reconsider.'

'Very well. And I suppose you saw that Mr. David Cochrane is now calling for an Inquiry. What was your opinion of that young man?'

Morton hedged his bets. 'He seemed straightforward. A good witness, I think.'

'Maybe so.'

Morton noted the tone of dubiety. 'Frankly I'm short of leads. Maybe something will suggest itself in the next few days. I've arranged a meeting with a man called Peter Stoddard...'

'The name is unknown to me. What is his connection?'

'He is...' Morton paused. How much should he tell Farquharson? 'He's, '...or he claims to be... a Customs Officer in the Highlands, involved in tracing drug smugglers. Claims McBain died at the hands of drug-dealers.'

'Ha! That sounds like a complete red herring, Mr. Morton. It's not the first time I've heard it but never from anyone with any credibility whatsoever. I would advise you to check the credentials of this man Stoddard.'

'I'm meeting him tomorrow.'

Morton's flat, untidy at the best of times, had been considerably neglected during the past few weeks. Heaps of damp towels and discarded shirts lay in, on and around the cane laundry basket. Dishes, pans and cutlery were piled high around the sink and a second pile had started on the floor. Two black rubbish bags had subsided under their own weight and leaned amorously together. The kitchen table was a chessboard of half-empty coffee mugs, plates, crusts of toast, used milk cartons and teabags squashed into saucers. Even the spider plants in the living room and the begonias on the kitchen window sill managed to look disreputable and the cheese plant in its shady corner in the hall was well out of order, the edges of its giant leaves paper-thin, brown and flaky.

Morton lay in bubble-bath foam, hot water lapping at his chest, trying to focus his thoughts. He was trying not to think about the fact that he had done no real work for several weeks, except for his two pieces on McBain for the *Standard* and a brief review of the new biography of George Galloway for *Politics Today*. He was, more or less, Scottish stringer for that monthly and uneasily aware of rumours that due to poor subscriptions and competition by its main rivals, *Current Agenda, Total Politics* and *Holyrood*, it was likely to fold in weeks. He needed to do better paid work but was getting more and more involved – entirely unpaid - in the McBain case. He heard the cordless telephone ringing in the hall. It was nearly midnight. It kept ringing.

Morton reluctantly clambered out of the bath and pulled on his robe and went into the hall, which was in almost total darkness. Picking up the receiver he realised his left foot had scattered some papers which he had piled neatly. He was therefore hardly aware of the voice at the other end of the phone as he stared in dumb irritation at the jumbled papers.

'Hello?'

'Beep. Beep. Beep.'

'Who's speaking please?'

'Beep... beep... beep.' The voice was unhurried, inhuman, unpleasantly near. Morton felt the water on his body turn to ice all the way up his spinal column.

'Who is this?' he blustered angrily.

Morton barely heard the brief and chilling message that the voice then imparted. The underlying menace, more than the words, mesmerized him. All he could subsequently remember was that it was a warning, and that his days would be numbered if... but in the extreme shock to his system he had already forgotten the rest of it.

The phone was dead; the connection between him and someone of malevolent violence was broken. He replaced the receiver very gently on its cradle as if it might attack him and rang 1471 but the calm female-robot voice informed him the caller had withheld their number.

He went to the bay window of the darkened living room and looked out but Shandon Place was as quiet and unassuming as ever.

9

And there the McBain story might have ended. Morton had never reacted well to threats of violence. Of course, he was no stranger to knocks and injuries. Playing rugby, he'd broken his nose once and had had all the usual strains and pains. But physical fear is a strong motivating force and fear suppressed, fear untreated, fear at the base of one's personality spreads like cancer into one's self-worth. Fear rationalised is worse for it consumes the personality entirely, alters character permanently. Sometimes, in the night, Morton would wake, sweating, naked, vulnerable, a perpetual victim of evil men who were ominously near.

That anonymous voice on the telephone brought it back to him. His horror of uncontrollable violence, of serious injury, the gut-wrenching nausea of personal powerlessness. A man out there who knew his phone number and his address wanted to hurt him. He could reason that it must be something to do with his McBain investigations. But why? The two stories under his by-line were innocuous, merely sketching the circumstances of McBain's extraordinary demise, the extent of his lengthy service to the nationalist movement, his success against the nuclear industry. There was a summary of his interview with Mortimer and quotes from individuals about the lack of proper investigation by the authorities plus speculation on the gun's location. They were not out of the ordinary run of things, basic journalism, neutral news investigation, hadn't pointed fingers in any direction. The phone call unnerved him. Morton felt that he could not quite write it off as the work of a lone crank. He'd had anonymous calls before but never death threats. Could it be some kind of psychopathic political extremist? Had McBain's role been more sinister? What if McBain had been involved in a faction fight between extremist fringe groups, say Vanguard and Clann Alba? Or had he been working all along for British Intelligence to investigate these groups? What if...? But this was in the realms of fantasy. McBain may have assisted some fringe nutters with legal representation but no more than that. He was - had been - a solicitor, a veteran politician, not a terrorist or a spy. He was 81, for God's sake!

Morton was aware that the number of political extremists in Scotland, eight years after devolution, was miniscule, perhaps even single figures, maybe even just one lone nutter out there. Scotland was a douce place, the Scottish political world too small for prolonged bickering. But he was also aware of rumours of secret policemen operating in Scottish politics to prevent devolution sliding into full-scale independence. As the SNP continued to dominate Scottish politics, as tension remained high between Scotland and London, it was quite likely MI5 were searching for a new role and were deployed hunting subversives north of the border. Allegations of Special Branch infiltration of the SNP and anti-nuclear groups, of paid informants and *agents provocateur* had surfaced many times in prolonged and sensational trials of Scottish 'terrorists' in the early days before devolution but there was always a lack of real evidence of their actual existence. No, the perpetrator had to be a lunatic or one of those persons whose paranoid delusions extended to imagining themselves 'spies' for one cause or another. Luckily, there were few of those outwith secure mental institutions. Or were there? Was someone watching him? For some reason, he remembered the Lord Advocate talking about *adversaries*, but he wasn't one of those... was he?

Sometimes the best thing was simply to get bladdered, so wrecked you couldn't remember all of the crap that covered you from head to toe, all of the official bureaucratic pointless politically correct bullshit. McGinley often felt a world-weary cynicism of such overwhelming magnitude that it almost engulfed him. His years of service in the Protectorate, so different from military service, had tainted him with an underground smell, a fugitive sense of being an outsider. So often he had to work an operation on his own for long periods, surveillance, living under assumed names, under cover, dodging around, chasing targets who seemed far from dangerous or even criminal, just ordinary people leading apparently blameless lives. And all of the methodical skulduggery had not improved things as far as he could tell. So getting wasted was the answer when he felt like this. Then he could let off steam, take the edge off his tension, get so blasted that he was out of it for days. It was an escape, a solace and increasingly a habit with him. There was only one rule – go somewhere well away from any of his operational zones. Tonight he'd broken that rule. After the evening tele-conference with his section chief, he'd driven from Saltisburn into the centre of Glasgow. He'd been lured by the lights of the Merchant City and parked on the street. Then he'd entered a wine bar and he was only a quarter of a mile from the Old Hundred. At first, he drank slowly, savouring the alcohol, looked around at the other patrons of the wine bar – largely an early evening business clientele – the drink after work crowd. It was a comfortable red lit place, soft music, soft lights, and attractive women. That offered one possibility. There were, he noticed, several showing interest in him. But he shrugged the idea off, and started to concentrate on drinking. After his sixth pint he gave up beer and switched to doubles. He liked the fiery heart of the malt whiskies reflecting in the panes of the shot glass he held up to inspect. And then it happened.

'You're McGee?' the voice said behind him as if it didn't entirely believe it.

'Eh?' He swivelled slowly on his stool.

'I said – you're Daniel McGee.'

'Who?' he muttered thickly. The name truly meant nothing to him.

The grinning man was his own height, long hair, thin face, leather jacket. He did seem vaguely familiar. 'Christ, I'm no wrong but. What are *you* doing here, laddie?'

'Bugger off!' Daniel muttered.

'You're going up in the world, eh, Daniel, this place… and you look… like a different man. Bloody hell, I believe you're a copper. That's it, eh? You're no Daniel McGee at all. You're a… well, what the hell are you?'

'Who the fuck are *you*?'

'No remember me, Daniel boy? It's yer pal, Desmond O'Leary.'

Daniel tried to think but his thoughts were too scattered. 'Nope. Means nothing. No hard feelings, pal.'

'This is a mystery then,' O'Leary said pleasantly. 'A man who hangs out at the Old Hundred for weeks on end, claims to be on the dole, a good comrade, disappears and then turns up in this smart wine bar in an expensive suit… Armani unless I'm wrong… you can see how it looks.'

'Listen pal – Dermod whatever your name is – bugger off, or…'

O'Leary laughed. 'Or? There's an 'or' is there? Well, I'll be waiting outside, Daniel boy, just me… *or* a few mutual friends. *Bon Soir*.'

Daniel began to sober up very quickly then after the man had gone and his predicament began to become clear to him. He went to the toilet and urinated. He returned to the wine lounge. He was drunk, no question, his head clouded with the booze, his body slow and unpredictable. But if he knew he was drunk then he couldn't be, not really. He had only vague recall of Desmond O'Leary, some operation. Must be recent. He seemed to remember that O'Leary had been dismissed as any kind of threat. Was that wrong? He had to think. As he stood in the doorway, he smelled food and suddenly realized his stomach was empty and growling. There was a restaurant in the wine lounge – and surely there might be a back door? It took him seconds to discover there was a kitchen and a rear corridor beyond with the evening sky framed in an open backdoor. No-one stopped him. He looked but couldn't see anyone, stepped out between drums of cooking oil, crossed a small yard and peered through the open gateway into a street. Seemed to be no-one about. He set off up the road, passing the darkened shapes of cars parked beyond the range of streetlights and came out into a little lane that took him back to the main street. He kept walking, not looking behind, until he turned into Queen Street station then he slackened his pace and took a deep breath of cool night air. He'd been stupid but he'd got away with it. Most likely nothing would ever come of it and he certainly wasn't going to report it.

Edinburgh is a capital city of Georgian splendour, of dramatic cliffs of windows rearing up out of the fog, of stone *poseurs* everywhere, but Waverley Station undulates like a grimy sea of opaque and filthy glass below the fortress of the former *Scotsman* building, at the eastern edge of Princes Street Gardens and the Waverley Shopping Centre.

The Victorian interior is a chaos of snackbars, kiosks, traffic cones, workmen's huts, parked taxis, railings, waiting areas and modern superloos, so that the platforms are all but invisible. Gaggles of bemused tourists, dodging black cabs, delivery vans and luggage trolleys, seek in vain some central information point to discover the whereabouts of the platform for the London train.

Morton bought a *Guardian* and once he had a seat, glanced at the front page. The concourse was busy in early evening. He was careful not to glance towards the snackbar window where Elizabeth McBain sat, head over a polystyrene cup of coffee.

A tall and cadaverous scarecrow-looking man was looking down at him. 'Morton?' he mouthed, and sat down at the circular metal table, nervous in his loose, greyish-green woollen suit and heavy brown brogues. The shaggy moustache was the first thing Morton noticed about him, that, and the fact that the man was clearly ill-at-ease in the noisy open spaces of the station. His face was like an animated skull, its yellow skin stretched paper tight over his high cheekbones. The moustache almost entirely concealed his mouth and lips and the hair on his head was a writhing mass of disorder.

'You're the Customs & Excise man?' Morton queried.

The man looked over his shoulder. 'Yeah. Stoddard. But I don't want you to use my name. That's important.' He seemed to gobble his words so that they stuck in his throat. It was a curiously unpleasant sound and Morton found himself smiling.

'Why the need for all the secrecy?'

'That will become apparent.'

'So what do you want to tell me?'

'I hope you won't dismiss it as hearsay or rumour.' Stoddard coughed and fingered his moustache. 'I've been running an undercover investigation into drug smugglers in the West Highlands for the past eight months. I've got good contacts and I know the area very well. All my contacts, including several in the police tell me the McBain case is a scandal. Badly handled. A botched job.'

'Go on.'

Stoddard leaned forward confidentially. 'The police and procurator botched the whole thing. Nobody believes it was suicide. The reason I've come to you is I think there's a drug link. When I saw your story, I thought you might...' he tailed off.

'Hard to believe,' Morton sighed. 'Drug smugglers in Scotland don't often kill anyone unless it's another dealer. Not that I'm wanting to tell you your business, but in Bolivia, perhaps...'

'But it is my business and the West Coast of Scotland is the main seaboard in Europe for South American and Far East drug-runs. Most of the money is fronted from Germany and Holland. McBain was a damned nuisance to them. A populist politician with attitude, good local contacts at grassroots level. You know he put an advert in the *Inverness Times* asking for information on drug-smuggling? He was willing to pay - from his own pocket - for it.'

'His own money?'

'It was more than an electioneering gimmick.' The Customs officer shook his head and expostulated: 'I'll tell you what it was - it was an absolute invitation to get his brains blown out! He defended two men in North Morar who beat up drug-dealers and during the trial made it plain he knew a lot about drug-smuggling in the Highlands.'

'A high profile stance? Yes, but all this was years ago?'

'Well, he put himself out on a limb, well out.'

'Okay, Peter,' Morton concluded, 'I get the idea but have you any specific evidence he was a target now?'

Stoddard leaned closer. 'A friend of McBain's claimed, only a few days before... before his death, that he was talking about a breakthrough. His precise words were: "I've got

73

them, I've got them!" - spoken in an elated tone of voice. I believe...' Stoddard faltered, choking with phlegm which he wiped out of his almost-invisible mouth with a large white handkerchief, 'I believe this referred to information he had received about a big cartel.'

Morton fetched his notebook from his inside pocket. 'Who was this friend and how can I get in touch?'

'I only have his first name and a phone number,' Stoddard said, sliding the torn-off back of a cigarette packet across the metal tabletop. 'But if you speak to McBain's neighbours at Arisaig you'll find most also believe he was eliminated by drug-dealers. The idea is that he was only to be warned off but produced his own gun and so upped the stakes and had to be done away with.' Stoddard produced his cloth handkerchief and blew his nose noisily.

Morton could see Elizabeth out of the corner of his eye above them on the pedestrian walkway to North Bridge and saw her focus the long-lensed camera. 'You mentioned you were conducting an investigation in the area,' he said. 'Do you know of any groups who might have felt McBain to be a threat?'

Stoddard nodded vigorously. 'But I can't go into details. I was on the trail of a large syndicate, gets its money from Geneva and has connections in a lot of other places. My job was watching the Scottish end and I had several suspected couriers here under surveillance. Then rumours started to fly about McBain. And, Morton, a funny thing, many people in pubs and clubs in Nairn and Inverness were talking about McBain having been shot hours before that *Sunday Mail* article appeared about the cause of death.'

'That sounds pretty inconsequential, Peter,' Morton said impatiently, 'I mean, rumours about rumours?'

'Yes, but the point is, people seemed to be in the know.'

'But which people? Where?'

Stoddard ignored this. 'At first there was talk that the shooting might have been accidental, something to do with poachers. It's a prime area for deer coming near the road. But of course, the poachers are even more tight-lipped than the police and there's no way of getting closer to that rumour...'

'Poachers?' Morton snorted, incredulously. 'McBain was killed with a revolver!'

'Yes. So I discounted it. And the Masonic connection.'

'I don't believe I'm hearing this! I'm sorry, but this is *crap*!'

'Oh no, Morton, the Masonic Lodges are very strong in the West Highlands. Most people I've come into contact with are sure that it's a drug-killing. But this is where it gets odd. I was in the middle of the investigation, as I said. Eight months in - and just beginning to get somewhere. We had a beach site, a possible vessel and two suspected couriers in Scotland. Interpol was keeping tabs on a German Swiss who'd made two trips to the area within the eight months. Then I was called in to my superior's office and told to call off the investigation. I wasn't pleased and I said so, but there was nothing I could do. Then two days later I heard I was to be transferred to a new posting -- in Bristol.'

'Yeah? But, um, what's this to do with McBain?'

'I'm just about to tell you,' Stoddard said.

'Well. Sorry. Go on.'

'Well, it *was* promotion and I had put in for promotion, but I did not want this particular job - especially not at short notice, in the middle of my investigation, but it was made pretty clear to me that I had to take it or resign. Anyway, the point is, this all happened two days after I'd interviewed the person whose phone number I've given you. Two days after I'd spoken to my superior about the possibility of a link with McBain and the two men who'd beaten up the drug-dealers of Kintail and two days after I'd requested copies of the court transcripts.'

'Interesting,' Morton said. 'Thank you for coming to me with this. I'll certainly check-it out. By the way...' he added as a sudden afterthought, 'do you know anything about a guy called Drysdale. Euan Drysdale?'

Stoddard stood up. 'No. Who's Drysdale? Anyway, look, Morton, if I can help in any way, contact me again. Also I'd quite like to know if you discover anything of interest.'

'Certainly,' Morton said, adding a silent 'not' to himself as he walked to his rendezvous with Elizabeth McBain. Why should Stoddard deny knowing Drysdale's name when his hooded eyes, by an imperceptible flicker which Morton had not missed, had made it quite plain that he did? Morton had never trusted volunteers and it was, he smiled to himself, a racing certainty that Stoddard was a volunteer. Morton just had that feeling that he was being manipulated. But it was too crude, too obvious. He took out the piece of cigarette packet and looked at it. Odd. He was fairly certain that Stoddard didn't smoke.

10

If the forensic report wasn't going to be made public, then maybe Morton could find another way in? That was his thinking as he sat in the car keeping a wary eye on the entrance of the cold store on the Kingsway in the city of Dundee, an hour north of Edinburgh. He had no idea what Professor Donald Blasher looked like. What do forensic experts look like? He imagined a weedy academic or a boorish boozer cracking sick jokes about the bits of bodies which were his stock in trade.

At 10.30am, he locked the Beetle and presented himself at the Reception desk in the glass podium. He was told Blasher was already in, in and working.

'Walk around tae loadin bay 5 and ask someone fur tae show you Freezer A,' the smiling bottle-blonde told him. Her eyes and smiles were all for the white-coated man in the white plastic hat too small for him who leaned over the counter and resumed chatting her up as soon as Morton reached the door.

In the first loading bay, men were humping pallets of frozen green bean packets into a lorry that was almost the size of the *QEII*. In the third bay, vast trays of turkeys in coloured cling film were being shipped out. In the fifth bay, two men lounged against a pillar, rolling smokes. They had large metal hooks dangling from their belts.

'Lookin for someone, like?' the older man asked warily.

'Professor Blasher.'

'Oh aye, police doctor boy?'

'Loading bay 5?'

.'Aye, he's in there. You need to go in by the side door. See the handle - gie it a bluidy good yank.'

'Mak shair ye pull it closed ahent ye, an a,' added the younger man with a cheeky grin, 'the Prof disnae like to be disturbed and a rush o cald air can disturb whit he's daein.'

The other man was unaccountably laughing. 'Sensitive work, see,' he explained. 'Detailed. Expecting ye is he?'

Morton frowned. 'Yes. Thank you.'

The handle was stiff but Morton, aware of being watched minutely by the workmen, exerted sudden pressure and it opened inwards. He tripped over something in the dark and fell headlong inside.

In the course of trying to get to his feet from the cold concrete floor in the dark, he groped something cold. Very cold and very dead. He scrabbled frantically for the door and burst out into the bright sunlight where the workmen were roaring their heads off.

'Very funny,' he said sourly, dusting his kneecaps.

'Hoy, you've left the door open!'

'You fucking close it. You work here.'

He returned to Reception. The blonde was still coo-ing with the man in the white coat.

'No find him?' she asked idly.

'No,' he grunted.

'Aw, I'd better take you myself,' the man said. 'The quick way, eh?' He winked at the girl. 'See ye later, Tracey.'

'Busy round here?' Morton asked pointedly.

'Yeah, all year round. This is the quick way. Through here.'

'No. After you.'

The man led him through a series of metal bulkheads at the end of a long concrete-floored corridor. There was a series of ramps leading off a central yard stacked high with pallets.

'This is the fire-escape, actually,' his guide told him. 'Runs the length of the building.'

They had reached a circular iron stair in a narrow well, down which they descended, casting dim-lit shadows on the white walls.

'Now, second on the right is the Prof's office.'

'You're not coming with me?'

'Na. Important business,' he winked, then, seeing the look on Morton's face, said; 'Don't worry he is in.'

Blasher turned out to be a quite ordinary - and youngish - man whom Morton thought he recognised. He stood in the doorway.

'Welcome to the Police Forensic Laboratory,' Blasher said grandly, offering his hand.

'How do I know you? Were you on TV?'

Blasher made a comical face. 'Indeed I was. I carried out the post-mortem in Kabul of three aid workers shot by British soldiers. But that was two years ago. Surprised you even remember. Shall we sit down?'

The office was a small, partitioned-off area. Through the open door, Morton could see what looked like large fridges.

Blasher had noticed his gaze. 'Yes, those are freezers. That's where we keep the evidence until court proceedings or burial. I've got some peculiar specimens in there. Poached deer, confiscated salmon, murder victims, my lunch...' He laughed pleasantly. 'All victims of some dastardly deed or other. Except my lunch of course. Anyway, what can I do for you?'

'I'm investigating a suspicious death and I'm looking for advice on the forensic side of things.' After a pause, he added; 'It's the Angus McBain case.'

'Oh ho, yes, I read about it. Who did the P.M.?'

Morton had to consult his notebook. 'Fishbourne, a Dr Henry Fishbourne, a consultant pathologist.'

'Pathologist? At Raigmore? Odd.'

'What's odd?'

'Well, the best forensic expert in the country - the man who trained me, incidentally - is based at Forresterhill, in Aberdeen. Just an hour and a half away by road. Would have thought he might have done the P.M. I've never heard of this Henry Fishbourne. Still, maybe old Jock McArthur was on holiday or something. He is the best man for a job like that.'

'Is it a highly-specialised job?'

'Very. Only about half a dozen chaps in Scotland have the skill to do a P.M. of that complexity. I did read about this case in the papers. Seems to me it was a pathologist's nightmare. Would you like some coffee? First, I'd better take these rubber gloves off.' He grinned and laughed lugubriously. 'Sometimes I forget I have them on. The wife's always complaining. Won't be a minute,' he said, stripping off the gloves and tossing them in the direction of a plastic bin. 'So you're a freelance you said?'

Blasher went to the sink and filled a beaker with water. He placed it on a metal stand above a bunsen burner which he ignited with a battery lighter and adjusted till the flame was bright blue and silent.

'Yeah. I used to be a staffer but although it's tricky making ends meet, I suppose I prefer the freedom.'

'In a way, I'm a freelance too,' Blasher told him. 'I'm employed jointly by the Health Board and the Police and I work some of the time with the University Teaching Hospital.'

'Sounds like three jobs to me!'

'Haha. Only one salary though.' He grinned. 'Death's my real paymaster. There's good money in it you know. So who are you working up the McBain case for?'

'The *Scottish Standard*, I suppose.'

'So how may I help you?'

'I was hoping actually you might be able to help me get a copy of the P.M. report,' Morton said tentatively, grimacing in embarrassment.

Blasher looked up slowly and his smile had faded. 'I doubt it. There'll probably only be two copies of it and they'll be under lock and key. This is a sensitive case. Did you think I could just phone up and order a copy as if it was the evening paper?'

'I thought... for research purposes...?'

'No way!'

'I suppose I could try his next-of-kin?'

'That might be a better idea.'

Morton decided he had liked Blasher and, as he walked to the car, was pleased that the Prof had been helpful enough to give him a twenty page file of detailed notes on the conduct of post-mortems and a file on handgun deaths and a page on suicides. Morton felt that it had been a worthwhile morning. He decided to continue on to Falkirk to speak again to David Cochrane. Driving somewhere - anywhere - was giving him the illusion of progress and he enjoyed steering the Beetle and hearing its reassuring puttering engine. He joined the ring-road, heading for Perth and the A9. He remembered Cochrane lived at Carronshore, near the Kincardine Bridge.

Once over the Kincardine Bridge, Morton easily located Carronshore and Castle Avenue but Cochrane wasn't in. As he was about to drive away, Morton saw him walking down the street.

'Remember me?'

'Sure,' Cochrane said, unenthusiastically, unlocking the front door. 'You're the journalist. Come in. Place is a shitheap.'

'You should see mine.'

The two-roomed Council flat was redolent of unwashed socks. Books and unwashed plates and mugs were scattered around the floors in both rooms. Approximately ten thousand ink-smelling copies of *Scottish Resistance* newsletters were stacked in a corner. Had no-one told him the SNP were in power?

Cochrane filled a kettle from the tap at the steel sink. 'I had the polis round a couple of days ago again - and they asked me about you,' he said. 'You been up to something?'

'Me?' Morton frowned. 'Why?'

'They wanted to know if I knew you.'

'What did you tell them?'

Cochrane found two odd mugs in a cupboard. 'Just that we'd had a wee talk about McBain. They were plain-clothes boys, not local. From London, I think. Probably Special Branch.'

Morton frowned. 'Oh? What did they want? I thought you'd already told them everything you knew, David? They weren't Customs Officers by any chance? There's a possibility McBain was on the track of some major drug-dealers.'

'Well, maybe,' Cochrane sniffed, as he spooned instant coffee in to the mugs, 'but they never mentioned anything about that sort of stuff.'

'No mention of drugs – or…' he glanced around at the pile of newspapers… 'or, say, Vanguard or Clann Alba?'

'No. Nothing like that. Believe me, I wasn't too polite. It was like they knew nothing at all about Angus. In the end I told them to go and read the files at Glasgow CID.' He grinned. 'They weren't too chuffed. But there is, you know, a limit to the number of times you can tell the same old story without getting pissed off. Sugar? No? Okay. Oh, by the way, I forgot something when we talked before.'

'Important?' Morton asked hopefully.

'Yeah. Remember when I told you that the policeman at the scene...'

'PC McGrath?'

'... handed me a holdall and asked me to collect up McBain's things? Well, I forgot to tell you about the pile of torn papers.'

Morton expressed incredulity. 'What's this?' He got out his notebook.

'Aye,' Cochrane explained. 'You're not going to believe this. See, I put my hand inside the smashed rear window and collected a couple of books, a Bible and a half-empty bottle of whisky and put them in the holdall he gave me. I told you that already, but I had a quick look around and about and it was then I saw the neat pile about fifteen yards up the slope from the car towards the road. How we'd missed it on the way down I don't know. There was a credit card, bits of a bill from a garage and a watch with a smashed face piled neatly. The watch was sitting on top.'

Morton exhaled loudly and closed his eyes. He ran a hand over his hair. He picked at a spot on his left ear and finally asked 'so, did anyone else see this?'

Cochrane shrugged. 'Dunno. I showed the policeman. In fact, the policeman only believed me that the body in the car *was* McBain when he read the name on the torn bill.'

'Did you tell the Procurator this?'

'I think so.'

'I hope so. Makes it look more like a suicide though.'

Cochrane protested. 'Not to me. No. I've thought and thought about this. McBain was jammed - totally stuck - into the car. The door was wedged into the ground, right? Now, there's no way he could have placed the neat pile there and then had the crash. And if the stuff just fell out when the car came down the hill, how come it was in such a neat pile? How come the bill was torn up and the watch was smashed?'

'What did the Procurator say when you told him? Assuming you did tell him?'

'Frankly, I can't remember, but he must have known about it from the policeman's statement. And... and when they were showing me the photographs, one of the yellow crosses marked the neat pile of torn papers.'

'You're sure? David, how many crosses were there?'

'A few. The car, the pile of papers, the gun probably.'

'They didn't tell you?'

'No, but what else could it be? It was some distance away from the cross marking the car's location. You've already asked me all this before,' he complained.

'I know, but maybe we can jog your memory. How far?'

Cochrane pulled a wry face. 'Ach, now you're asking me to guess. Some distance.' He thought hard. 'About maybe two or three times the distance from the cross marking the car's position to the cross marking the pile of torn papers. That's the best I can do.'

'So - that would make it about... thirty or forty yards away from the car?'

'Well – maybe,' Cochrane said doubtfully.

'They've more or less admitted that it was thirty yards or so. Very far if this is supposed to be suicide. You'd expect someone throwing the gun that distance to end up with their arm outside the car. The window was fully wound down?'

'Yes.'

Well, David - Mortimer told me - indirectly - that the gun was about thirty yards away.' Morton closed his eyes tightly in an effort to remember. 'What did he say exactly...? He said: "further away than if it had just fallen from his grasp..." those were his exact words, though he didn't disagree with thirty yards, which I mentioned several times.'

'I'm amazed he even agreed to see you,' Cochrane said, 'not that you seemed to have got much out of him. I wish he would decide to hold a Fatal Accident Inquiry and get everything over and done with once and for all.'

'It would be better if he did,' Morton agreed, talking to himself in his empty car, ten minutes later as he headed back to Edinburgh. Then he suddenly remembered he'd forgotten to ask about Euan Drysdale. 'Damn it to hell!' he cursed loudly, then rolled down the window to let the rush of cold air cool him down. He hated to have proof of his own inefficiency.

McGinley had been forced to own up to his cover being blown but had managed to make it seem accidental. The incident had been transposed to Queen Street station. No mention of alcohol in any shape or form. And it had now occurred in the afternoon, not the drunken night. McGinley knew that O'Leary wasn't about to contradict him.

Jo Haines took the news calmly when he phoned over his weekly report. 'These things happen. Anyway, you were on secondment to the Department at the time. Nothing is going to come back on us. I'll pass this on to them. With any luck, this O'Leary will assume you were from Special Branch anyway.'

'It's the first time I've been made,' Daniel agreed. 'Irritating, all the same.

'We're not perfect individually Daniel. It's teamwork that makes us winners. Teamwork. Not your forte exactly, is it?'

Daniel started to react before he detected that she was teasing him. That was almost worse than being ballocked. Anyway, there'd be no more need for Daniel McGee – he could grow his moustache back and return to normal duties.

Morton was still feeling out of sorts and irritated with himself as he parked the car a few streets away from his home in the first space he saw. He noticed a dark estate car double-parked outside number 13. There was something intent about the head of the man sitting behind the wheel, staring ahead of him. Morton turned and walked back down Shandon Place and loitered at the corner behind the phone box then he went in and pretended to use the phone and kept an eye on the car.

But he couldn't keep up the pretence for ever. Nobody used public phone boxes anymore and it looked odd him being in there so he put down the receiver and returned to his car and sat inside. He gave them quarter of an hour and returned to the corner. The car was still there. He began to feel rather annoyed and his empty belly was complaining audibly.

It was another hour before he saw the car leave, heading out to Slateford Road.

As he stepped round into Shandon Place, he spotted the other man standing just inside the doorway of the tenement opposite his and also noticed that the car had turned and was coming back!

Morton fled to his car. He studied the mirrors for some minutes before driving off and heading down into Morningside where he found a quiet street and parked. He sat wondering what to do. Who were these people and what did they want? He remembered Cochrane telling him about the plain-clothes policemen from London asking about him. Then there'd been that awful threat on the phone. What did they want from him? Eventually, he got out his Blackberry and called his solicitor's home number.

Archie MacDonald was senior partner in his family's firm of solicitors. Classmates at George Watson's, where they hadn't been great friends, but MacDonald lived well in Morningside and had often invited him to dine with his wife and three children. Or was it four? Morton had so far avoided this and one of the reasons was - he couldn't remember the name of Archie's wife. Archie had handled the divorce and various related property transactions. Morton was parked only three streets away, so he easily found the address.

MacDonald opened the glass door of the inner hall and ushered Morton into the parlour.

It had been a year or more since Morton had seen him and he thought Archie was looking old and stooped, bowed beneath the kind of responsibilities which he himself didn't have. Family and business worries, employees.

'Always happy to help, Willie, you know that.'

'I have a bit of a problem.'

'Fire away, old bean.'

'You're sure you're not too busy...?'

After outlining the situation to Archie, Morton phoned his downstairs neighbour, Philip Barron, and asked him to give a message to the two men in the car outside. Philip was an acquaintance and no fan of the police but he was a decent chap and he and Morton had had long chats on the stair.

'Thanks a bunch, Philip, it's about a story I'm working on. Tell them to meet me at my solicitor's office tomorrow at 2pm. Halbron, Finlay & MacDonald, Torphichen Street. Then ring me back.'

In ten minutes it was accomplished. Barron had relayed the message and the men had apparently agreed to the arrangement, though without identifying themselves. They had driven off. Who *were* they? And what business did they have with him, Morton wondered, as he drove to his parents' house in Merchiston Crescent, reluctantly accepting the necessity of spending a night there.

He phoned Elizabeth from his parents'. He was feeling drained and listless. He wished he could see her in person. He liked her company and missed her reassuring common-sense. She reported the details of her interview with Euan Drysdale but it didn't sound promising.

'Drysdale seemed more interested in me than in my uncle's death. Mind you, when I finally got him on the subject, I felt that he knew more than he was telling me.'

'Knew what?'

'I don't know it was just a feeling that he was being cautious. I wasn't there long enough to find out. My first time inside a prison. I'd always wondered what they would be like. Useful experience.'

Even although she'd volunteered, Morton suspected that the visit had shaken her a little. He was surprised to find he didn't like the idea of her being anywhere near violent men.

11

During the hours of darkness while Willie Morton's body lay inert, he sank into ever deeper fathoms of narcosis. Peculiar things were happening to him with a vividness rarely encountered in daily life. Angus McBain, a puffy red demon in crumpled suit was his guide through an underworld of febrile imaginings. He awoke with the terror of the fugitive and by the time he had opened and closed his eyes a few dozen times he knew the paranoia would remain with him.

He felt his caffeine addiction kick in and went down to the kitchen. His parents' kitchen. Home, but no longer his. Being at his parents' house reminded him of his juvenile days, made him feel insecure.

The voices susurrated in the muffled gloom of the New Town office.

'My client is concerned that you are apparently attempting to impede him in his business as a freelance journalist,' said Archie MacDonald wearily. 'He has no extra information - except that which he has gleaned from freely available sources, all of which you have already consulted. He has, quite simply, nothing whatsoever to tell you.'

The solicitor's face was laden with occupational gravitas, the effects of overeating and under-exercise. Large reddish pouches hung beneath the eyes which were faintly pink and glistened in the dim natural light. It was hard for Morton to believe Archie was his own age. They had spent their schooldays each unaware of the other, having little in common. MacDonald had been in the middle-to-bottom of the Latin stream, while Morton had topped the bottom half of the year which had been streamed into Woodwork. Later divisions between history and geography, science and arts had confused the social divide but that first cruel segregation by supposed academic ability at the age of 12, had left Morton with an almost imperceptible inferiority complex.

The police solicitor, whose name Morton couldn't remember, pursed purple lips. There was the look of a predator about him, the prominent nose, nest of dark hair lying flat at the back of his bony skull. 'Why then does your client seek to avoid an interview? Hardly the actions of someone who knows nothing?'

'This *is* the interview.' MacDonald raised his ponderous eyebrows in exasperation. 'Really. Mr. Morton is a busy journalist attempting to make a living. He has no time to brief all and sundry on stories which he is researching. The local police here and in Glasgow are fully aware - fully aware - of the details of the McBain case. The matter was the subject of a thorough and lengthy investigation by a Procurator Fiscal and even the Scottish Office. Mr. Morton is attempting to obtain *some* of the information which the authorities already hold. I suggest you consult them if you wish to pursue this matter. Unless you leave my client alone, I shall pursue, on his behalf, an action for harassment. Do I make myself clear, gentlemen?'

The tension in the room was rising. Morton had not spoken, and neither had the man called McGinley, described by the solicitor as a "special investigator", code, Morton suspected for Special Branch. McGinley sat impassively on the other side of the room. He had the face and physique of a good prop forward, Morton thought, and the manners of a suave brute. He wondered if it had been his voice on the telephone that night.

'Very well, let us come to specifics,' the police solicitor said. 'The particular subject area which we wish to pursue with Mr. Morton concerns Euan Drysdale.'

MacDonald glanced at Morton, who shook his head and scowled.

'I believe that my client...' MacDonald began, 'does not...'

Morton interceded. 'Never met anyone called Euan Drysdale.'

The solicitor said, 'Drysdale is presently being held on remand in Shotts, facing charges of sending incendiary materials through the mail to various government ministers.'

'Sorry. I can't help you,' Morton said. 'But what's his connection to McBain?'

There was no reply. The police solicitor shifted in his seat. 'I find it hard, given the evidence I have, that Mr. Morton can claim to have no knowledge of Drysdale?'

Morton recognised the danger ahead. 'I knoweth not that whereof ye seek,' he said jovially, wondering whether Elizabeth could give him chapter and verse. He wondered if Special Branch knew about his meetings with her and Angus and her mission to Drysdale in prison. They probably would.

The hawkish man was looking expectantly in his direction. 'You have heard of him, though?' he asked, frowning deeply.

'Have you also met him? Or is it just that you've heard of him?'

MacDonald coughed behind his hand and intervened. 'To reiterate, my client is perfectly happy to assist the police with inquiries relating to matters under investigation and is willing here and now to answer any specific questions put to him. He has answered your query of Drysdale. He does not know of such a man and has certainly not met him. Since the man concerned is in prison, it is unlikely that he will meet him. Now, my client is not prepared to co-operate with lengthy and pointless interviews repeating information already held by the police. This would clearly intrude upon his civil liberties. Unless specific reasons can be given now, I will raise an action. I am suspending this interview.'

McGinley was on his feet and coming across the room. 'Take care of yourself now, especially on the roads,' he said jeeringly.

Archie MacDonald looked aghast. 'What the devil is that supposed to mean? Is that a... a threat?'

The police solicitor hastily intervened, ushering McGinley out. 'No, no. Merely a solicitation for the welfare of your client.'

'Goodbye. See you around,' McGinley jeered.

'Not if I see you first,' Morton said, quietly.

'Nasty!' MacDonald opined, when they were alone. 'Who would think we actually pay the wages of those barbarians. They were, quite frankly, little short of being out and out thugs.'

Morton returned home, a little warily, but there was no-one waiting to waylay him. He'd have to buy a bottle of something good for Philip. The phone rang. It was Elizabeth McBain.

'I've managed to have a chat, rather brief, with my father and have some information and some photographs,' she said. 'We were intending to come round this evening... if you're not busy.'

'About seven,' he agreed. He still felt a bit jittery.

He felt a sudden compulsion to tidy-up the flat and got out the hoover, which he could barely remember how to operate. He dusted ledges and nooks and crannies and even dragged a limp cloth around the window panes and did the dishes. As a last-minute gesture he squirted an air freshener around the flat. Elizabeth McBain was half his age, well, sixteen years younger, but he didn't want her to think him a slob.

She arrived almost an hour late and she was on her own, wearing jeans, white tee-shirt and brown suede jacket. 'Angus could not come,' she explained. 'I hadn't checked with him and he had another engagement. After what you told me on the phone, I was wondering all the way over here whether I was being followed.'

He stared at her. 'Do you think you were?'

She laughed. 'I wasn't being entirely serious, you know. Still, I suppose it is a possibility... goodness knows why.'

Morton walked to the window and stood looking down at Shandon Place and the junction with Merchiston Grove through the blinds. 'Well, there doesn't seem to be anyone there now.'

'Anyway, what do the Special Branch want of us?'

Morton frowned and ran a hand through his long hair. 'It was more a sort of warning shot across the bows. But it convinces me, even if I wasn't convinced before, that something's going on. I didn't tell you before, but I got an anonymous phone call - threatening me. Sounds stupid, I know, but there it is.'

Elizabeth's face coloured. 'Oh, that's awful,' she said.

He told her about it while he got out a bottle of wine from the fridge and poured two glasses.

'Anyway, that's enough of that. Have a glass of this. Now, what have you got for me?'

'I asked my father straight-out whether he had seen the post-mortem report. He said he had. So I asked him if I could see it. He simply said "it's not for your eyes" and walked away. I can't ask him again. I don't want to push him. He's on the edge, emotionally. I simply can't do any more. And if he won't even talk to me now, there's little chance he'd speak to anyone else - especially not a journalist.'

'Right. You tried. So we're back to square one. We don't know if he has an actual copy of the report, although what he said seems to imply he does.'

'I still think he doesn't. More likely he had a meeting where he saw it.'

'You don't think that somebody's got to him?'

Elizabeth started. 'Threatened him? No. You don't know him. He'd never ever be intimidated. No more than my uncle would be.'

'He seems unduly scared of publicity. They were very close, I believe?'

'Very.'

Morton sat back and sipped the wine. 'I wish I could get a clear picture of Angus in my mind. What kind of man he was. His mind-set, to use the jargon.'

Elizabeth pushed her hair back behind what he noted were small and delicate ears. 'I don't know what I can tell you about my uncle. I loved him dearly.'

'Well, what was the best thing about him?'

'Best thing... generosity. Not just with money. He was generous with everyone. He always had time for people. He was patient - but he hated anything that wasn't the absolute unvarnished truth. Hypocrisy, white lies, euphemisms, half-truths. He was a plain speaker, dealing in hard facts. He liked to cut the flannel and get to the bottom line. Sometimes perhaps, he was a little...'

'Tactless?' Morton queried gently.

'Blunt. The devious use of language to create mystification or obfuscation enraged him. He was always coming across it - legal jargon.' Her voice softened. 'Of course he himself liked to throw, right into the middle of a conversation, the occasional obscure Scots word which no-one else understood. I think the power of language attracted him. He always talked about writing a book.'

'Oh! And did he?'

'I don't think so. He had all the cuttings, the Knoydart Inquiry, his school photo, war service records, pictures of him in India after the war. But I doubt whether publishers would have been terribly interested. Poor Angus. He'd maybe left it a little too late.'

There was nothing for Morton to say. He had the mental image of McBain, cigarette in hand at his desk, poring over yellowing cuttings with time passing, years going by. *Where had the excitement gone?*

'I always thought of him as being a big man,' Elizabeth continued, 'although he was only five feet seven, heavy though. He was always around our house. Lived on his own, always had done but really he wasn't much good at the domestic life.' She smiled wistfully. 'Sometimes he'd wear shirts until they were black with grime, then he'd throw them into the laundry basket but since he often forgot to go to the laundry, the shirts would often appear out of the basket for a second coming. Or he'd buy a dozen new shirts and simply throw them out when they got too crumpled and dirty.' She pushed back into the sofa. 'I suppose he was a fairly good cook when he wanted to be but mostly he lived in restaurants and cafes.'

'He never married?'

Elizabeth sensed the implication behind the question: 'Oh, he had female friends and I believe that he proposed to at least one of them but she had second thoughts or something. He often used to say "who would have me?" or "I like women too much to inflict myself on one of them." He was always putting himself down. It was just his way.'

There was a long pause. The wine was finished. Morton stood up and began pacing the room. 'Okay, Elizabeth, what do we have so far? Firstly, Angus was stuck fast in the car which rolled or was pushed - down the hill but failed to go into the loch. Its location on the small plateau might have been a result of not enough speed to run it into the water. Secondly, he's shot in the temple, with what we must presume was his own gun. Gun found two days later an impossible distance from the car. Yes? Impossible distance because both his hands are inside the car.'

'But of course, Willie, the car had been removed before the gun was found, so there is scope for considerable inaccuracy, isn't there?'

'True, true, but even the Lord Advocate agrees it was found suspiciously far from the car's location, so I see no reason to doubt that as a fact. Then there's the neat pile placed where Angus couldn't have been. Who would bother to break credit-cards and watch and dump them in a pile up the hillside? Surely if there was someone there at the time they would have either have stolen them or left them in the car?'

'It's very odd,' Elizabeth agreed, smiling faintly.

'Then there are the background facts. No alcohol in his bloodstream. Given what had happened previously in his flat and from what I know now about your uncle he'd have been sure to have a *deoch an dorus* before excuse me - topping himself.'

She winced. 'I think so.'

'Agreed, the road is tricky, especially in the dark, but Angus knew it well. Then there's the fire episode. Does that suggest a suicide attempt or an unfortunate accident?'

'Accident. He liked his neighbours and there's no way I see my uncle recklessly endangering their lives. I think we can rule out the fire in the flat as a suicide attempt. And the crash. That's not suicide either,' she concluded firmly.

'*Can* we rule it out, entirely?'

'Almost no-one who knew him closely can even begin to believe it,' Elizabeth said quietly, chin thrust forward. 'Even my father. I think his attitude has a lot more to do with a sense of betrayal - that Angus might have done something behind his back - and shame that further investigation could lead to dishonour or embarrassment to the family than to a real belief in his brother's suicide.'

'Let's move on. What did he mean by "I've got them! I've got them!" Got what, who? What had he found out?'

'Who heard him say that?' Elizabeth asked.

'Acquaintance of his, a man called Mackay, whom he met in Sauchiehall Street, on the Wednesday. I spoke to him on the phone. Stoddard gave me his number.'

'What did it mean?'

'Wish I knew. Mackay took the trouble to write to the *Scotsman* to bring it to public attention. He doesn't know what it meant, or why Angus should select him as a confidante. Those were his only words, in response to Mackay's greeting, and he hurried away without elucidation. Mackay says Angus was intensely preoccupied, sort of elated. Stoddard, mentioned the use of the phrase in a drug context but Mackay doesn't believe Angus's death was a murder by drug-dealers. He does think it possible Angus had information on drug-smuggling but doubts whether it was important-enough to lead to his death.'

'What do you think about Stoddard anyway? He was rather peculiar wasn't he? Odd-looking, too.'

Morton grinned. 'Ugliness isn't a crime, but there *was* something furtive about him. Shot out of the station quick-enough too, yet what he gave us wasn't really such a big deal. Not enough to have him disciplined. I'm still not sure what to make of him. Don't trust him of course. Then there's the mystery about the post-mortem at Inverness when the top man was at Aberdeen? We could make too much of that of course. May just have been procedural problems.'

'But there is no easy explanation for your harassment by the Special Branch - or for the death threat you received.'

Morton combed his fingers through his hair. 'There certainly isn't. You're right, Elizabeth. But what am I supposed to find? What do they think I might stumble on?'

'What did my uncle know?' Elizabeth wondered. 'What did he know that they think you might find out? And who are "they" anyway?'

12

Elizabeth's question remained unanswered. In the meantime, Morton's daily existence seemed to become increasingly hindered by minor unexplained irritations. His answerphone had begun to receive lengthy but utterly silent messages. The dial would reveal that he had six messages waiting but each would prove to be completely blank. He had no option, after a few days of this, other than to switch off the machine altogether. He couldn't see what was wrong with it.

One morning his car wouldn't start and he spent half an hour patiently pressing the accelerator, clutch and choke, to no avail. He waited for the garage to send round a mechanic to look at it. When the man eventually arrived, it took him half an hour to discover the problem; a large quantity of sugar in the petrol tank.

'Happens,' the mechanic assured him. 'Not very often though. Probably just vandals.'

Morton was unconvinced. 'But the petrol cap is still locked. There's no sign that it's been forced.'

The mechanic smiled at his naivety. 'Lots of people make keys. Beetles have been around for nearly forty years.'

'But why didn't they simply steal the car?'

'I dunno. Maybe somebody has a grudge against you? It's hard to tell. Whoever did it must have been standing here in the street for at least five minutes. Somebody might have seen them. You'd better go to the police and report it. For insurance purposes at least. It'll not be cheap to sort it out, I'm afraid.'

'I need the car. It's essential for work.'

The mechanic nodded, wiping his hands on a rag. 'I'll speak to my guvnor. Maybe we can take it in as an emergency.'

These were irritations, nothing more, but, taken together, they began to suggest conspiracy - or paranoia. Was he being paranoid?

At least he now had legitimate reasons for continuing to investigate the McBain case. He had begun to write a book about it. An unexpected message left at the *Standard* for Hugh Leadbetter by Bob Cameron, the messianic boss of Rannoch Books, had turned out to be a commission to write an 80,000 word manuscript on McBain's death. Morton had not previously written a book but Cameron had surprising faith that he could do it. He went to see him. Fingering his virile black beard as he leaned back against dangerously overstacked shelves in his third floor office in Great Frederick Street, Cameron expounded this belief to a dubious Morton.

'It's not a book about a mysterious death, Willie. No, it's to be a book about a *murder*. Or at least, it's a book about a murder investigation that may prove to be a suicide. See what I mean? We need a new angle. Its great material, the biggest unsolved mystery in modern Scottish politics.'

'Well… hardly…' Morton demurred. 'McBain wasn't an elected…'

'But the book must be definite, forceful, not waffle. I know you can do it.'

'Well, I hope I can,' Morton said.

'It's only a matter of scale. You went to university didn't you, wrote essays, what, three thousands words, probably a dissertation in your final year…?

'Uh-huh. That's long ago.'

'Ten thousand word dissertation?'

'I think so.'

'And I know you've done features about three thousand words.'

'Four or five times.'

'Well, then. Get to it, m'boy. The key is in the timing. You've got a full two months.'

Morton almost fell off his chair. 'You're joking?'

'Well, you can have eight weeks if you prefer...'

'Eighty thousand words... in two months? I'll never manage it!'

'Och, easy! Some advice; start by making a full cuttings file, collect all the pieces that have appeared about McBain. Do a solid background biographical chapter, then a chapter about the crash-scene based on witness testimony, mainly David...'

'Cochrane.'

'Yes, and any others you can find. Then it's a question of a chapter on each stage of your investigations, preliminary, the interview with Mortimer, use quotes from Stevenson... and so on. Then, if you like, we can collaborate on the first and final chapters and the various blurbs we'll need. Think tabloid values, Willie. We must have something new, a new twist of some kind. Revelations. Scandals. Names must be named. I see this book in the Scottish bestsellers chart for months.'

And so Morton switched on the angle poise lamp and word processor in his study and sluiced his palate with a mouthful of milky Nescafe. Then wandered back into the kitchen and then into the lounge and switched on the TV. There was a news report about some event... the one o'clock gun and the saltire flag which hung above Edinburgh Castle. Why did it have to be so big? He wondered how many yards across it measured. Bloody boastfully enormous. We *arra bloody peepul!* Except we aren't, he thought, not really or not yet. And then he returned to the spare bedroom and sat, fist clenched around the mug of coffee, dreading that the story was going cold on him. What he was engaged upon was nothing less than the disinterring of Angus McBain. He was walking at midnight in bone orchards, stepping through skeletons, probing layers of ossification and deceit.

So he went back over the old trails, wearily, but with more thoroughness, looking for the important piece he'd missed first time around. A second interview with Nicholas Mortimer QC was out of the question and Dennison's phone was out of order, but he spoke again to the elderly Donalds by telephone in their chintzy sitting-room and learned nothing new. The First Minister's office refused his request for another interview on the grounds that McBain's death was a private family matter. The only people Morton could still find to talk to were Malcolm Farquharson, David Cochrane and Elizabeth and Angus McBain. But he needed to get deeper into his subject. He needed to connect with the living spirit of Angus McBain if that was possible, get inside the man's skin.

After a few phone calls and a fast train through to Glasgow, he sat in a stuffy, subterranean-smelling projection room at BBC Scotland. As his eyes adjusted to the coffin-like dark, light suddenly filtered down from the projection room at the rear. The technician's voice was muffled by his ever-present cigarette (against regulations).

'Can't hear,' Morton shouted.

'That better? I've stitched the clips back-to-back. I can copy it onto a DVD which you can take away with you. So here we go.'

'Magic.'

Soundless marchers, pale vague figures moving in strong sunshine, old-fashioned banners with black and white homemade saltires and uneven lettering. Tillicoultry Branch, Dingwall, Aberdeen. A lot of kilts. Early sixties? Near the head of the procession, McBain smiling broadly in a tweed suit, narrow tie undone, shirt collar open. His hair was short at the back and sides but lanky on top. He talked animatedly to ladies on either side who wore respectable coats and bonnets. One was possibly Wendy Wood, the other had a poodle on a leash. The picture stuttered in the gates of the projector and the screen cleared.

'SNP Annual March to the Borestane, Bannockburn, 24 June 1962,' Joe read off the notes. 'That's all there is.'

A second clip. Colour, though insipid, watery orange-yellows, pale greens. Washed-out Lion Rampants, broader white bars in the Saltires, seventies lettering on larger banners. Open-necked shirts, tee-shirts and flared jeans, thick sideburns, feather-cut hairstyles. Falkirk West, Argyll & Bute, Dundee East. Folk singers, the massed ranks of Scotland's anoraked middle classes plus bearded urban revolutionaries in anoraks. McBain slightly further back, a row or two behind the leaders, Wolfe, Wilson, Stevenson, McRae and Rosemary Maclean. McBain seemed shorter, broader, perhaps simply older and he walked in the midst of a group of leather-jacketed, kilted men. The Vanguard group - or its forerunners.

'SNP March, June 1978,' Joe said. 'Almost four minutes of footage includes McBain. The next pieces are much shorter but I've stuck them together in a loop.'

McBain in a clinch of journalists outside the High Court, vigorously no-commenting as he passed the camera, then on the steps, with a different tie modest over a famous triumph, his client, Anthony MacIntosh unconditionally freed from a charge of bombing a BBC pylon at Alva. Then a series of brief interviews from the 1992 Knoydart Public Inquiry, humorous, ironic, bombastic. His bullish neck noticeably red, his hair disordered. What looked like the same pin-striped suit. His habit of ending sentences on Scots words which caught the attention, tossed like grenades into whimsical English. His right hand semaphoring with a smouldering cigarette, his nervous habit of cocking his head to one side as he squinted truculently into the camera lens, the breathy moistness of his speech - almost expostulations - his tone scandalised, indignant, yet somehow schoolboy-ish. He looked like a naughty schoolboy. Morton knew he was descending into subjectivity, anathema for a journalist, but he needed to get a grip on something closer to the real man. But he suspected that to grasp hold of McBain firmly, to predict his behaviour, was like grappling with a chimera, attempting to befriend a ghost.

13

As soon as he had his car back in working order, Morton faced the task of confronting Iain McBain. There was no denying the necessity of speaking to him, at the very least to counter the danger of subsequent legal action over any inaccuracies of fact that might appear in the book.

Elizabeth had given him the address of the surgery, a rambling two-storey building in a quiet street near Falkirk Technical College, but could not be persuaded to come with him. So Morton drove to Falkirk by himself on a rather damp and gloomy day.

The small front gardens had been grievously neglected and the stone wall had tumbled onto the scrubby grass amongst a collection of empty crisp packets and Irn-bru cans. The front steps were worn and flaking and hosted a matching pair of push-buggies.

In the dim waiting room, a rosy-faced, rather blowsy receptionist held a prolonged and intimate telephone conversation on an antique Bakelite phone in front of a crowded room of docile patients. The décor of the place was early 20th century, Morton decided.

'Be with you in a minute, love,' she mouthed, her eyes not quite meeting Morton's, indicating with her pink fingernail varnish, the one vacant place in a row of dilapidated wooden chairs.

Morton sat and listened to half of a conversation about an operation then went into a corridor, following a sign marked 'Toilets' but stopped outside a consulting room with a small plaque marked Dr I McBain, listened briefly, then pushed open the door and looked in.

Iain McBain was examining a patient's neck and looked up in surprise. Morton had a strong impression of *deja vu*. He felt as if he was seeing the dead come to life. He apologized and left.

He returned to wait in the car. He found a news programme on the radio and listened to a discussion of Nigels and Jeremys about financial affairs in the city. It was so boring that Morton listened, deeply fascinated. What planet did these aliens inhabit, he was thinking.

It was almost two hours before Dr McBain emerged from the building and got into his car, a pale blue Citroen.

Following him was an easy task despite lunchtime traffic, for the doctor was driving home and Elizabeth had given him the address. It proved to be a substantial detached house in a tree-lined avenue in the suburbs near a golf course.

Morton rang the bell. After a longish pause, a woman appeared and silently held open the door for him to enter. Morton's eyebrows arched and a smile tightened his face. The doctor continued to neatly dissect his steak as his wife ushered Morton in.

'I had a feeling we'd be having a visit from yourself,' he said phlegmatically, motioning the journalist to a chair. 'Cup of tea?'

Morton saw the moistness of wry amusement in McBain's eyes, which he found disconcerting. The similarity in appearance was startling, except that the doctor's hair was a uniform light grey. There were dark, deeply-etched lines under his eye sockets, but it was essentially the same face, the same genetic imprint.

'I have seen you before,' McBain said. Gratified by a puzzled glance, he explained: 'Outside Bute House, some days ago. I was meeting Donald for lunch, arrived early and saw you leaving. I'm good with faces. I knew you straight away this afternoon at the surgery. And I'm afraid I could hardly ignore your car as you followed me here. Volkswagen Beetles are rather distinctive.' He chuckled dryly, and added, 'reliable cars, I understand.'

'I'm sorry to have to resort to such subterfuge.

'Tush, tush,' McBain cut Morton's apology short with a peremptory gesture of his fork. 'I'm merely a little surprised that you're still pursuing the case, but you're here now, so I suppose I'll have to see if I can help you.'

'I'd be grateful if you would.'

The doctor leaned back and the seat creaked. 'What still concerns you about my brother's death?'

Morton looked closely at him. 'Have you no doubts yourself? You're absolutely convinced it was suicide?'

McBain carefully laid down his knife and fork and pushed his plate away. 'I can't say I'm absolutely convinced but there is no other explanation.'

Morton nodded. 'On balance, it is the most logical conclusion, but there are a number of peculiarities which defy that explanation.'

'But nothing which materially affects the cause of death? There are always unexplained circumstances. We'll never know exactly what was in poor Angus's mind when he died but there is no evidence of anything untoward happening to him. Nothing, I mean, involving other people.'

'Hmn, well, there's the neat pile of papers on the hillside fifteen yards above the car. That seems to suggest at least one other person.'

McBain frowned, his bushy eyebrows meeting in the middle of his brow. 'This is news to me. What was supposed to have been in this... neat pile?'

'Torn pieces of paper, a bill from a garage at Fort William, in fact, which had Angus's name and address on it, some snapped credit cards, again belonging to Angus, and a broken watch, which was sitting on top - which had been placed on top. The pile was neat and had not been dropped or thrown down casually. Someone must have devoted time to doing so and that someone could not have been Angus because he was trapped, stuck fast in his seat and the car-door was jammed into the side of the hill.'

While he had been speaking, Morton had been observing McBain and knew that his words had had a strong impact. He could see the confusion in the doctor's face. He sat silently while McBain sorted himself out.

After a few moments, when he responded, his voice was slow and reflective, as if he was mastering his emotion. 'I see. But who could possibly have been there with him?'

'I presume that the broken watch did belong to Angus?'

'I beg your pardon?'

'The broken watch. Did you get Angus's possessions back from the police and was his watch broken?'

'It was. I believe so. I presumed that was a result of the crash. There were no torn papers or snapped credit cards returned to me. In fact, there were relatively few things handed back. A half-bottle of whisky, some cigarettes - well, one packet of cigarettes...'

As a trained journalist, Morton knew when to be silent. McBain squirmed in his seat and fiddled with his watch strap. His seat creaked.

'You see, Mr. Morton, one of Angus's bad habits was smoking. I was never able to get him to give up. He was a chain smoker, smoked about fifty cigarettes a day. He always had a large supply - a carton of packets - in his car. Gold Flake was his favourite brand, and yet...'

'And yet?'

'Well, there was Angus heading off for a working weekend at Morroch Point and he had only one packet of cigarettes with him which wouldn't even last him the journey. Why didn't he have his usual carton with him? Or if he did, where did it go? Many times he set off for Morroch and he always had a good supply with him. I know he hadn't left them in his flat because I myself checked the flat and they weren't there.

Morton scribbled in his black notebook. 'Perhaps someone purloined them after the crash? Or maybe some dishonest policeman removed them in the police station?'

'Possibly. There could be several explanations. I got back his Bible, personal possessions, wallet, pens, that kind of thing.'

'In my opinion, the neat pile of papers and the missing cigarettes are inconsistent with the idea of suicide,' Morton said. The doctor made no reply. 'Angus was completely trapped,' Morton reiterated. 'He couldn't have got out of the car to deposit those papers and the watch. That must have been done by someone else.'

There was a long pause, almost a minute. 'Perhaps,' the doctor began, 'perhaps these items came out of the window of the car as it turned over, and... only looked as if it was a neat pile.'

'The pile was described by Cochrane and PC McGrath.'

'David Cochrane? You might give him my regards next time you see him.'

'You know him then, personally?' Morton said. *Small world.*

'Of course. But not very well. He used to live at Grahamsdyke, not far from here. Haven't seen him for years. His father was a patient of mine. Morton, I must say I'm very surprised that this so-called neat pile wasn't mentioned to me. On the face of it, such a pile would seem to indicate suicide - were it not for the unusual circumstances of the car's positioning.'

'Is the pile mentioned in the post-mortem report?'

McBain blanched. 'Ah, no, I don't recall it. No, it couldn't have been.'

'You do have a copy of the PM report?'

'Confidential,' McBain muttered. He cleared his throat.

'That's confidential.'

Morton was astounded. 'It's only as confidential as you want to make it.'

'Exactly. I do want it kept confidential.' He stood up.

Morton pocketed the note-book and stood up. 'I had several chats with your son and daughter on this subject.'

McBain looked discomfited and cleared his throat.

'Yes,' Morton said apologetically. 'They came to me with a number of concerns which they told me are shared by other family members.'

'I... what? Other family members? And Angus and Elizabeth told you this?'

'They feel that not enough information has been given out to the family.'

'They feel that? Do they really? I had no idea.' McBain's chair creaked under him. 'In such tragic circumstances, you know, one doesn't wish to dwell on such things. It's true I haven't actually discussed Angus's death in detail with my family. But what is there to say? It's all too tragic and upsetting.' He looked up at Morton. 'I'm surprised to hear this from you – from someone outside the family. If they feel this way I might have expected to have been given an indication of their feelings.'

The Grandfather clock in the hall wheezed and struck the half-hour. Both men looked at each other earnestly. McBain seemed so uncomfortable that Morton began to apologise.

'I was unaware that they hadn't discussed the matter with you,' he said, colouring slightly at the lie. 'I assumed...'

The doctor sighed at last. 'Don't worry, Mr. Morton. We each have our cross to bear.'

Morton wondered how he could manoeuvre the conversation back to the gun and the post-mortem. 'I don't wish to intrude but I do have a couple of questions more.'

'Perhaps you could leave these for a later time? What you

have told me has been distressing. I feel that I must discuss the matter with my family before we can talk again.'

'Of course. But in the meantime, a sudden thought. Might not the cigarettes and the papers have been returned to Angus's business partner along with his briefcase and other work-related items?'

'You mean Mr. Dennison?' McBain said, frowning heavily. 'I would rather not speak about that individual, if you don't mind. At least not today.'

'But it is a possibility?'

'Nothing you could tell me about Mr. Dennison would surprise me very much, but I doubt that anything belonging to Angus would have been returned to... to... him.' McBain turned and thrust out his jaw. He seemed to have come to a decision. 'I never understood what Angus saw in that unreliable young man. He let my brother down so often - so often - and yet Angus always, generously, foolishly in my opinion, forgave him. Frankly, I wish to have nothing to do with him and you would be doing well to give him a wide berth.'

'You will see me again?' Morton said. 'I mean, you're not looking for an excuse...'

Iain McBain smiled for the first time as he ushered Morton out. 'I'm a man of my word, just as my older brother was.'

14

Morton drove westwards towards Glasgow on the M8. It was raining heavily. The car sloughed deep trenches of water at the sides of the roadway. It was a typical early autumn day for which 'dreich' was the only accurate descriptive. The Beetle puttered at an even 55mph, windscreen wipers soothing him with their regular rhythm. He exited at Charing Cross, traversed Sauchiehall Street and parked on the third level of the Wellington Street multi-storey carpark.

The white bonnet steamed and rain, dripping from the concrete roof, lay in dusty, oil-stained pools. Wet tyre marks wound round the parking bays. Morton fetched his raincoat and umbrella from the back seat and proceeded in the lift to street level. Rain whipped round the corners in wet blusters on the short walk to the offices of Angus McBain & Co.

The DPM Shipping Office across the landing was closed for lunch according to an ornate notice on the glass doors but the crudely hand-lettered cardboard sign above the letterbox of McBain & Co advised: 'Closed Until Further Notice.' Morton lifted the heavy brass letterbox and peered inside. The hall doors were slightly ajar and there was an unmistakable smell of disintegration and abandonment. He could see the offices had been closed for some days. He was aware of mail lying on the linoleum floor of the hall.

A more pushy reporter would have slipped the lock with deft use of his NUJ card but Morton had never learned how to do that or if it was possible outwith the pages of fiction. Instead, he returned to the wind and rain-scoured street, located a Chemist in the Enoch Centre and hurried back, noting that it was 1.45pm and the Shipping Office was due to open at 2pm.

He knelt in front of the door and angled the small shaving mirror which he had bought through the letterbox and used it to study the mail on the doormat inside.

He found that he had to remove his jacket in order to be able to get his left arm inside the letterbox. He fed in the fully-extended pair of compasses, face pressed hard against the door. Using the mirror in his right hand, he directed the compasses to push away what was clearly junk mail and began to spear the others, bringing them up to his right hand and pulling them through. It was a knack that took him a minute or two to master. He soon had a little pile at his knees.

The sudden thrumming of the lift wires startled him and he dropped the mirror. His left arm seemed to be stuck inside the letterbox but he knew that he had the last letter stuck firmly on the point. He felt it fall back to the doormat and redoubled his efforts. The lift was whirring in motion, ascending. He could see the letter. He had it. He jerked it through the letterbox and simultaneously, as the lift gates flew open, snatched it, the pile of letters, his jacket and umbrella and sprawled down the steps around the corner of the lift shaft. Voices. Keys in the lock of the Shipping Office, but Morton was silently slipping down to the ground floor.

After that excitement, and with his fingertips still tingling from the high blood pressure which it had provoked, Morton sat quietly in the car and fumbled through the mail. Nearly all bills. Some of the letters postmarked early July. So Dennison had continued to practice, although Morton had discovered that he'd been struck off in May. The Law Society of Scotland had refused to divulge why Dennison had been struck off nor whether they were aware of any winding-up or de-registration of the company. But Morton had spoken to him in the office in May when Dennison had claimed to be the sole partner. Was he already, even at that time, disbarred? And who was the Mr. Andrew Laing, who appeared to be 'acting for your client'? One letter, thanking the company for its prompt and effective actions, was addressed to Mrs. Edina Cuthbert. The receptionist?

Morton braved the rain to reach the Central Post Office and asked for a telephone directory. There was no number listed for a Brian Dennison anywhere in the Greater Glasgow area and only two Dennisons. Although both of them were in, neither admitted to being related to, or knowing, Brian Dennison, the solicitor. He could be anywhere, Morton said to himself, in any one of the thousands of pubs within a forty mile radius. By contrast, there were scores of Cuthberts and seven E. Cuthberts in the telephone directory, whose addresses he jotted down in his notebook.

He walked to the Mitchell Library and was given a pile of the electoral roll registers. It took him half an hour to find there was only one Edina Cuthbert and she lived alone. He could find no solicitor called Andrew Laing registered with the Law Society of Scotland or listed in the Yellow Pages.

It was a quiet street in Cathcart, a neat semi with a trim crab-apple tree in a tiny front garden of pink gravel chips. Morton immediately saw Mrs. Cuthbert's blue-rinsed coiffure moving about above the net curtains as he parked alongside the box hedge.

He knocked at the white UPVC front door. 'Hello! Mrs. Cuthbert? We have met, at McBain & Co. My name is Morton. Sorry to bother you at home... but I need your help.'

Her face resumed that severe, pinched meanness that Morton remembered, which he presumed she reserved for working hours. It was a transformation triggered by mention of her employer's name. The door began to close. Morton tried to put her at ease.

'I'm a friend of Iain McBain - Angus's brother...'

The door was close-in to Mrs. Cuthbert's cheek.

'I very much need to speak to Mr. Dennison, or Andrew Laing. Can you give me an address where I might reach either of them?'

Morton was amazed at the transformation occurring to the small segment of her face that was visible. The door slammed shut. From behind its whorled glass panels, he heard the small, insistent voice telling him to go away.

He moved a few steps from the door, then had a sudden idea and returned to the letterbox, and spoke through it:

'This will shortly be a police matter. I might be able to keep you out of it.'

He heard her retreat from the door and wondered whether she might phone the police herself. It seemed unlikely. That look on her face indicated fear. Who was she scared of? Dennison? Or was it something to do with Laing? And who was Laing?

Morton looked into the kitchen window and simultaneously saw in its reflection that he was being observed by an elderly couple on the pavement. He pushed through the wooden gate into the rear courtyard and to his surprise, saw that the backdoor was open. He went in.

'Mrs. Cuthbert!' he called from the hall as she retreated in front of him. Suddenly, he confronted her in the sunny living room. She had armed herself with a full bottle of Irn Bru. Morton laughed, and raised his arms in mock surrender. 'I give up.'

The elderly lady moved towards him, threateningly.

'Come on, don't be ridiculous. I just want to talk,' Morton protested. 'Look - ye daft old bat - this is my press card. I'm a journalist. See this picture. That's me. Go on – have a shuftie.'

She snatched the card and looked at it. He could see her spectacles on the mantelpiece behind her. He moved over to the sofa and sat down.

'My son is due home any minute,' she said.

'How about a cup of tea?'

'Cheek!'

'Okay, yes, well thanks for offering. Now, look, I visited the office and the people next door said it's been closed for two weeks. I know Dennison's been struck-off. What was the reason for that, by the way?'

'It's got nothing to do with you.'

'Can I speak to him? Do you have his address?'

'He's left Glasgow.' Her face assumed a malevolent sneer. 'To get away from nosey parkers like you. He's not well.'

'Is he in hospital? Or a clinic?'

Mrs. Cuthbert glared at him.

'Are you still employed by the company?'

'You're wasting your time. I've said all I'm going to say. My son will be here any minute.'

'You must have something to hide. What have you got to hide?' Morton was losing his temper. 'What is going on? I've checked up and there is no-one with that name registered as a solicitor in Scotland. Yet I've seen letters that prove he - whoever *he* is - was working as a solicitor out of your office.'

'Letters? How did you get hold of letters, unless by thieving.'

'Maybe. But I have them here.' He pulled the letters out of his breast pocket. 'Let's see…. A. G. Ashley Ltd, 35 Renfrew Street…. 13 June… reference to letter… Mr Andrew Laing who acts for your client… Ring any bells? I see that the typing reference is AL/EC. You wouldn't be EC would you?'

Mrs Cuthbert had gone very pale and Morton knew that he had the truth of it. He began to feel a little sorry for the poor old soul.

'I was just the receptionist. I had no right to interfere…'

'But I'm sure the police will be able to sort it all out.' Morton assured her with a sarcastic grin. 'You know what I think? I think our alcoholic friend has been passing himself off under another name and working after he was struck-off. If I'm right, he's heading straight to jail. It's known as conspiracy to defraud. And you'll be in trouble too if you knew about it, as I suspect you did. But I'm not here because of Dennison's petty little scams. What I *am* interested in is the death of Angus McBain'.

He saw her startled look. 'Mr McBain?' she quavered.

15

The *Standard* used his story on Friday's front page, continued inside. It had taken just one phone call to A.G. Ashley Ltd to establish that Dennison, address presently unknown, and Andrew Laing were one and the same. The Law Society of Scotland was launching its own investigation. It was a useful little story and Hugh Leadbetter was pleased.

'You've earned yourself some dosh, Willie, lad', he rumbled, 'take the whole weekend off.'

'It's only Friday!' Morton grinned. 'Are you trying to get rid of me or what?'

'Or what, probably,' Leadbetter grizzled.

On the way out of the building, he ran into Danny Stark. Stark was 24, an ambitious, football-mad Dundonian who'd gone over the wall at D.C. Thomson and was already Senior Political Reporter of the *Standard*. 'You spoke to Dave Cochrane,' he said, 'so what's your angle, Willie?'

'Look, Danny, sorry, but I'm doing the piece myself. Need the money.'

Stark stroked the thin moustache, which, with his jet-black hair and olive complexion, reminded Morton vaguely of El Zorro. He'd been growing it for a fortnight, the subject of jocularity. All he needed was the sombrero. He already had the small gold earring in his thick sideburns. Someone had put a wee cactus on his desk.

'Yeah. Nice wee piece, Willie, I was wanting to talk to you…'

'I'm in no hurry.'

'Something I want you to see. Come upstairs.'

Back in the pressroom, Stark unlocked a drawer of his desk and handed some papers to Morton. 'Here you go. List of

Statutory Objectors for the forthcoming Gruinard Inquiry in Dingwall.'

Morton gaped. 'I'd forgotten about that!'

Stark smirked. 'Uh-huh! Inquiry to allow AtomTech to construct a deep storage shaft facility on Gruinard Island. You'll note that your man's name is second-top of the list.'

'Jeezo! I see,' Morton said, reflectively. 'That's one hell - one hell - of a bloody coincidence.'

Stark nodded. 'Hard to see how we can use it though, as yet. Unless we had some direct evidence of a link. But the anti-nuclear angle is compelling. I keep coming back to it.'

'Yeah,' Morton agreed. 'Could be, but we need something more.'

'There's a few bits and pieces, rumours... and the like...' Stark said, 'nothing much...'

'About McBain?'

Stark looked up at him oddly. 'No, no, man. Dounreay and the nuclear industry. Rumours that something big is going on with AtomTech Ltd. I haven't been able to get it all into a coherent story. It's just bits and pieces at the moment.

Morton took a guess: 'More reprocessing deals?'

Stark nodded. 'Since the row about that contract with Kraut Nuclear, there's been no further information about any more reprocessing, and you know they are presently prohibited from doing any more foreign deals, yet the workforce, according to a mate of mine who works on the *Wick Observer*, is not being run-down at all, it's being *increased* and more workers seem to be doing overtime. The plant is working round the clock. So what work are they doing?'

'You tell me.'

'Obvious isn't it?' Stark said. 'The plant is doing other reprocessing...'

Morton said: 'You mean *illegally*?'

'Well. Put it this way, mate, every time news of foreign deals leak out, no pun intended, Willie, there's a furore. You're talking about a Westminster government - and nuclear matters are still under their authority - which is jittery on the whole issue, and a Scottish Parliament which would shut the plant down tomorrow if it had the authority. What would you do if you were in AtomTech's shoes? You can't keep the place open without foreign reprocessing deals. The answer is you try to keep the bloody lid on things. Absolute secrecy.' Stark made a wry face. 'In the interests of commercial confidentiality, of course.'

'You don't have to convince me, Danny. But how could they get around the Inspectorate?'

Stark laughed. 'Don't be naïve! The Inspectorate are scared shitless to do anything without UK government authority. And the Scottish government couldn't care what is really going on, just as long as it doesn't get into the papers! They've an even bigger desire to keep things quiet. Of course, if it does become public knowledge, the SNP will hold their hands up in horror and blame it all on Westminster.'

'So you think McBain could have stumbled on to something like this?' Morton suggested.

'Look, Willie - if your man's death is proved to be anything other than suicide, then I'd say there could - must - be some kind of link. Too much of a coincidence otherwise.'

'That's putting it… I mean no one person could be that dangerous. Not even McBain. He was 81 you know.'

'Of course,' Stark concluded, 'knowing is one thing, proving it another…'

Alan Bailey, the Senior News Editor had stopped to listen in. A bespectacled, frail little man in a yellow and blue bow-tie and red velvet waistcoat, with a permanent expression of disapproval and the corners of his mouth always turned down. Everyone knew he was the proprietors' man, the bosses' spy. 'What are you two hatching?' he inquired suspiciously. 'Nothing libellous, I hope?'

Morton's and Stark's glances met. 'The McBain story,' Stark admitted reluctantly.

'You're a freelance, Morton? Are you working a shift with us today?'

Morton laughed derisively. 'No, don't worry, you've already paid me.'

'Good, good,' Bailey nodded. 'So - any new leads?'

'We're looking at the coincidence of the death given that the Gruinard Inquiry is about to start.'

Bailey's mouth sagged lower. 'Ah, I'd be really worried if you were to start slinging allegations at the nuclear industry. We can't afford to be sued. I mean, there's news value there, but we'd have to be sure of the facts, damn sure. Probably better to shelve it for now. There's easier angles.'

'Yes?' Morton queried.

Bailey puffed out his cheeks and emitted a low wind. 'The drug angle, always a good read. McBain had a seamy past. Use it. The gay connection. Did he use gay bars, that sort of thing?'

'He wasn't gay,' Morton said, but Bailey had moved on, so he exchanged meaningful glances with Danny Stark.

'He's just such a caring human being,' Stark said sarcastically.

'He's right though,' Morton conceded. 'If we go at this half-assed, the nuclear industry and their paid hacks will blast us out of the water.'

'Yeah, agreed, so let's collaborate.'

'Okay, Danny. Hugh will be happy, no doubt.' Joint by-lines are better than no by-lines, he added, to himself, on his way out. And Danny would be useful to have onside. Reminded Morton of his own younger self.

The Vaults is the gloomy, nicotine-stained howff halfway down a steep flight of stone steps between George IV Bridge and Candlemaker Row. It was where, in the early months of the minority SNP government at Holyrood, the employees of various newspapers mingled with other lowlife elements. As usual for an early Friday evening it was crammed with reporters, printers, tipsters, sporting gents, police grasses, tourists, French dancing masters, tarts on the razz, merchant bankers and nickety-nackety-the-noo-salesmen.

Morton located Leadbetter and the others in one of the booths, squashed bums together onto one wooden bench and indicated by semaphore that he'd get a round in. It took him ages and then some of the beer slopped onto the tin tray as he pushed back through the crowds. He landed the tray on the table. 'Manager's obviously not heard of fire regulations,' he grumbled.

Leadbetter was talking to Roger Freeman, *Scotland's Mirror*, who greeted Morton by gleefully belching in his face. 'We're about to knock our tartan section on the head, Willie. Aye, it's just been sanctioned by HQ. We can sell as many in jolly Jockland by putting a kilt on our London edition.' Putting a kilt on – Morton knew – was a term used to indicate an attempt to make it look like a Scottish edition was actually coming from Scotland. Usually these attempts were gloriously hilarious failures.

Morton pondered this over the frothy head of his pint. It didn't affect him at all. Interesting though. 'Anyway,' he said, 'I'm following up the McBain story, even though its four months old now. He was the leading anti-nuclear campaigner in Scotland, you know. That should count for something.'

Freeman grunted. 'Anti-nuclear is a non-story now, old chum. Nothing to focus it. Now if a bunch of weird women were to set-up camp outside Dounreay and got their tits out for the lads...'

'That'd be a cracking lead story!' someone behind him said. There was sniggering at this, but Morton just ignored it.

Leadbetter sipped his pint ruminatively. 'Aye, McBain was an interesting character. If I can think of anything to help I'll pass it on. It's all a bit well, bygone days, isn't it? Mind, the party hierarchy didn't like him... Nae chance of him ever being appointed to a Ministerial brief. Way too old... and since the SNP got in there's been a certain weeding-out of the hairy brigade so as not to frighten the horses in the new Scotland.'

'Indeed, shiny new faces.'

'Now that I remember, Willie,' Leadbetter said, carefully placing his pint on a nearby wooden ledge, 'there was a good story from when your man used to be a candidate for some god-forsaken place in the Heilans far from civilised pubs.' He tugged heavily at his beard, 'now *where* was it...?'

'Maybe Assynt, Wester Ross?' Morton prompted.

Leadbetter slapped the tabletop. 'Aye, that's it. The Euro Elections. Nearly won if I remember right. Good second place. Anyway, he used to tell this lovely wee story about canvassing in the remote villages on the... Applecross peninsula, where half of the villagers, you see, were strictly teetotal, but the other half would be mortally offended...' he assumed a mock Highland lilt... 'if the candidate himself, chust, as it were, refuses the hospitality of a *deoch-an-dorus* – a wee dram. So your man concluded, Willie, he said, you know, that a good parliamentary candidate in... it was Lochaber West, I think... needs to have two basic skills. One,' Leadbetter wiped beer froth sideways into his beard, 'the skill of appearing sober to the teetotallers without offending the drinkers. And two: the skill of finding the bloody car in the dark after an evening of canvassing! Aye! He was a character and a half was old McBain.' He raised his pint ceremonially 'may he rest in peace, and it's your round, Willie. Aye - *again*!'

As he stood at the busy bar, Morton did a bit of thinking. The nuclear industry link... He found himself reminiscing about Angus McBain... at the high rostrum on the final day of that Annual Conference in Dundee more than a decade ago. Hair bunched lopsidedly... gleam of absolute sincerity in his eyes, meaty fist punching the full hot glare of the spotlights and TV cameras and the unbearable heat of three and a half thousand roused activists. The Garibaldi of the SNP in a crumpled, soup-stained navy-blue suit, tie already awry around his great bull neck... on the platform behind him, MPs, MSPs, MEPs, elected and prospective, scenting power, the breakthrough long awaited... on the cusp... his voice booming to the ornate ceiling of the lofty Caird Hall. What was it he'd bawled...? "Turncoats, toom tabards and tallymen all aboard Westminster's gravy train... and Scotland's no even in their vocabulary!" Inflammatory, passionate, totally off-message - but in the midst of his hard line bombast a couthy, self-deprecating humour. Held himself up as an object of ridicule, a wee politician, surely the lowest of god's creatures. That was why he was so damn dangerous, Morton concluded. He'd had the common touch, the ability to inspire immediate empathy and his unvarnished and undiluted sincerity. Incorruptible. And when his speech ended, Morton recalled, there had been a stamping, clapping, cheering, standing ovation, greater than that for any other of the party's leaders. And now of course, that they had power, everything had gone rather quiet. Their radical edge blunted. They had been trapped in devolution, unable to convince the Scots to move forward to Independence, doomed to ruling the colony on behalf of their imperial masters. Reduced to being bystanders on the many issues where Westminster still ruled: the nuclear industry. Although the SNP Government was anti-nuclear to a man and woman, they had no authority to do anything about it. All energy policy was controlled in

124

London. There was no doubt McBain's death was convenient for someone. He was a man to be feared, Stark was right. But did it mean that McBain had been *murdered*? And how could that be... but then it wasn't a simple car-crash either. There was a heck of a lot unexplained and nobody really seemed bothered.

It was late when Morton walked home from the pub under the streetlights. There were few people about on the quiet streets. Shoulders hunched against a light drizzle that seeped from the dark sky, he had reached the end of Johnston Terrace and was turning down into Castle Terrace when he saw - or comprehended without seeing - a shadow detach itself from the high darkness of the wall and accost him. He flinched instinctively, expecting a blow, but the shadow had a face and it was the face of someone he truly did not want to see. McGinley! When he realised there was to be no blow, he swore out loud, relieved but fearful and stepped backwards.

McGinley, formidably tall and bulky in a tweed cap and waxed jacket, restrained him firmly with ease and grinned down at him. 'Well! Fancy us running into each other again, old boy! And so *soon*!' Around the corner slowly and ominously came a large black vehicle, its headlights dazzling on the wet cobbles. There were men inside it. While McGinley restrained him effortlessly with one hand, Morton heard a door open in the vehicle.

'Quite right, William, our transport is arriving,' McGinley beamed, his face uncomfortably close to Morton's own. 'No expense spared, eh, old boy?' And he began to propel Morton towards the vehicle.

One of the men reached out and pulled him in. He was wedged in the back seat between two of them while the door shut and the vehicle began to move out towards Lothian Road.

'Just a friendly chat,' McGinley said affably, 'we're not going to fit you for concrete overshoes. That was a joke, or it was meant to be.'

'Ho ho,' said the man in the driving seat wearily. 'Must be the way you tell them.' Morton could only see the thickness of this man's neck and the tip of his nose. He felt as if he was sitting high up and his back felt stiff. He was sitting between two men and one had his arm around him. Morton could smell bad breath. At the back of his mind, he didn't really believe it was happening. It could possibly turn out, he believed, to be a bit of a prank.

The vehicle, which he knew was a Range Rover Discovery, sped through the Edinburgh streets and didn't seem to be impeded in its rapid movement by traffic congestion or traffic lights. It glided along smoothly at well above the regulation speed, breathtakingly fast at junctions, halting, when it needed to halt, quite suddenly, so that Morton felt completely powerless and fearful. The streetlights and shop displays were a colourful blur and Morton caught odd snapshots of ordinary people going about their ordinary lives within inches of where he sat imprisoned and helpless. And the silence and impassivity of the four men in the car became more ominous with each passing second.

McGinley turned round. 'Morton, m'boy, I'm beginning to worry about your unhealthy instincts. Having a nose for a story is one thing but there are limits, certain boundaries which must not be transgressed.'

'Oh are there?' Morton said in a brave attempt at being sarcastic. 'Such as?'

'The laws of these islands, William, made in the name of the Queen. God bless her and all who sail in her!'

'I haven't broken any laws,' Morton said. 'As well you know!'

'Well! Temper, temper, William. But what are laws *for*? The protection and security of the greater majority, yes? That's what a democracy is all about and that's why we have laws, don't you agree?'

'Of course. What's your point.'

'Laws like the Defence of the Realm Act, the Official Secrets Act for example, and there are plenty more. They give people like me lots of authority to take action against possible... now what's that word.... Ah yes, *subversives*. Not that I'm saying you definitely are one, Morton. In fact that's why I've arranged this little chat.'

'Where are you taking me?' Morton asked. 'Am I under arrest?' They'd left the streetlights behind and he was amazed to see that they were already breasting the rise of Morningside Road, heading south. He didn't like it that they were leaving the city behind. The city of ordinary people. The car slowed to take a corner and Morton seized his chance. He leaped for the door and flailed at the handle but the door was locked and the two men who hadn't moved at all, easily pulled him back into his seat. They began to laugh at him.

'Who the hell *are* you?' Morton shouted, struggling to evade the encircling arm around his neck. 'Special Branch?'

The man on the left chuckled and pinched Morton's cheek. The bad breath intensified around him.

'If that's who you think we are, Morton, then that's who we will be,' McGinley said.

The driver swerved the vehicle off into Braid Hills Drive, which Morton knew from weekend walks, and drove past the farmhouse. It was a dark area of golf courses, open space all around, and Morton knew there were a few disused quarries nearby. His mind was racing. If McGinley and his men had had a hand in the death of McBain, how far were they prepared to go? But his thoughts were breaking down into one vast amorphous gut-wrenching fear. He couldn't think straight.

'Why are we stopping?' he asked, in a fearful voice, though he feared that he didn't want to know. It was impenetrably dark outside but McGinley was getting out! Then Morton felt himself being shoved out and he was outside, sprawled on his hands and knees on the wet grass and all he could see was the tail lights and the dim light from inside the Range Rover and the impossibly distant lights of Edinburgh like the Milky Way. He suddenly realised he was in the hands of people who didn't care, who didn't need to care. The law was on their side.

A torch beam played on his face. One of the men sniggered.

'Look at his face! He thinks he's going to be rubbed out! Hey, Morton, we're not the fucking IRA you know.'

'What's happening to me?' Morton heard his own voice ask, a puny, embarrassing voice. The light was dazzling him.

'I just want you to consider this, Morton.' McGinley said.

'What? What is it?'

'Hold your hand out. Feel this.' McGinley's face loomed closer to Morton's.

And Morton felt something wet and cold put into his hand. It took him a moment to decide it was a handful of earth.

'Smell it, Morton,' McGinley said. 'Go on, inhale that nice clean smell. Now do you know what that is?'

'Of course, it's....'

'Exactly. Now how would you like to have a suit of pyjamas made out of it? And how would you like to wear them *all the time*?'

128

'What… do you mean?'

McGinley chuckled. 'You're not stupid, Morton. I don't think I have to repeat myself. Now, Angus McBain? What do you think happened to him?'

'McBain? Eh, he had a suit of…'

McGinley roared with delight. 'You're a fast learner, William. I'll give you that. It's not exactly what I meant. I'm looking for your opinion. Suicide - or was he murdered? What happened to him, in your opinion?'

'I've no idea,' Morton said cautiously. He felt wetness seeping into his trousers and around his ankles but wasn't sure if his bladder had given way or if it was the wet grass. 'Suicide, probably. Who'd want to murder him? He was 81.'

'Not good enough, Morton. Not good enough. You must have had thoughts about who might want to murder him? About enemies he might have made? What - maybe drug-smuggling gangs? Extreme republican fanatics who felt he'd grassed them up? Anyone else?'

'Eh, no, that seems to be….' Morton faltered, shivering. The presence of these grim men around and above him and the suspicion they were enjoying this, the darkness and the helplessness he felt and the handful of wet earth. Never had he felt so vulnerable.

All he remembered about the return journey was the creaking of McGinley's waxed jacket and the certainty that he had urinated himself. They pushed him out in Polwarth Terrace. He'd never been so pleased to see the pavement and the streetlights. He felt as if he'd been orbiting Saturn for a hundred years but his wristwatch showed that it wasn't even midnight and when he looked at its welcome and familiar face, he realised he still clutched the handful of earth, which his hot hand had crushed into a round clay ball. He looked at it with acute distaste and let it drop onto the pavement. The streets were silent and free of traffic. It was a peaceful night.

Morton felt such a mixture of emotions. His life could never be the same again. He had learned something about himself. He did not want to die.

16

The dark gradually gave way to daylight and Morton, who'd barely slept, began to feel more positive. But a sense of foreboding and terror wasn't far beneath the surface. He pondered that as he prepared a cup of tea and wholemeal toast and marmalade. Work was the last thing on his mind, but phoning Danny Stark was a kind of insurance policy. He caught Danny at a bad time, having forgotten about the early morning Editors' meeting.

'Danny, I've been warned off by McGinley I was telling you about.'

'Yeah? *Really*? The Special Branch guy? What happened?'

'Can't go into it just now, I know you're busy. I'm going to make myself scarce. I won't be around for a few days. I'm thinking of taking a trip.'

'Text me or call me,' Stark agreed. 'And, Willie, take care on the roads.'

The very words McGinley had used! A cold shiver ran through Morton's shoulders and the back of his neck. He felt an overwhelming desire to get away from the city, where he could be easily observed, where, even now, McGinley and his thugs might be watching him like a cat watches a mouse. He threw some essential items into a weekend bag, stuffed in a spare shirt, some underwear, a notebook, camera and voice recorder and left the flat after carefully observing the street for some minutes from his window. He found the car, parked some distance away, in Harrison Gardens, and stowed the hold-all in the boot under the bonnet.

By lunchtime he was speeding around the west bank of Loch Lomond. The sun was phosphorescent through the trees, scorching the surface of the loch and dazzling him with rainbows across his windscreen. Walkers and cyclists appeared suddenly like ghosts or mirages around the sharp bends. He rolled down the window to swallow great gulps of cold air, drawing it deep into his lungs. His fear was beginning to subside.

The loch petered out at Ardlui and the road turned inland to Crianlarich, then Tyndrum and Bridge of Orchy before the long run through the mountains of Glen Coe to the Ballachulish Bridge and the banks of Loch Ness. At Fort William he found a parking space in a supermarket car park near the pier. He was feeling safe now, relaxed, as he walked away from the car.

While Fort William in the tourist season is discordant and noisy, like a frontier trading post, in the spring it is cold and dreamily peaceful. Encouraged by the lack of crowds, Morton took the opportunity to stretch his legs and spent an hour in the tourist centre and the adjacent museum. To his surprise, he remembered the collection of Jacobite relics, the rusty, notched blades of basket-hilted claymores and broadswords, studded leathern targes, scraps of 'authentic' tartan, although he remembered vaguely that tartan was a Victorian invention. Fragments from a childhood holiday - one of few - with his parents. How many years ago? Museums were the kind of place they visited only when it was wet, because they were free. Morton couldn't remember any more than that he had been here before. He bought a sandwich and a carton of orange juice and sat on a bench in a small grass area in front of a hotel. The mountains across the loch looked benign, cool, faintly blue, reflecting upside down in the water. He took deep breaths of the colder air.

He resumed his journey, catching glimpses in his rear-view mirror of the scarred grey bulk of Carn Dearg, the westernmost col of Ben Nevis. He'd climbed it as a teenager. Reflections from the water burned incandescent patterns at the back of his eyes and he felt the need of sleep. He planned to find a quiet B&B somewhere in Arisaig and catch up on sleep. Somewhere McGinley couldn't trace him. But the fear of McGinley was turning itself into anger. After all, how much of it had been bravado or bluff? And if he could get evidence of the harassment, where might it lead? At the very least, he should find out who McGinley worked for, then the connection with McBain's death was there to be made.

Morton stopped at Glenfinnan and parked in the empty carpark. He sauntered across the quiet road and down to the base of the commemoration tower and looked out over the quiet, steep-sided fiord called Loch Sheil. The shore was pinkish sand. It was a quiet, peaceful place, watched over by the Highland Chief statue high above. Morton wondered if American tourists believed it was Bonnie Prince Chuck himself. He studied the inscriptions on the wall plaques, English, Gaelic and Latin, the badges of clans in the rising of 1745.

He walked back towards the road and breasting the rise was a black Range Rover. Instinctively, he ducked behind a concrete litterbin as it swept past. Two men inside. He didn't think they'd seen him and because a coach was reversing into the car-park, his Beetle had been obscured from view. But there could be no doubt that it was McGinley. They were following him!

He could see their car taking a bend up ahead. Several cars passed as the coach driver terminated his engines in a splutter and wheeze of hydraulics. Early-season tourists began to step down onto the gravel. Morton returned to the car and sat and considered what to do. There had been long periods when his had been the only car on the road. It must therefore be a coincidence and there was a chance anyway that it wasn't McGinley at all. He started his engine and drove out of the car park and continued the way they had gone, heading west.

He kept a sharp eye to the road ahead but there was no sign of the Range Rover.

Passing the railway halt at Lochailort, a wide expanse of open sea appeared on his left, a sea-loch, then the road began to twist and turn, climbing into dense forest. There was a glimpse of water somewhere far below after a tight bend protected by aluminium chicanes but he was too absorbed with the task of keeping the car on the narrow road to do more than register it as Loch Dubh, where Angus McBain had met his death. Then he was descending towards a widening shine of water through the thinning screen of trees ahead and soon saw the road sign for the village of Arisaig.

Slowing to take a bend before the tiny village, he saw the Range Rover, stopped, or idling, just in front of a white van which was indicating to overtake it. Without hesitating, Morton swerved the Beetle off the road and into the open gate of a grass field behind some trees. He got out and stepped cautiously over the dried rutted mud and watched the black vehicle up ahead. Then its tail lights glowed briefly and it accelerated off to the left at a junction and Morton lost sight of it. He returned to his car and reversed and continued on to the junction and read the sign: Rhumach. Morton remembered, from his scrutiny of the map that McBain's house at Morroch Point was less than quarter of a mile along that road. So it *was* McGinley. And he was going to McBain's house!

The last thing Morton wanted was to encounter him on a narrow road in the middle of nowhere, the day after he'd been warned off. Not for the first time, he cursed his ex-wife for purchasing such an obvious vehicle. He'd be safer travelling on foot, in the trees, where he could hide if need be. He drove slowly along the main road through Arisaig looking for a parking place, noting a hotel, shop, post office, café. He turned off at the end of the houses, turning up a hill track which ended on a flat plateau on the edge of the moor behind a low hedge of gorse. Safe here. He locked the car and took out his jacket and binoculars and found a narrow footpath that led down to the back of the hotel. He saw some people in the café but no-one in the street and quickly crossed the road and returned to the junction.

Closely lined with overgrown hedges and brambles, the narrow road out to Rhumach was in a poor state, pitted and pockmarked and disintegrating at the edges where it met the thick weeds of the bank. Moreover, looking down it he could see the road was full of twists and turns. The Range Rover might appear at any moment and he would be trapped. He stepped into the bushes and found a narrow track, probably a sheep track, that picked its way through the thistles and nettles parallel to the road. He spread the map out on a mossy tree stump and saw that, further along, where the road turned was where McBain's holiday home was located, amongst a small group of houses on the headland.

Morton heard an engine and a curious swishing sound. There was a vehicle coming along the road. He crouched in the undergrowth. He found a viewing point through a clump of hedge through which to look down at the lane.

He'd expected to see the Range Rover. The oncoming vehicle was white. An estate car. Towing a caravan. The swishing noise was the sides of the caravan brushing overhanging foliage. It proceeded very slowly heading out to Rhumach and Morton could see that it was taking up most of the width of the lane. No other vehicle could get past.

Morton slithered and struggled out onto the lane and, walking quickly, was able to keep behind the caravan as it jolted along. Then after a hundred yards, it suddenly came to a halt.

He clambered hastily back into the bank through a gap in the hedge and crouched low. He was proved correct. The estate car had encountered another vehicle, which was having to back-up. The caravan resumed, slowly following this other vehicle, which Morton could still not see. Then the caravan lurched heavily, scraping itself into the ditch and the other vehicle appeared, nosing forward.

The black Range Rover! And McGinley's face, looking directly at him. But it drove past, back to the village. Morton had covered his mouth with his hand and thrown himself flat. He hadn't been seen. He was almost certain. McGinley had no idea that he was there. As he lay still, the smell of wet earth clogged his nostrils and reminded him... But nothing happened. He found himself chuckling aloud in glee - and relief. Then he stood up and brushed himself down.

He went out into the empty lane and jogged along, past one, two, three and four driveways on the right and entered the fifth, the last, into a little grove of trees whose trunks were overgrown with ivy. Then he saw the house outlined against the sky.

Built, as Morton knew, in the 1920's, McBain's large white house stood foursquare, shaded by enormous yet wizened trees, facing the sea and small rocky islands off the headland. Ivy was devouring the lower portion of the gable end and the garden was seriously overgrown, several white garden chairs being almost entirely submerged by an upsurge of bracken and nettles.

Morton circumnavigated it quickly, observing that a stony path led down fifty feet or so to a pebble beach through a bank of stones and weeds and low trees and beyond that, were two or three yachts lying on their sides at low tide, among wet clumps of seaweed.

The windows were dark and empty in the shadow of the trees. Morton stepped onto the porch and tried the back door. Open! Folk in the Highlands were so trusting, he thought, but strange that none of the family had been north to secure the property. He tip-toed from dusty room to room, smelling the staleness of disuse and neglect. The kitchen and a small dining area showed the most recent signs of use by McBain. The entire surface of the table was taken up with scattered, jumbled papers and newspaper clippings, some of which had spilled onto the floor.

He studied some of the papers. Legal work. A layer of dust lay everywhere. As he searched, he became aware of the faint staleness of cigarette smoke. An over-full ashtray lay on a chair and inside -- was a smoking cigarette stub...

Morton ran out into the hall and stopped dead, listening. Nothing except his own tumultuous heartbeat. He returned to the kitchen. Someone had smoked a cigarette in this room recently. It must have been McGinley. Morton calmed down then and continued his search of the house, upstairs, creaking stairs. Considerable disorder, clothes flung about, drawers left hanging open. It occurred to him that it was too disordered even for McBain. It was the result of a search by McGinley's men. What were they looking for, four months after McBain's death? He sat on the edge of the bed and casually glanced out of the window. The Range Rover had entered the driveway and was parking beneath the trees.

17

Elizabeth McBain got off the bus on Slateford Road, crossed the road with care and continued to the junction with Shandon Place. At number 13, the blue door, she had to step out of the way of two men exit-ing in a hurry, who barged past her and careered down the steps.

'Sorry!' she said, pointedly, since it was the two men who should have been apologising. They had barely glanced at her. Then she had to bite her lip to stop from shouting out. One of the men was Peter Stoddard. She knew his features well from staring at them through a telephoto lens at Waverley Station. She stared after their retreating backs as they hurried down the street and were lost from view. She had a sudden misgiving about Morton and rushed up the stairs to the second floor.

She knocked, but Morton wasn't in. She remembered then that he was friendly with his downstairs neighbour, Philip, but he wasn't in either. She went back and looked through Morton's keyhole but couldn't see anything. She kept thinking about Stoddard. What was he up to and why such a hurry? There was something not right about him. She didn't trust him at all.

She walked slowly back to the main road and there, leaning against the door of a dark blue estate car which was illegally parked on double yellow lines at the junction, was Stoddard, talking animatedly on a mobile phone.

Elizabeth walked straight up to him, an elegant figure in grey trouser suit, her long black hair tied in a ponytail with a red ribbon.

As soon as he saw her, Stoddard snapped his phone shut and turned his back to her, to get into the car.

'Excuse me,' she said angrily, 'You're Mr. Stoddard aren't you?'

He half-turned and Elizabeth found herself staring at his deep eye-sockets and the overgrown moustache. 'Don't think I've had the pleasure,' he said in his curious muffled voice.

'Oh yes, we have, we talked on the telephone. I'm Elizabeth McBain.'

'Ah, charmed,' he said, smiling wanly.

'So what are you doing here?' she asked.

'Eh, um, ah,' he stuttered. 'I'm working. In fact, sorry, if you don't mind…'

Elizabeth persisted. 'You were at Morton's flat just now,' she said. 'What were you up to?'

He frowned and all the loose lines on his forehead gathered tightly together. 'Ah yes, Morton wasn't in.'

'Do you need to contact him? If so I could pass on a message to him.'

Stoddard leaned forward, his hands clasped together. 'Ah, you know where he is?'

'Yes. Why do you need to see him? Have you found out something new?'

'I'm afraid I can't discuss that. But when is Morton due back? Have you arranged to meet him here?' Then Stoddard smiled again, and it seemed almost too much of an effort, his teeth remaining entirely hidden beneath his heavy moustache. 'Ah, no, but of course, you expected to find him in, so your visit is… unsolicited?'

'It might be.'

'Why make a mystery, Elizabeth? I have offered to help Morton. I didn't have to. It's not part of my job to help him.'

'And just what is your job, I wonder?' Elizabeth said, but he didn't answer and got into the car which was driven away.

Later, Elizabeth phoned the *Standard* and during a discussion with Danny Stark, discovered Morton had gone north. She had been on many holidays to Arisaig and knew that her uncle always left the house open. She began to wonder if Morton would be there. It was 4pm, so she rang the number of her uncle's house at Morroch Point.

Morton, crouching behind the dusty bannisters at the top of the stairs, heard the telephone ring in the kitchen. McBain's telephone receiver, being of the heavy old-fashioned Bakelite type, had a particularly insistent ringing tone. He heard McGinley and his colleague tersely discussing the call but they let it ring. He could hear them moving about, the scrape of chair legs on the bare wooden floor. What were they doing? Why didn't they answer the damn phone?

The phone stopped ringing. He heard McGinley instruct the other man to do something and heard a single bell tone as if the phone receiver had been picked up then he heard clearly the words "Edinburgh number". He dared not move a muscle and strained to hear the voices. A few minutes later, there was another ringing noise which he suspected was a mobile phone and he heard more conversation. The word "Morton" came distinctly upwards to his ears. He felt sick. One man went into the hall and he heard the voice, much louder, say the words: "she just rang here... the bastard must be nearby..." *They were talking about him!*

McGinley was at the front door, and Morton very clearly heard him say: "but he couldn't have it" and the other man said "that's what they're paying us for - to put out the fire before it spreads" and then something about "unicorn" and Morton heard them move out onto the porch. It became clear to Morton that they thought he had something, perhaps belonging to McBain that they were searching for. Something perhaps which they couldn't find. It must be something important if they were being paid to retrieve it. And maybe even it was something so important that McBain had died trying to keep it? Morton heard their voices out in the garden but he didn't trust them. Did they suspect that he was already in the house? He raised himself very gently, aware of his creaking knees and very slowly tip-toed back into the bedroom whose window overlooked the drive. He crouched beneath the window sill and gingerly raised himself by inches until he could see out. They were at the Range Rover, both of them. So it was safe to move. He slid away from the window and rushed to the top of the stairs. He ran blindly down the wooden stairs, deaf to the creaks. He raced across the hall and peered through the open door, around the door jamb. He crawled across the threshold keeping low and slumped off the end of the porch into the cold overgrown grass. He got to his feet then and fled around the side of the house into the trees and got over a low stone wall onto the shingle. There was a gap in the wall and he could keep the two men and their vehicle in view. He felt a lot safer now he was out in the open and he could see them, McGinley and the shorter man. He felt sure they had no idea he was so close.

He tried to make himself comfortable on the shingle and prepared for a long wait. It looked as if it might rain and he had only the sparse shelter of the mossy stunted trees and the dilapidated wall. He looked around to see if he could discover a better shelter. A small boat which he had earlier observed standing off the nearest of the islands was coming in and he observed it idly for a few minutes. He took out his binoculars and focused on the craft. It wasn't a fishing boat. It looked like a police cutter or a Customs & Excise launch. And it was heading straight for Rhumach Bay. It was coming in fast. Morton could see several figures on the boat and felt a sick ominous feeling in his guts. He squirmed back into the low trees, keeping very low in the shrubbery, his earlier elation dissipated. He heard the voices of the men at the Range Rover. Then he saw them come back to the front of the

141

house to look at the boat. He was seeing them clearly for the first time in daylight. The other man, whom Morton didn't know, a younger man, in his twenties perhaps, whose hair was merely a grey shadow on his skull, wore a brown leather jacket but the wax jacketed man was McGinley. They acted silently and swiftly, their guns out, darting inside the house, separating, checking each room. Suddenly he understood. *They had been told he was there!*

Morton didn't wait for them to find that the house was empty. He hurried around the gable wall into the drive and fled headlong up the lane. He ran until his lungs forced him to stop, then he climbed into the hedge and continued more slowly to the village along the sheep track in the woods.

He made it to his car just before the heavens opened and a thunderstorm lashed his windscreen. He sat there in the safety of the hawthorn hedge and the deluge, almost hidden from view. When the rain lessened, he got out and peered over the hedge. Over in the west, rain clouds sagged nearer and in the bay he noticed that the black launch had tied up at a pier near McBain's house on the Point. He got back in the car with the windscreen steaming up, and the rain too heavy to allow him to open the window.

Iain McBain sipped a whisky and soda and watched as the head-waiter brought the young journalist over to his table at the plush Jacobite Grill in Hanover Street. He had surmised that the neat young man in the olive-green raincoat in the hallway was the person he was expecting.

'I'm Danny Stark,' the young man said, thanking the head waiter, as he arrived at McBain's table in the corner beneath the stained-glass window.

'Iain McBain,' he said, half-rising to shake hands.

'Nice to meet you at last. I'll have another whisky and… for you?'

'I'm alright for the moment, thank you.'

Stark sat down at the table, spread with white tablecloth and gleaming silverware. 'Nice place,' he commented. 'First time I've been here. I usually dine at the chippy,' he explained.

'Quite so,' Iain McBain muttered, looking at him from beneath his bushy white eyebrows. 'Now, Mr Stark, as you know, I had a meeting with your colleague, Mr Morton, and since then, I have been prevailed upon, mainly by my daughter, to alter my decision with regard to a Fatal Accident Inquiry.'

'Good,' Stark said, nodding, 'I think you're doing the right thing. It's important that everything is brought out into the open.'

A hovering African waiter in tartan waistcoat deposited shiny menus in front of them.

'Very nice,' Stark commented, 'but I'll just have the fish and chips, otherwise I'll get the sack. We've to watch our expenses, but of course, you have what you want, on me, of course.'

Dr McBain frowned. 'I won't hear of it. This must be on me. I insist.'

'Oh well, I accept,' Stark said, 'but I'll stick with the fish supper.'

'I had expected Mr. Morton actually, but Elizabeth told me he might not coming.'

'Willie's up north, looking over the crash-site and he's attending a small commemoration service there tomorrow.'

McBain pursed his lips and sipped his whisky. 'Ah yes, I was invited but I have had to turn down the invitation. I find it rather…. rather intrusive. Although, of course, I have known Malcolm Farquharson for many years. I believe – am persuaded - that his interest in pursuing the matter is genuinely a result of his friendship with my brother.'

143

Stark agreed. 'Willie said he'd formed that impression when he spoke to him on the phone.'

'Indeed,' said the older man, 'ah, the waiter.'

The opulence of the polished wood and gleaming brass and the sobriety of the stained-glass windows afforded a touch of luxury to the restaurant, which was sustained in the deference of the uniformed waiting staff.

After they had ordered, Iain McBain unfolded his napkin and placed it upon his lap. 'I hope that the Lord Advocate will accept my change of heart and agree to institute an FAI,' he said.

'Legally, I'm sure he must,' Stark said. 'But don't be surprised if there is a long delay. Are you going to write to the Lord Advocate, or go and see him?'

McBain looked closely at Stark's face. 'Oh write, I thought, I mean, I would imagine obtaining an interview may take some time. Writing will be quicker.'

'Could I have a copy of the letter,' Stark asked. 'As I discussed with Elizabeth, doing a story on your call for an FAI in the *Standard* is likely to give the whole issue more weight.'

The doctor ran his left hand wearily through his iron-grey hair. 'I have to say, I'd prefer it to remain a private matter. Could we not keep the story under wraps until an FAI has been authorised.'

'If you do that, Doctor, then, in my experience, it would be much easier for the Lord Advocate to refuse.'

Dr. McBain frowned, seemingly genuinely confused. 'Refuse? Mr. Stark. How could he refuse?'

Danny Stark smiled ironically and his teeth gleamed in his piratical smile under the thin moustache. 'I'm afraid he does have the power to refuse, if he perceives that it is not in the public interest. He doesn't have to give any more reasons than that. He might very well refuse, if, as I suspect there is something sinister about your brother's death, which he doesn't want revealed. Like for instance, that your brother was the subject of an intensive surveillance operation.'

'I am to take it, Mr. Stark, that you think there is something sinister?'

'Personally speaking, yes, but, as far as the *Standard* goes, we only print what we can prove. I think, and Willie agrees with me, that Angus's anti-nuclear stance had made him a target. Angus was to have been the major objector at the Gruinard Inquiry in Dingwall which starts next month.'

'Oh, that's surely simple coincidence? Angus had been a well-known opponent of the nuclear industry for many years.'

'I have suspicions that he may have latched on to something, some new information that the nuclear industry didn't want made public...'

'But my brother had already done that...'

'All I'm saying is that there is something going on, and I think Angus got to the bottom of it, no more than that. So we must take the story a step at a time. First, the FAI. We must publicise your decision in such a way that the Lord Advocate is not backed into a corner, so that it seems that your call is not in any way a product of political pressure. Make it clear that it comes from the family and for purely family reasons and is not related to other groups which have already demanded an FAI.'

'Those *are* the reasons why I've changed my mind. Hearing some of the circumstances.... The pile of papers and broken watch, the distance of the gun from the car... but principally what affected me was the realisation that I had been selfish, that I had been keeping it all to myself and that the rest of the family wanted more information.'

145

'On the subject of the gun, Mr. McBain, is it true that this was a small handmade weapon made by Afghans and presented to Angus when he was in India?'

McBain shook his head firmly as the waiter brought their entrees. 'I saw all that nonsense in the papers. No, no. There is no such gun. The gun the police found at the scene, albeit after considerable searching, was Angus's own Smith & Wesson 45. He'd had it since the war. That part is correct, and it was unlicensed. That's true, too. It sat in his garage for decades and then he cleaned it up for some reason and I remember occasionally seeing it thereafter in his desk drawer. He began taking it with him - without ammunition - on his weekend trips north. Made jokes about being attacked by wolves or bearded in his lair by unhappy clients. I don't think either of us ever really imagined the gun was capable of firing. I'm not sure it even had a firing pin. Certainly, I didn't think you could get ammunition for it - it dated back to the forties after all. But the bullet which killed him came from that gun - his own gun.'

'How can you be sure?'

'Because I myself examined the bullet which the surgeon recovered.'

'Was this the second or first bullet?'

'There was only one bullet found.'

'But the gun had been fired twice.'

An expression of pain flitted across Dr McBain's face and he closed his eyes momentarily. 'Ah, you're quite right. A test-fire, I suppose, quite common.'

'In suicides...' Stark completed his sentence for him. 'But if it is not suicide, where is the other bullet?'

18

Morton drove into the trees with an acute sense of foreboding. The rain had been holding off but the skyline was blotchy with impending cloudburst. With the window rolled down, the car was cold with the raw wetness of mountain air and the forlorn sound of the bleating of sheep among high crags, the salt wash of the rough tide beneath. Morton was travelling between the worlds of sky and sea, and on both sides of the car, dense foliage threatened to obliterate the very existence of the potholed road.

He saw the gap in the rowans, the open patch of heather, pulled over and parked off the road. Through his window he could see that the narrow verge he was parked on descended after a yard or two to a plunging ravine and at the bottom was Loch Dubh, whose water looked very cold, as it darkly shivered and stiffened beneath the sea-breeze.

Standing on the rim of the ravine, Morton noted the narrow plateau which had arrested the plunge of McBain's Volvo down the slope. It was a long way down. With the city-dweller's reluctance for wild countryside, Morton began the tortuous descent, using his hands to grasp heather clumps and to balance himself when he felt himself slipping in the boggy ground. He heard, but could not see, a car pass up on the road.

When he got to the plateau, he examined the ground and was astonished at how easily he accumulated a handful of glass fragments and flakes of what looked like maroon paint at the base of heathery tussocks and clefts between rocks. This was a real connection, of sorts, with the dead man and the car. The case was no longer merely philosophical, an abstract investigation, now he had seen, he had touched... he had been there.

Morton gazed up at the slope above and then down to the loch. The car must have crashed off the road and run straight down to lodge itself on the small plateau. Yet those who had found the crashed car said that it must have turned over because it had come to rest on its side, pointing back upwards to the road. It had also slewed round. So, unless the car's speed was much less than supposed, with the engine off and freewheeling, how had it failed to go all the way down to the water? How had it stopped here, just halfway down? As Morton stood with one leg higher than the other on the slope, conjecturing, a shadow flitted across an unseen place at the corner of his eye.

He turned quickly, his spine squirming under the skin – and lost his footing. He tumbled headlong and rolled, grasping desperately at anything and succeeded in halting his movement. He gripped tight and waited till his head cleared.

He saw a familiar, squat, stocky figure, head drawn in and cocked to one side, in a small cloud of cigarette smoke.

'Ye'll no be findin an answer if you're aye arselins, man!' The unspoken words carried in a burst of ironic laughter in the wind.

There was no-one for miles. Morton knew there was no-one standing where he saw or almost saw – or had he seen – the figure of Angus McBain? Of course not! It was his bad conscience - or his fear. He looked around in all directions. Nothing. Not a bloody thing! The machair grass whistled, the black water stiffened its shadows. No-one. He had a sore elbow where it had made contact with a stone and he rubbed it ruefully. As he climbed to the road, he heard a car passing above.

He was still jumpy. He began to have the feeling he hadn't looked thoroughly enough... had he missed something? He had the palpable sensation of another presence. He resisted the urge to look round. When he reached the rim of the slope

148

he whirled round. Nothing. Unconvinced, he hastily unlocked the car door, his spine freezing over his neck joints and clambered in and drove to Arisaig, straight through the village and carried on at a steady pace to Mallaig.

The West Highland Hotel, where Morton checked in, sits on top of the hill that overlooks Mallaig Harbour and affords a great view on clear days over the Sound of Sleat. Morton indulged himself in several pints of beer and packets of crisps in a corner seat in the wood-panelled lounge bar. His enthusiasm for the McBain story was waning somewhat. Apart from being chased by superannuated hoodlums like McGinley and his skin-head pal, now he was the victim of his own frightened delusions. Get a grip, he told himself angrily. But he seemed to feel the need of reassurance, to know that he was not alone, and since Stark was unavailable, he dialled Elizabeth McBain on his Blackberry.

'I couldn't remember if you said you were coming up for the commemoration,' he said.

'No,' she said. 'Sorry, Willie, I can't make it. I have something to tell you though, about our friend, Stoddard.' Elizabeth told him in detail of her suspicions. It suddenly became clear to Morton how McGinley had learned of his trip north. Stoddard and McGinley were working together!

'So really he doesn't know for sure where I am? It's only because they traced your call to Morroch Point. I had a narrow escape there.'

'Do be careful, Willie,' Elizabeth's voice, close to his ear, leaked sympathetic female concern. Morton liked it. He told her of his suspicions that McGinley was searching for something in her uncle's holiday house.

'Willie – um… I have my father here with me. He'd like a word with you.'

'Really? Well, put him on.'

'Mr. Morton? I hope everything goes well with you? I have decided now to request a Fatal Accident Inquiry into my brother's death and I have discussed the matter with your colleague, Mr. Stark.'

'I'm very pleased to hear it,' Morton said. 'I don't know whether Elizabeth has told you but I seem to have become the subject of surveillance. In fact, I've had a bit of a nasty experience... which I won't go into now but which leads me to believe something is going on. I also know that these secret police... Special Branch or whatever they are... are searching for something which they seem to think your brother may have had. In his house at Morroch Point, they have turned the whole place inside out. The contents of his briefcase were all strewn around...'

There was a long pause before Dr McBain came back on the line. 'Briefcase, did you say? I have been looking for that. I had come to the conclusion that that particular item was missing, which was odd as Angus took it with him everywhere. I mean everywhere. He would undoubtedly have taken it with him from Glasgow on his final journey. It wasn't returned to me with his effects and it wasn't in his home or his office. Apart from anything else, Mr Morton, it is an item of some sentimental value. Almost a family heirloom. I bought it for him about... good grief, would you believe, almost forty years ago, out of my first salary as a junior houseman in the infirmary?'

The next day, Morton returned to the narrow road above Loch Dubh. The sky had cleared somewhat but rain was not far off, only kept at bay by a strong wind. As he drove, he tried to imagine the bulky solicitor driving recklessly in the dark, chain-smoking, brusquely flinging the butts out of the window, jaw set firmly, lighting another cigarette as the maroon Volvo spun around a hairpin bend in fourth gear. But McBain was inscrutably dead and in a cheap plywood coffin (according to the stipulations of his will), annihilated, extinct, his battles over, oblivious, sleeping with a Saltire on his face, the old warrior, beneath a mountain. And Morton recalled that his was an unmarked grave! How histrionic. That was McBain and his choice, but Morton wanted to know what had really happened, and why. Not knowing was starting to bug him.

A few cars were closely parked on the roadside verge, a black Saltire, flapping furiously from a pole embedded in a small cairn of stones that someone had erected on the grassy rim of the ravine.

Malcolm Farquharson was supervising a group of youths constructing a substantial cairn on the plateau halfway down the slope. He stood bent over in the wind, his beard blowing in white tails over his face, green-blue kilt swirling around his legs, revealing the silver hilt of the sgian dubh in his green stocking.

Morton slowly descended the hillside, battling against the bullying wind. 'Good day, Mr Morton,' Farquharson roared at him, holding firmly to his pale blue glengarry. 'It is good to see you.'

'Are you planning to have the ceremony down here...?'

Farquharson studied his face closely, then he nodded. 'Ach, no, no, we'll have to have it up on the roadside. In this weather...'

The rest of what he was saying was lost to Morton because of the howling wind which had suddenly sprung up, scattering heavy drops of rain. Sea-mist too was already billowing like shrouds through ghostly trees as they scrambled back to the road.

About a dozen cars in all and a camper-van, Morton saw, all crammed in to the tiny verge and some almost blocking

151

the road. There were now several banners ripping against the wind and Morton recognised some prominent Vanguard supporters but also Jacobite Monarchist flags and badges from the Nationhood cultural fringe group. All shades were there, Morton reckoned, many axes to grind. A cold-looking teenage Vanguard supporter in kilt and black sweatshirt thrust a small card into Morton's hand. Beneath the red celtic knot logo of Scottish Vanguard, the card read, "On this spot, on 7th April, Angus McBain, friend of the Scottish nation, was assassinated. His spirit lives on. "

About thirty persons assembled by the main road around the black Saltire now flapping so wildly that it looked ready to take leave of its pole and go into orbit. Morton stood on the outskirts, chaffing his hands together. He noticed a bearded man across the road, filming the proceedings with a video-camera and wondered idly whether he was from Special Branch. He had half anticipated McGinley would appear and felt that in daylight, with others about, he wouldn't feel so scared.

Malcolm Farquharson held a megaphone and began to speak. His gentle voice even with its electronic aid strove to make itself heard against the gale from the sea. He was saying kind words about McBain and telling of his pointblank refusal to accept the suicide theory: calling upon all patriots to strive to obtain a Fatal Accident Inquiry. It suddenly struck Morton than Farquharson did not know about Iain McBain's change of heart. And then it began to sleet, coming down in slow white diagonal lines, wetting the faces and hands of the audience. Farquharson was winding things up in his dignified manner, hatless, for his glengarry had blown off and been retrieved by someone else. 'All that remains is for the piper to play the coronach which he has specially written for this ceremony...' his voice took on an edge of unaccustomed ferocity... 'and we will come back here next year and the next if needs be until we get answers and find out who is responsible for Angus McBain's death.'

The pipes' shrill notes perfectly suited the harshness and bleakness of this place, Morton reflected, rubbing his hands and desperately waiting for the moment when he might be able to return to the warmth of his car. Bagpipes were an instrument for mountains and mist and grandeur and personally he had always preferred them in the next glen, rather than six feet from his ear. The slow lingering lamentation of each note and its successor, a weird, dreeing, keening, mournful sound, a dirge for a nation steeped in defeat, and how appropriate, Morton thought that such a farce was occurring just a mile or two from the spot where the last Jacobite rising had begun and ended. That was irony!

Morton returned to his car and sat there until everyone except Farquharson had left, then went over to the ancient yellow Ford Escort and sat in the back on the fake tiger skin upholstery behind him. Rain was thrashing the windscreen beyond the blue fluffy dice. Farquharson told him his son, Duncan, had gone off to the nearest pub with some friends.

'It looks as though there will be an FAI after all,' Morton said, 'Iain McBain has changed his mind and is taking that up with the Lord Advocate and the Fiscal's office.'

Farquharson nodded. 'Thank you for telling me, Mr. Morton, that is good news.'

Morton agreed, 'but what I'm concerned with at the moment is locating the briefcase. I think that is what McGinley's thugs are after. Must be something important inside it.'

'I hope the contents are crucial,' Farquharson said solemnly, 'crucial. If they are what Angus died for. But I remember the briefcase in question. Indeed, quite an antique it was, a beautiful tooled-leather job. Given him by his brother decades ago, as I recall. Went with him everywhere.'

There was something about the hesitant note in Farquharson's voice that made Morton ask the question. 'I don't suppose you'd have any idea...?'

'Where it is?' Farquharson finished his sentence. 'As a matter for fact, Mr. Morton, I might be able to make a suggestion... an unlikely possibility... a longshot as they say...

'Go on,' Morton said. 'Anything that might help.

'You see Angus and I were old friends,' the Highlander began, 'and we'd shared many walks and talks together in this area. He had certain worries... some of his clients were... perhaps unscrupulous is the word... and we decided, that we might...' he paused and tugged at his beard and glanced over into the back seat at Morton. 'This might seem highly ridiculous to you, Morton?' he suggested.

'Not at all, but what were you going to say?'

'We both reached the conclusion that it might be wise to have a safe hiding place where we could keep certain documents from prying eyes of... well, gentlemen like your Mr. McGinley. This was long ago - maybe ten years ago - and as it happened, we never did use the hiding place. Or at least I never did.'

'You think he might have?'

'Well now, that's just what I'm wondering.'

'And it is near here?'

'It needed to be somewhere easily accessible but safe from accidental discovery.'

'Where is it?'

The Highlander smiled broadly over at him. 'Patience, Mr. Morton, I'm coming to that. You see, at the time, we were walking upon the beach at Loch Ailort and we saw a team of British Rail engineers working at the station. That was what gave us the idea you see.'

19

Danny Stark had spent most of the morning browsing the Internet, collating information on Special Branch, the Security Intelligence Service (SIS) and the Atomic Energy Authority Special Constabulary. Not much of that kind of information is available, even under the Freedom of Information Act, but Stark knew that each Police Authority and some government departments had to produce Annual Reports. Most were now on-line and among the statistical appendices, could be found manpower numbers. Adding these together could establish an approximate strength for the Special Branch. But numbers of personnel of the British Security Intelligence Service which includes MI5, are impossible to ascertain, or even guess at. They are not listed anywhere for reasons of state security though they have 'shoot to kill' powers, as do the armed nuclear police force, within a 15 mile radius of nuclear facilities or nuclear convoys travelling on public roads. Nor is there public information about the other secret police units, the MOD police, who have powers to investigate suspected saboteurs; the crack anti-terrorist, para-military forces who operate in plain-clothes; the special military units who specialise in infiltration of all sectors of the population, whose very existence is not even acknowledged. Other units whose remits are more of less unknown include D11, the Defence Intelligence Agency; and the numerous American security and intelligence operatives working in Scotland alongside the British SIS. It is a sinister alphabet soup of acronyms and Stark had to concede that McGinley could be from any or none of them. He'd spoken to Archie MacDonald, on Morton's advice, and to the Assistant Chief Constable of Lothian & Borders Police but was no nearer finding out precisely who McGinley was and why he was harassing Morton. Stark had to curtail his search at lunchtime. He had hoped to construct a carefully-worded piece probing links between McBain's death and the harassment of a journalist by a 'secret policeman', which would consider the various shadowy security agencies and also give details of the odd meeting in MacDonald's office. He planned to use Morton's name in the piece in order to safeguard him from further harassment, but the solicitor completely refused to comment or to be mentioned in the story. He would have to be used anonymously, if at all.

'Ach, without the lawyer ye've nothing,' Leadbetter concluded bluntly, leaning back in his swivel chair in the glass-walled office in the corner of the pressroom. 'You could use Willie's account of the meeting but stories about journalists by other journalists is too far up its own arse.'

Stark didn't want to let the story go. 'But if we could get a picture of McGinley and his accomplices, we could send it to the Home Office and demand an explanation,' he argued, fingering the smooth upper lip where his moustache had been. He'd taken it off the previous evening just for a change. 'There must be a way to stand this bloody story up.'

'We'll get the story, whatever it is,' Leadbetter said. 'Even after all this time. But tittle-tattle about the police hounding a hack is not news. What we need is the link - if there is a link - with the death of your man, McBain. Wait and see what Willie comes up with in the next few days. Meanwhile, Danny, get some real work done, eh?'

Willie Morton drove through the birch woods on the steeply twisting road which descends to the shoreline of Loch Ailort, the wide sea-loch, whose tides were lapping at the rocks ten feet beneath the side of the road. He parked in the deserted hotel carpark. The lights of the hotel were on, although it was only early afternoon, since there was a pall of sea-mist hanging low over the loch which spilled up into the hillsides. It was so thick that once Morton had walked fifty yards back along the road in the drifting cone of his torch light, and crossed onto the grass verge, he could no longer make out the lights of the hotel. Just ahead he saw the rusty iron gate Farquharson had told him about. Just the gate - no fence or wall attached - and behind it, a strip of old tarmac, breaking up and already mossed-over and weedy, leading into the woods towards the railway embankment on the West Highland Line.

Morton hurried into the shade of the trees and began scrambling on his hands and knees up the steep sides, impenetrably thick with brambles and drenched weeds and nettles. At the top he came upon a wire fence. But there was nothing on the other side except a sheer drop of thirty feet into a railway culvert somehow free of the fog. Morton didn't at first notice the drop because of a clump of bracken on the other side of the fence. He had almost vaulted headlong into nothingness. He stood peering down through the bracken, feeling the wet vegetation with his left hand, searching for the edge. The railway line at this place had been blasted out of solid rock and it looked dank and dangerous. Once down there, Morton knew, he'd have a job getting back out. On the far wall of the culvert he could see the orange wetness seeping through the shiny black rock face. The mist was infiltrating the hillsides above and on all sides.

Morton found easier access and carefully lowered himself down onto the single track. It was narrow, about fifteen feet wide. He now bitterly regretted not having checked the railway timetable at Lochailort Station. He would have to take a chance.

He began to walk on the rusted clinker between oily railway sleepers towards the tunnel. Farquharson had told him the tunnel was two hundred yards long. If a train was to come from Fort William it would hit him long before he heard it. He nervously switched on the torch and hurried into the glistening mouth of the tunnel, hearing only the muffled scuff of his sodden brogues on the greasy stones. It was echoingly empty as he moved into the darkness. Morton counted his paces, eighty-two, eighty-four, ninety, ninety-six, one hundred. Here it was. Or should be. He felt along the wall for the cavity. The torch beam raked the glistening walls and illuminated the limy-green scale. There was a small square brick-lined vent. As he went down onto his knees to feel inside, he began to wonder if he was hearing twanging noises. He strained to hear but the noises were certainly coming from the railway line, metal noises, unmistakably - of a train somewhere on the track!

He lunged deeper into the hole, cheek pressing against the wetness of stone and his fingers felt something at last that yielded to the touch. He grasped it and pulled it out into the torch beam. The briefcase. But the twanging steel on steel noises were intensifying. Grasping the leather case, he ran for the tunnel entrance, his lungs bursting, stumbling on the tricky surface, and fell headlong. A brilliant glow was suffusing the tunnel. Oncoming train lights! The briefcase had fallen and he'd also dropped the torch. He hauled himself to his feet hearing only the shrieking violence of the train thundering through the tunnel towards him. His scrabbling fingers found the briefcase and he was out, crashing into the daylight.

He had no time to get out of the culvert, saw a space at the front of the tunnel face, about two feet wide, dived into it, flattening himself against the embankment.

The train smashed out of the tunnel, inches from him and he endured the endless brutality of its noisy onrush. He dared not look down. Only when the train had gone and the stinging sounds on the iron track had subsided, almost completely silenced, did Morton look down to see that the torch lying at his feet was now two-dimensional.

Morton was still nervy as he climbed out of the culvert and stepped over the wire fence. He happened to look up at that moment, leaning on a fence post and saw a man with a rifle moving swiftly towards him.

Stark was working up a piece speculating on the likely victims of an impending reshuffle, when the whistling copy boy with the big feet and raging acne carelessly tossed a manila envelope into his in-tray. An official letter with the royal crest of HM Customs & Excise. Stark read it quickly, grunted in mild disbelief and continued working on his story. After a few minutes, his brow corrugated, he reached for the letter again and re-read it. Odd. He took it through to Leadbetter, who was lounging on his swivel chair, feet up, chomping a pie, looking even more than usual like Desperate Dan.

'Have a look at this, boss. HM Customs. Stoddard.'

'Stoddard?' Leadbetter said through a mouthful of mince and pastry, leaning over to take the letter. He read it and looked up at Stark. 'See what you mean,' he said. 'It's the kind of letter ma mammie used tae write to get me off maths homework.'

Stark grinned. 'I mean, okay, it's only a letter confirming Stoddard's credentials as a bona fide Customs & Excise man but, I mean to say…'

'Yeah, it's unheard of,' Leadbetter agreed, swinging his legs back to the ground. 'If the guy is genuinely an investigator, working in a dangerous world of grasses and major-league drug dealers and the like, why would his boss write a letter to the papers telling us his name? So what else do we know about this loon, Danny?'

'Well, we've now got a picture,' Stark told him gleefully. 'Taken when he had a meeting with Willie at Waverley Station. I only just received it.'

'Nice one! And is it good and grainy?'

'Yeah. Taken by a real amateur with a long lens. Makes him look really shifty, like a Nazi war criminal.'

'Better and better. So the angle is: "Possible Drugs Link to McBain Death?"'

'No, boss,' Stark said carefully. 'Sorry and all that, but that's a load of crap. That's what we're meant to believe.'

'Ye cheeky wee get!' Leadbetter growled in disbelief, extracting a large lump of grey gristle from his mouth and flicking it accurately into his paperbin. 'I've been doing this job longer'n you've been alive. I wasn't asking, I was telling. Whether the story is wrong or no it's a good story. We've been wanting to use it for weeks but this guy with the funny name finally gives us our chance.'

Stark expressed his misgivings. 'It's Willie's story. The picture is down to him.'

'Ach, well, do it under a joint by-line, if it bothers you. Where is he anyway?"

'I'll need to check with him, about the meeting. You know, the details.'

'Well, see to it, laddie,' Leadbetter wiped his beard with a paper tissue. 'And look, Danny, even if this guy is phony and shootin us a line, well, we can do another story about that. There are eight million stories in the naked city.'

'Gee, thanks boss!' Stark moaned to himself, returning to his crocodile eat crocodile screensaver and his cold cup of coffee.

20

Morton steadied his nerves with a pint and a packet of cheese and onion crisps in the dismal wood-panelled lounge where long-dead salmon and speckled brown trout gazed disinterestedly from glass cases above the gantry to the collection of antique fishing rods bolted to a wooden panel on the far wall. The edges of a half-eaten sandwich curled up on a plate on a formica-topped table beside the dregs of a pint of Guinness and two cigarette stubs in a metal ashtray.

The gamekeeper, Murdo McLachlan, swung through the doors just as Morton was about to leave.

'Drinking on duty?' he exclaimed jovially, leaning his shotgun against the bar and deftly removing his tattered wax jacket. 'It was you I saw, wasn't it?'

Morton smiled sourly and quickly drained his pint.

McLachlan rapped on the counter. The barman appeared in the archway that divided the lounge bar from the hotel's interior.

'Afternoon, Murdo, your usual?'

'And another for our friend here,' he nodded at Morton,

'Thanks, but I was just leaving.'

The gamekeeper looked incredulously at him. 'Ach man, you'll no refuse a nip? A wee apology for giein' ye a fleg on the hill.'

Morton accepted defeat. 'Well, go on then, but there's no need.' He raised the glass he had been given.

'Cheers!'

'Aye, *slainthe!*'

After a gulp of whisky, the keeper turned towards Morton, a wry smile turning up the corners of his mouth. 'You'll be thinking that I'm the devil of a nosey bugger?'

'It's your job. I can see that,' Morton said, reluctantly, holding up his glass for inspection. Pale, an old single malt then, possibly twelve years. He wanted to get away.

'Ah that's good of you to say, man, good of you to say,' the keeper said and there was a long pause. 'I like to keep an eye on strangers. We get just all sorts here you know.'

'I'll bet.'

'Not so much of the poaching nowadays but we still lose a few 24-point stags each season. Mind, I could see right off you weren't one of those.'

'No,' said Morton, 'no antlers at all!'

'Funny man you are. Hah!"

Morton didn't want to prolong the conversation. 'No. I get my meat at the butchers.' He downed the remainder of his whisky and began to sidle off his stool.

'So what's your verdict then?' the keeper suddenly asked, looking closely at him.

'Eh?' Morton grunted in alarm.

'The tunnel man, the tunnel, will it have to come down?'

Morton smiled in relief. 'Oh, ah, no, it's…' he searched his memory… 'it's structurally sound, as far as I could tell.'

'Trust Scottish Rail to send an architect all the way from Edinburgh when I could have told them that over the phone,' the keeper grinned, his jaw hanging slackly, revealing tobacco-stained teeth.

Morton turned back at the door. 'Who told you I was from Edinburgh?'

The keeper tapped the side of his nose and grinned. 'Told you I keep an eye on strangers. I thought maybe you were with that other lot that were here yesterday.'

'No, I always work alone,' Morton said. 'They couldn't have been from Scottish Rail or I would know about it.'

'Well, well,' McLachlan said, putting down his drink. He leaned over the counter and called for the barman, who appeared in the archway. 'Jimmy, mind those two fellas you was telling me about, yesterday?'

'Oh aye, Murdo, the blokes in the big black Range Rover.'

'That's the chaps. Now, Jimmy, they did say they were from Scottish Rail didn't they?'

'Didn't believe a word of it myself, Murdo. Funny kind of blokes. A gin and tonic for the big lad and the wee chap was on the orange juice. But you get all sorts up here in the season.'

'That you do, Jimmy, that you do,' the keeper agreed and turned back only to see the door closing behind Morton. 'Ah, he's gone. Well, will you have one yourself, Jimmy?' he inquired, flipping banknotes from the top pocket of his padded jerkin.

'I will, Murdo. And I think that was another of them funny blokes,' the barman said, nodding at the door. 'From Edinburgh, you say? Didn't like the look of him myself.'

'We get them, we certainly do,' the keeper ruminated. 'I caught him poking about in the railway tunnel. Claimed to be an architect for Scottish Rail. Some cock and bull story about checking the tunnel to see if it was safe. Couldn't have been more than a minute or two after the 3.45 train to Mallaig had gone through.'

The barman laughed. 'And wasn't that where the other two were just yesterday?'

'Ach, no, Jimmy, them two fellas was down at the station, hanging around, like they were looking for something. They were up the bank and in the trees on the other side of the road. God knows what they were up to.'

'Aye, the world's gone mad, Murdo, that's for sure.'

Morton resisted the temptation to examine the briefcase and its contents, although he unlocked the boot to check it was there. Still feeling jumpy, he set off on the road back to

Edinburgh. He imagined his route: Fort William, Glencoe, Tyndrum, Crianlarich, and then either east through Glen Dochart to Lochearnhead, to Crieff, Perth and down the M90 and the Forth Bridge or south through Glen Falloch by the side of Loch Lomond to Dumbarton, through Glasgow and then the M8 to Newbridge Roundabout. It was a long way whichever route he decided on. He'd better petrol-up at Fort William. It was after 10pm before Morton found a parking space near his home, switched off the engine and stretched his neck, feeling the lump of tension in his collar bone that he always got driving long distances. He stretched his legs, collected the briefcase from the boot, locked the steering wheel immobiliser, and walked the few streets to Shandon Place.

Before he even unlocked the front door, he could hear his phone ringing. Stark.

'I've been ringing you all night, Willie, everything okay?'

'I'm just in the door. You in the pub?'

'Yeah, the Vaults, coming down?'

'Nah,' Morton said. 'I've got things to do. Listen, I've got McBain's briefcase and I think this is what McGinley is after. I'll see you tomorrow.'

Stark didn't seem to hear him. 'Look,' he said urgently – 'Hugh's insisted we do the Stoddard-drugs link story. It'll be in tomorrow, picture and everything. Sorry.'

'Don't worry, Danny. Might be a good decoy, give us cover on the story we're really doing.'

'That's what I thought. Keep McGinley off your back. I've given you a joint by-line, and you're name-checked in the story as well. Hope that's okay. Did you say you found the briefcase? Well…'

Once Stark had rung off, Morton rang Elizabeth McBain to give her an update then made himself a coffee. Now was the moment. There was McBain's antique leather briefcase on his sofa. Morton approached it with trepidation. What was going to be in there? Most of all, he feared there would be nothing. He undid the brass clasps and snapped it open and began unloading the contents onto the carpet. A folder of re-typed newspaper cuttings and the yellowing cuttings themselves, which related to a book he was working on; papers about the Knoydart Public Inquiry, documents from his years as SNP Spokesman on Nuclear Issues. Personal effects: a crushed empty packet of Gold Flake cigarettes, a Law Society of Scotland diary with no writing on any of the pages, old-fashioned fountain pens, a red toothbrush still in its cellophane. A photocopy of his will. *His will?* Nine large but closely-typed legal pages; an extract from the Registers of Scotland. Morton noted the receipt from Glasgow Sheriff Court, dated the 3rd of July but two full years before his death. It was an extremely detailed document, bearing, at the bottom of each page, the scrawled signature of its progenitor. But that was all.

The doorbell rang. At this late hour? Carefully he tiptoed to the door and peered through the spy-hole. Elizabeth stood outside. She was alone. He undid the bolt. Ushering her inside, he locked the door. She looked at him curiously.

'Just a precaution,' he said, and smiled grimly, 'don't worry, I'll let you out.'

'So what is in it?' she asked, nodding at the briefcase.

'Not much,' he told her. 'Just personal stuff. Nothing of any importance that I can find.'

'Then why would my uncle have taken the trouble to hide it?'

'I'm really not sure.'

Elizabeth picked up the briefcase. 'Yes, I remember this. He used to take it everywhere, even when he came to visit us.'

'The only thing that might be relevant are these old clippings, but I doubt it...'

She looked quizzically at him. 'And you said that McGinley had been seen near where it was hidden? You don't think it has been tampered with...?'

'The only other person who knew of the hiding place was Malcolm Farquharson,' Morton said. 'And he wouldn't - couldn't - have told them. He would have told me if they'd approached him. Also, they were seen at Lochailort on Friday on the same day that I overheard them discussing whether I might have it. So clearly they didn't have it then.' A new thought struck him. 'Unless, of course, they returned after the gamekeeper had gone, but frankly, I simply can't see them leaving it in the tunnel if they had found it.'

Elizabeth was sceptical. 'That would have been the clever thing to do though. Remove whatever was in there of importance, replace irrelevant things like these items, and leave it for you to find.'

'Yes, that would be clever,' Morton conceded, but the problem with that is, firstly - if I found it, there would be nothing worthwhile inside, so it would make me suspicious. Secondly, they couldn't be certain that I would ever find it, so for them, in their attempts to throw me off the scent, it would be a wasted opportunity. No, I don't think they've had this.'

Elizabeth carefully re-examined the contents and studied the pages of her uncle's will, while Morton made fresh coffee in the kitchen. As he was pouring boiling water into the mugs, he heard Elizabeth exclaim loudly.

'Willie!'

He rushed through. She pointed at the inside of the briefcase. 'Have you seen this?' she said. 'There's an extra row of stitching here. Now why would that be?'

166

Morton went down on his knees to examine it. 'That is odd.' There was a double row of stitching along the top of the briefcase on the inside where there was only one row at the bottom. The extra row was neat but not neat enough. It had been done very carefully but not by a machine.

'Very devious. It fooled us at least,' Morton said. 'Of course it might have been added for reinforcement. After all, it is over forty years old. We'll soon know.'

Elizabeth took out a pair of nail scissors from her leather handbag and began to remove the stitching. After a few loops had been removed, she pulled the loose end and it all came easily then. There was a secret pocket and inside were three flimsy folded pages, photocopies of poor quality. From a cheap old-fashioned Xerox machine, thought Morton, handling them delicately. The typescript was grainy and blotchy and smelt of chemical. The pages were shiny and thin and they crackled as he opened them out and flattened them onto the table top.

'What are they?' Elizabeth asked eagerly.

'An official stamp,' Morton noted. '*Streng Geheim*, that's German isn't it?'

'Not sure, I'll look it up...' Elizabeth told him. 'Oh... *top secret*!'

'Ye gods! And the logo at the top is the International Nuclear Energy Authority. Address in Vienna, and it's dated... February this year!' Morton exclaimed, his voice rising in excitement. 'Elizabeth! This is... is...'

McBain had written an English translation, word-for-word between the typed lines in a broad-nibbed fountain pen whose ink had separated and gone slightly green. McBain's scrawl was never easy to read at any time, but, with effort, Morton slowly deciphered the message. 'Some kind of nuclear accident,' he concluded... 'at a reactor in the Czech Republic, a place called Bohunice...em, let's see, severe structural damage to exterior and interior fabric… large cracks in steel vessels…' He stopped and ran his hand through his hair at his left temple. 'Jeezo!'

'What. *What?*' Elizabeth demanded, scanning the second page.

'Meltdown,' Morton said quietly. 'Or partial meltdown, the rest is too difficult…' He looked at her and felt a hot rush of anxiety and of fear. This couldn't be real, could it?'

'My uncle died because of this?' Elizabeth said softly, adding, 'was *murdered* because of this?'

It was almost too much to take in. Morton read the rest of it. No emergency back-up systems… the scientists who built the plant had been dispersed… the reactor was a Soviet-built VVER 230, built in the late 1960s.

The second paragraph outlined the damage. Workforce staff and several local residents seriously ill with radiation sickness. Estimates of volume of radioactive material which leaked into atmosphere vary from 200 to 1,000 litres… reactor floor flooded, three feet deep in contaminated cooling fluid…

'I can't read any more of it,' Morton said. 'Too much of a scrawl. It's catastrophic.' He sat down on the sofa. 'I need a drink.'

'Not now,' Elizabeth protested. 'We need to think clearly about what to do.'

'Yes now,' Morton said firmly, going into the kitchen and pouring himself an inch of Glenfiddich and adding a few drops of tap water. He took a sip and rolled the rich 10 years old single malt around his tongue. 'Ah, better,' he muttered.

'So *what* are we going to do?' Elizabeth demanded.

'God knows! Finish reading this,' Morton said, 'to make sure we've got the whole story right. The first thing is to establish when all this took place. If it did. I mean, can we really believe it?'

'February,' Elizabeth said. 'Clearly it was just before, maybe a few days before, this INEA minute was drawn up. So could be about six weeks before Angus' death.'

'He had this for six weeks,' Morton mused. 'So what was he going to do with it? I never heard anything about a nuclear accident.'

'I didn't either. But we can check.'

'According to this, the INEA seems to have decided to keep the whole thing quiet,' Morton said.

'Nothing new there. We only know what they tell us.' Elizabeth was reading the second page. 'They have all eventualities covered. If the Austrian government monitors picked up the high radioactivity at Vienna 80 km away, a statement would be issued that a minor incident – minor incident - had occurred but that the public were in no danger. All INEA member nations were to collaborate in this... deception. '

But it was the final page that was the clincher that rendered Morton and Elizabeth speechless with rage and fear for their own safety. They barely had time to think about their next course of action when the doorbell went.

21

The ringing of the doorbell was terrifying and unexpected. Morton and Elizabeth looked at each other, at the items on the floor, the pages spread over the table top.

'Who the hell...?' Morton whispered. 'It's almost midnight!'

'Wouldn't be your friend, Danny, would it?' Elizabeth suggested hopefully. They were fearful and grasping at straws. Morton shook his head.

'He's in the pub. Won't be seeing him tonight.'

Then, as abruptly as it had started, the ringing stopped. They began to breathe again. Morton tiptoed out into the hall and heard footsteps going down stairs.

'Whoever it was, they've gone,' he said jubilantly. He went into the kitchen and poured himself another inch of Glenfiddich and drops of water. It went over the back of his throat and brought a soothing warmth.

Morton had just returned to the living room when the doorbell went again, insistent, very loud.

'They must have just gone down to the street and seen the lights,' Morton whispered. 'We'll have to see who it is. Let's get this out of the way first.'

They hastily gathered up the briefcase and its contents and took them into the bedroom in the dark.

'Shove them under the duvet! Elizabeth, you stay in here, and I'll see who it is.'

Morton hurried to the door, discarding his shoes and socks and sweatshirt which he bundled into the cupboard. 'Just a minute,' he called. 'Who is it?' He couldn't hear a reply. He unlocked the door and gingerly opened it and peered out.

It was Peter Stoddard.

'What on earth…?' he began, through the gap in the doorway. 'It's midnight. And how did you get my address?'

'Forgive me,' Stoddard said in his curious gobbling voice, 'I know it's late, but I wanted to show you this.' He brandished a rolled-up newspaper.

'What is it?'

'Your *Standard* article.' He held it up. 'The front page story you did… I'm not happy… can I come in?' Stoddard looked rather forlorn, standing out in the hall.

'I was almost in bed, I've had a long bloody day. Can this not wait?' But it occurred to him that maybe he could ask him about McGinley, see if they were working together. He didn't feel any fear of Stoddard like he did of McGinley.

'Well?' Morton demanded.

'Your article has my picture in it,' Stoddard complained. 'That's hardly fair. It's going to cause me a lot of trouble with my superiors. But it's the tone of the piece, sceptical, as if what I told you is a pack of lies…'

There was something almost plaintive in his tone which persuaded Morton to let him in against his own better judgement.

'Okay, but just so that I can see the piece,' he explained. 'I didn't actually write it, you know – it was my colleague - and I've been out all day.'

Stoddard glanced quickly around the living room, as if searching for something. He would have noted the two coffee mugs, and, Morton, realised, could hardly have failed to spot Elizabeth's suede jacket on the armchair. 'Sit down,' Morton said. And excuse me a minute.'

Morton left the room, closing the door behind him and went across the hall into the bedroom without putting the light on. He couldn't see Elizabeth at first. She was crouched down on the far side of the bed.

171

'It's Stoddard,' he hissed. 'Just stay hid and I'll get shot of him as soon as I can. Keep the door ajar so you can hear what's going on.'

He returned to the living room. Stoddard was standing beside the glass-topped coffee table. 'Sit down,' Morton said. 'Now I'll have a quick look at that *Standard*. You were pretty quick off the mark, old boy. How did you know it was going to be in?'

Stoddard sighed as he sank into the sofa, his eyes seeming to droop downwards with the lines of his face. 'No, of course I didn't know. I picked up a copy at Waverley station by pure chance. You get Sunday papers there from about 8pm,' he said, adding, 'as I'm sure you're aware, so I came up to discuss it with you. I'm not happy about several things in it…'

Morton held up an admonitory hand. 'Hang on, I haven't read it yet.'

There was a pause of almost a couple of minutes while Morton read Danny's cleverly written attempt to milk the sensationalism of a 'drug-link' whilst distancing himself from the sources of the stories. There were plenty of 'he claims' and 'it has been suggested' and the article contained strong statements by several individuals denying the credibility of any drug-link.

'Well it seems okay to me,' Morton told him. 'As I said, I didn't write it.' He handed the newspaper back, and as he did so, noticed a sheet of paper lying underneath the coffee table, very close to Stoddard's black shoes. It was one of the photocopied pages of the INEA document. Morton froze and Stoddard's complaints washed over him. All he could think about was how to hide that piece of paper. He had to get Stoddard away from the table. His eyes fell on the empty whisky glass. Of course!

'Like a drink?' he offered, getting to his feet. 'I'm on whisky.'

'Well, I, ah, ehm, yes,' Stoddard chortled in his curious manner. 'Don't mind if I do. Long as HM tax duty has been paid on it.'

'Huh.' Morton went into the kitchen. Stoddard followed him as Morton had hoped he would. 'Nice place you have here,' he said appreciatively.

Morton led him to the area of worktop where there were several bottles of spirits and cans of beer. 'Choose your poison,' he said, 'I'll just get my glass.' He darted back into the living room, snatched his glass and the paper, dropped the paper safely behind the armchair out of sight, and returned to the kitchen. 'Ah, Glenfiddich 10 year old?' he mused. 'Don't worry, tax has been paid on it. That was a weak joke wasn't it?'

'Somewhat.'

'One Fiddich coming right up.' He poured a shot of whisky into a tumbler and turned round. 'Neat? Or…?'

'Soda, if you have it. No? then a little lemonade will be fine.'

'In 10 year old?' Morton winced.

'You'd think, that being based in the Highlands for five years, I'd have acquired a taste for it *au naturel* but I'm afraid my stomach won't allow me.'

'So what is your problem with the story? Seems to me we've done exactly what you suggested.'

'The picture, mainly. That was completely unnecessary to your story,' he peered at Morton over the rim of his whisky glass. 'A bit sneaky. And how you obtained it I don't know. You must have had someone concealed in Waverley Station somewhere…'

Morton shrugged. 'That's irrelevant. But having your boss confirm your identity to a major national newspaper now that… that virtually invited this kind of publicity.'

'I accept that,' Stoddard said quietly. 'It was, in hindsight, a blunder. Luckily I'm no longer working in the Highlands.'

Morton raised an eyebrow. 'Oh, you're not? You didn't make that clear before.'

'No. But if I was I could have been put at considerable risk, but what annoys me is the tone of the piece, as if… as a public servant I am not to be believed. I volunteered the information I gave you out of my conviction that there is a drug-link to McBain's death. I still believe that.' Stoddard put down his whisky and sat on the stool, leaned back and crossed his legs. 'And what do you believe, Mr. Morton? Have I been wasting my time? Is it all for nothing?'

Morton didn't answer. Instead he went on the attack after throwing back his whisky. 'Exactly what are your motives?' he asked. 'You must see that it looks odd when somebody who is some kind of a secret policeman volunteers information and goes to the trouble of having his identity confirmed.' He brushed the hair back behind his ears in his habitual manner and patted it reassuringly. 'You must see how odd it looks. As though someone's trying too hard.'

'I'm sorry if you wish to misinterpret my actions,' Stoddard said wearily.

Morton stood above him. 'I mean, you turn up here at this time of night… and how *did* you get my address by the way… and make such an effort to convince me McBain was on the trail of drug-gangs. Then, when we use your story, you're still not satisfied. What is it you actually want?'

Stoddard rose to his feet. 'If this is what you feel, well…'

'I don't think you've any right to claim wounded pride, either, if I may say,' Morton told him. 'You've given me nothing but rumours, in fact you given me so little to go on, that I was forced to use you as the source of the story just to have something stand up. Unless you can give me something more… tangible, the story ends here, with you.'

'Well, yes,' Stoddard said, becoming more animated, 'of course, that's just what I do hope to do... but getting my picture in the paper doesn't exactly help.'

Morton led the way into the hall. 'I'd welcome any further help you can give me, but only if it is definite information that leads somewhere.' He had a sudden thought. 'Oh, and since you know *my* address, how can I contact you? Do you have a card?'

'Of course,' Stoddard abstracted his wallet and slipped out a small white printed card, which he handed to Morton. It had the HM Customs & Excise crest on it. Morton deliberately fumbled the card and it fell at Stoddard's feet, who instinctively bent over to retrieve it. As he did so, Morton snatched his wallet and stepped back into the living room, before Stoddard could do anything.

'What... give me that!' he gurgled angrily, coming forward just as a photograph fluttered out of the wallet and landed on the carpet. Morton saw that it was a photograph of himself.

'Ha! How will you explain that, I wonder?' he said calmly. 'Was that taken by your pal, McGinley?'

Stoddard looked at him, the harsh light illuminating every pore and crack in his face. 'Who?'

'I think you know very well...'

Stoddard said nothing, pocketing the wallet which he had snatched back. He glared at Morton, strode to the door and marched down the stairs indignantly.

'It proves something,' Elizabeth said later, once the door was locked. 'It's been taken in the street, by a telephoto lens. Looks as if it has been cut out of a larger picture.'

'Yes, Morton agreed, 'a long tom, probably 300mm zoom, a professional job. The cheek of him, complaining about *us* taking *his* picture!'

'What on earth was he doing with it?' she wondered.

'What it proves,' Morton said, 'is what you told me before, that Stoddard and his friends are watching me. I'm under surveillance. Question is, Elizabeth, is Stoddard working with McGinley... or what is their connection?'

Elizabeth had been re-reading the photocopied pages of the INEA memo. 'I think we both know,' she said, 'that the connection is this stuff. Even just holding these pages is making me feel scared. I've got the feeling that we could be in great danger if they find out we have these.'

'Assuming they don't already know,' Morton muttered, mainly to himself.

22

Angus McBain stood jubilantly on the steps of the High Court in Glasgow. The solicitor's bucolic face pulsated with an almost demonic energy. Kneeling in front of him, Willie Morton minutely searched the blotched grainy features on the screen for traces of a sardonic smile. Was it possible - even remotely - that he could have faked his own death - to make it look like murder and pin the blame on the nuclear industry? Morton pressed the play button and watched McBain come alive, the famous triumph, congratulatory handshakes, the broad impish smile, the ebullience. Was he enjoying a joke at everyone else's expense? It hardly seemed likely that, having obtained such an astonishing coup by acquiring - however he *had* acquired - these secret minutes, he would tamely commit suicide. And even if he had contemplated faking his own murder, surely he would have made the secret minutes more accessible? No, Morton decided, his death had to be the result of foul play. Perhaps 'they' had expected him to have the papers on him. Going by the statements of friends it would have seemed likely, even certain to them that he would have had them with him on that fateful journey.

So it all came back to the personality of McBain. According to the testimony of Iain and Elizabeth, to the evidence of party members and the public record of his activities, Angus was a determined, forthright and positive activist, a driven and determined individual, used to adversity, already prepared to be the subject of surveillance. Anyone who knowingly took on the entire nuclear establishment, as McBain had, would know the risks. Given his past record, McBain would have relished the trump card he had been dealt. These secret papers which he had spent time

177

translating, were dynamite in the hands of someone like McBain. Yes, but he had had them for six weeks, six full weeks, and had apparently done nothing with them. What was he waiting for? Surely the very existence of this secret memo… Morton felt a cold finger lifting the fine hairs at the base of his spine. Of course! The memo by itself was useless. Could be denied, disproved as a fake, just like that earlier memo back in 1992. McBain would have been painfully aware of that. This time he was waiting for absolute proof. And that could only mean… *The convoys!*

Morton retrieved the third page and reread it carefully. The British Nuclear representative at the secret INEA meeting in Geneva had suggested Dounreay as the preferred destination for the storage of the contaminated machinery due to the "minimal risk of interference by anti-nuclear protestors" in the UK. This had been accepted unanimously and a bracketed phrase added that the machinery would be "transported as normal road freight with minimal security presence." That was the most damning part of it! It wasn't coming for reprocessing, merely for storage and it was coming disguised in traffic, alongside mothers taking kids to school, commuters going to work, food delivery lorries. Morton tightly closed his eyes and opened them wide. Morning light was filtering through the orangey material of the curtains. He couldn't face any more coffee. He had a sick feeling in his guts and was developing a headache. It was just after six o'clock. He was desperate to share the information, to blurt it out, to pass it on but he had another three hours to wait.

The main entrance to the *Scottish Standard* building is in George IV Bridge but there is an obscure side entrance in a grimy windowless wall in the Cowgate. This is unmanned and only accessible to those with the five-digit entry code.

Morton had the code, which was changed every week. He booked a taxi to take him from the Slateford Road, into Dalry Road, Morrison Street, Bread Street, West Port into the Grassmarket and along the Cowgate to stop right outside that door. It was a journey that could take him about ten to twelve minutes, depending on traffic. Just to be safe he was going to meet the taxi outside a shop on Slateford Road, not at his own house, and he used a false name.

Danny Stark's ambition was perhaps most clearly shown by his willingness to arrive in the office well before 9am. Unkind wags said this was because he hadn't long been out of school and was still not adjusted to the adult world. When Morton entered the press room, he was already going through the mail.

'You look bloody awful,' he said, as Morton slumped down into the adjacent chair and helped himself to a digestive biscuit from the opened packet near the screen. 'I thought you were having an early night after your travels.'

Morton smiled wanly in the middle of his chewing. 'In theory.'

'What, couldn't sleep? Guilty conscience?'

'I had a visit from Stoddard, complaining about his picture being used, compromising his security. He was not a happy man. Anyway, whoever he really is, he has had me under surveillance. I asked him about McGinley. He said he didn't know him, but I still think they're working together.'

'Figures,' Stark said, nodding. 'Soft cop, hard cop. So that'll be the drug-link idea dead in the water, then?'

'Absolutely,' Morton was reluctant to tell Stark about the INEA memo. Where to begin?

The journalist looked at him closely. 'You alright? Something up?'

'You could say that.' Morton moved himself nearer in the swivel chair and rotated himself in one direction then the other. 'Bailey not around?'

'Of course not. Way too early for his nibs.' Stark grinned like a Mexican bandit and lowered his voice to a stage whisper. 'You've got my attention, Willie, fire away. There was something in McBain's briefcase?'

'Danny, this is...' Morton said, leaning forward confidentially. 'Not - as yet - to be shared with Hugh or anyone else. *Seriously* - okay?'

'Of course,' Stark agreed, entering eagerly into the confidential mode. 'What have you got?'

'Hand me those papers on your desk.'

'What? Sure...'

Morton slipped the three pages out of his inside jacket pocket and placed them between Stark's sheets. 'Take these over there, Danny, and photocopy them. Don't read them, or look at them - yet.'

'Anyshing you shay, Mishter Bond.' Stark winked and sauntered over to the photocopying machines by the far wall. When he got there, he turned round and winked conspiratorially across the vast empty space of the newsroom. There were few staff around. But he wouldn't be surprised if Alan Bailey suddenly walked in. He had never trusted the man. Bailey could go either way, take the story away from him so he'd only get some of the credit, or rubbish it and prevent him from following it up. Or get him removed from the list of 'preferred' freelances.

Stark returned and put the pages on the desk. Morton replaced the originals in his inside breast pocket. 'I'm going to put these somewhere very safe.' He nodded at the photocopies. 'Now, can you scan those into a file?'

'Yeah, there's a scanner in Hugh's office.'

'Well, make sure no-one sees you when you do it. There are three sides, it's in German and the English translation is handwritten between the lines so it probably won't copy well. That should help in case anyone else opens it accidentally.'

'Exciting…' Stark enthused. 'Can't wait to see what it's about.'

Morton pulled a face. 'You won't believe. Anyway, after you've scanned it, read the paper copy and meet me in… better not be The Vaults, too public… meet me in the City Library, just inside the door, at 11am, and bring everything you can find about AtomTech.'

'AtomTech? Oh boy!'

'Yup.'

Morton left the pressroom and exited the building by the Cowgate side entrance. He was already behaving as if he was a fugitive with something to hide.

He used the intervening time to visit the offices of Halbron, Finlay & MacDonald, where he deposited the INEA memo, with an affidavit, taken by Archie MacDonald, of his dealings with McGinley and Stoddard.

'Possession of this document led to McBain's death, Archie – in my opinion - so you see I have reason to believe that I could be in danger,' he said. 'You do see that?'

MacDonald wearily collected the documents into a large buff envelope. 'Ordinarily, old chap, I'd think you were away with the whats-its, but having seen that brute, McGinley, up close, I'll give you the benefit of the doubt.' He straightened up and Morton could see the tiny spots of sweat on his balding head. 'I must say though, what exciting lives you journalists lead. Compared to mine that is.'

'Archie, you're probably on three times what I make and you're home every night with your wife and family. I'd swap you.'

'When it came to it, I doubt if you would,' MacDonald said. 'At school, you were always the unconventional type, Willie. Me, I really just went into the family business because it was expected and because… well, because, I couldn't think of anything else.' He stopped at the door and adjusted his dark blue tie. 'That's not actually true, I had hankerings to be a horticulturist, which I rashly mentioned one day to pater.' The solicitor grinned sourly at the memory. 'Hit the roof. No son of mine etc etc poncing about with bloody flowers. He actually said that, "bloody flowers". Think it was the first time I'd ever heard him swear. A shocking experience. Blighted my young life.'

'Anyway, there it is, Archie,' Morton said, 'I leave you in charge of all particulars, in case anything happens to me.'

'Understood, old man. But try to avoid trouble if you can. I need more fees out of you in the next few years if I'm to have a decent pension.'

The commercial activities of AtomTech Ltd, had been the subject of headline-making stories since the company was formed in the aftermath of the privatisation of the Atomic Energy Authority. AtomTech had acquired three nuclear facilities in England and two in Scotland - Dounreay and Torness, both of which, by 2004, had been extensively run-down. Torness was closed within a year. Dounreay had been in the lengthy process of decommissioning when it was purchased by AtomTech but was mysteriously given authorisation by the Energy Department to return to full production to fill a perceived 'energy gap'. The Scottish Government did not want new nuclear plants in Scotland but the UK Government called the shots and its revenge was to allow the moth-balled Dounreay to return as a fully functioning plant. The UK government had set up a body called the Nuclear Research and Manufacturing Association

– NuRMA - to oversee the development of a new generation of privatised nuclear power stations in the UK. Morton discovered that AtomTech's CEO, Dr. Reginald Matthews, was also the Chair of NuRMA. The company from the first had courted notoriety with its pro-active marketing strategy and it was said by industry analysts that they were only in it for short-term profit for directors who were of course allowed to hide behind a special anonymity clause. They made little attempt to upgrade or improve the facilities and governments did not seem to want to probe too deeply into their affairs, in case they were implicated in scandal. When the SNP took over as a minority administration, Ministers expressed outrage on a monthly basis but could do nothing. With the apparent approval of the UK Government and a toothless Scottish Parliament which could not intervene, AtomTech were free to scour the world for reprocessing deals. The lucrative deal with the German company Nukem brought bomb-grade uranium (enough for 29 nuclear bombs) to Dounreay. They accepted 363,000 used uranium fuel rods from a reactor at Hamm in Germany that had had to be shut down because of a poor safety record. Several other deals, like the attempt to accept Pakistani nuclear waste while the UN were monitoring the nuclear stand-off with India over Kashmir, went sour when details were leaked to the press. Morton knew that public opinion was a slender weapon against the combined lobbying efforts of Euratom, the European Commission's nuclear agency, and the INEA which acts to ensure secrecy - or as some called it - confidentiality and the UK Government's Department of Trade and Industry and NuRMA which as far as he could see was a kind of super-pimp for the nuclear industry. But nuclear scandals or secret deals or radioactive leaks were potentially big news stories and it was obvious to Morton that AtomTech Ltd, which depended on commercial reprocessing, might have had to use extraordinary methods to safeguard their business. With a sizable number of armed security police on their payroll they could probably call on the assistance of the armed police establishments of Euratom and the INEA and even, if circumstances were propitious, the MOD police, the RAF and the army. In fact, Morton thought, there were probably so many secret policemen swimming in the alphabet soup that one of their biggest operational problems would be inter-departmental rivalry.

He had worked out that the potency of the story which McBain had rumbled was not AtomTech's dodgy deal, there had been many of those -- not even that a major European nuclear accident with real fatalities had been hushed up, nor that the dangerous convoy was to be transported on public roads. The real killer punch was the UK Government's collusion and its willingness to keep the Scottish Government in the dark. Political tension between Scotland and England had been rising for years. This deal reeked of UK Governmental complicity at the highest levels. And if that was true, then it was just one more step to the idea of government involvement in McBain's murder to suppress the story. Morton was in a very dangerous place. What he now knew - or suspected - made him feel very alone.

Consequently, Morton was already seeing shadows and spooks on every street, and listening to the hesitant tread of his shoe-leather along pavements as he walked to his rendezvous with Danny Stark. Even in daylight in the pleasant and peaceful surroundings of the General Reference section of the Edinburgh City Library, he felt ill at ease. Part of it, of course, was that he was exhausted, physically and mentally and lacked sleep. Stark arrived on time, exuberantly swinging in through the doors and tripping up the stairs. He immediately began to talk volubly and loudly.

Morton was appalled. 'Not here!' he hissed, grabbing his arm and leading him back out onto the street.

They mingled with the lunchtime crowds. The sun was shining directly above their heads. Morton felt happier out in the public eye, where they were fewer shadows.

'There's a good lunch place, just around there,' Stark said, when they reached the corner of Chambers Street. 'An Italian place, with a beer garden. Just off Nicolson Street.'

'Alright.'

Stark punched Morton on the shoulder. 'Willie. It's incredible! What a scoop! This is the biggest story of our careers, no question.' He stared at him, desperate for a reaction as they waited to cross at the lights. 'Isn't it? It's fucking gorgeous, man!'

Morton winced as an elderly couple looked in their direction and shook their heads. 'Danny. Shush!' They crossed over onto the pavement.

But Stark was hyper, couldn't stop himself. 'This convoy contravenes just about every regulation going. The regs for the safe transport of radioactive material, labelling regulations, the UK Nuclear Industry Road Emergency Plan, blah-di-blah and of course,' he was walking too fast and turned back to Willie... 'this speaks volumes about the cause of McBain's death, eh?'

'Wait till we're off the street, can't you,' Willie hissed.

'Okay. You're right.'

'Danny, I'm not being paranoid but we've just got to...'

'Yeah, right. You know Willie, you have to doubt if the Scottish Government – as the appropriate roads authority – have even been told. If this stuff is as radioactive as the memo says, then it should be transported in purpose-built transporters, correctly labelled, in vessels which have been exhaustively tested. Water spray test, water immersion test, free drop test, compression test, thermal tests and loads of other kinds of fucking tests. Shit! It's just so *illegal*...'

'You're missing the point, Danny,' Morton said quietly. 'The whole thing is illegal. Right from the start, so of course, they've made no attempt to conform to any of the regulations or standard procedures. The thing is, for them to get away with it - even to try - proves that they must have top-level government and military backing.'

Danny Stark stopped and looked at him. 'You're right. This goes way beyond parliament. Westminster's control over the nuclear lobby has always been purely theoretical. We'll get nowhere asking politicians to intervene. And so, the best way to stand the story up is to go right to the top and get words from the top man...'

Morton grimaced. 'Who'll deny everything - even if you can get an appointment?'

Stark beamed. 'Already have, man.'

'You - *what*!' Morton grabbed his sleeve. 'With who?'

'Whom. With whom. Relax, Willie, I've not said anything about the memo.'

'Jesus... what the hell?'

'It's okay. Really.'

'But who with?'

'Matthews?

'Matthews. Of AtomTech? As in – Dr. Reginald Matthews, also chair of NuRMA? You know he's chair of...?'

'Willie! Of course I know.'

'Well. He's certainly the top boy, as you put it. Jesus. And he's agreed? But *why* did he agree?'

'I've asked him to comment on a story about a proposed French reprocessing deal. He's quite keen to do an interview on that.'

'Is he? I can't imagine he ever wants to say anything publicly about... well, anything.'

'Well, he wants to get public opinion on his side. Wants to boast about getting a special licence to do the deal, flaunting their top-level connections. Reminding folk how crucial AtomTech is in keeping the lights of Britain on. You know… nuclear vital part of the energy mix, blah blah.'

'Wasting his time. Nobody really believes that anymore.'

'Maybe… Anyway, once we've got him at his ease, then we'll spring him some questions about this. Gradually. I mean, obviously he'll deny the lot but it'll give us the chance to print the whole story. I mean, we have to offer him the chance to give his side… We need to be able to put the allegations to him. We should get a double-page spread with a teaser on the front page. We can use a picture of the memo pages, the story about how they were found… the McBain link… and some background on Bohunice. Damn it man, the story is so big that it will be syndicated to almost every paper in the world. Even bow-tied Bailey couldn't knock that.'

'So who's the interview *actually* with?'

'I told you. Matthews himself. The Director. And - get this - at his home, near Inverness. Tomorrow.'

'Away up there?' Morton said quizzically. 'A long way.'

'So we'll drive up. A couple of hours tops.'

'What time have we to be there?'

'1pm. And by the way, I've not mentioned you. I've kept you right out of it. Just in case he's aware of the surveillance on you.'

'Well. That's a good idea. I don't mind at all. Thinking about it, we should be safe there. I mean, surely he's above suspicion? They wouldn't dare to nobble us there, would they? He's the numero uno nuclear guy in the UK. So who have you told about it? Leadbetter?'

'He knows. No-one else. Although Bailey will have to be told soon enough.'

'Fuck Bailey!

'Hugh said he'd tip off the Editorial team tomorrow lunchtime.'

Morton nodded. The cat was out of the bag and he wasn't sure whether he felt reassured or more scared. They had reached the Trattoria Venezia, and pushed through its swing doors and walked straight out into the crowded and noisy walled beer garden, colourful with its array of Neapolitan sunshades and white tablecloths. 'Over in the corner,' he suggested. 'There's a table free.' He turned to Stark and smiled grimly. 'I'd prefer to have my back against the wall.'

23

Returning to his flat, Morton got a text message from Elizabeth. She was coming round at 7pm with some important news. He wondered what more could be going on.

Morton had perhaps unwisely imbibed most of a bottle of Lambrusco, and this, on a lethargic afternoon which was warm and sultry. The fresh air he had breathed on the walk home helped and he had made himself a coffee and reclined on the sofa to wait, watching the early evening news. But then he had fallen asleep, his coffee almost entirely untouched, and in his troubled sleep he had imagined silent figures flitting purposefully through the flat, could almost feel the cold draught of outside air as they entered from the hall. They were not here to kill him, he knew with the certainty of a dream, they had other purposes, perhaps they were searching for something...

He snapped awake, hotly terrified. Knocking? There was nobody... his head cleared. Only a dream? Somebody at the door.

Elizabeth. He had been asleep for three hours.

'Have you had visitors?' she asked anxiously as he opened the door. He stared at her while rubbing his eyes. She was looking crisply efficient, her long hair tied back into a single ponytail, wearing a loose white blouse and a light grey trouser suit. He found himself regarding her and had to tear his eyes away.

'Visitors?' Then the shock hit him and his mouth went slack. 'God no!' he moaned. 'I don't think so. A dream...'

'It's just that there were three men... policemen types... hanging around outside. They have a blue van. As I came round the corner, I saw into the back just as they were closing it. It had seats in it and sort-of technical equipment, you know, like a TV detector van.'

Morton rubbed his eyes to wake himself up. 'In my dream, there were men in the flat, here, searching… Anyway, forget that,' he said, 'That was just a dream, it wasn't worth mentioning.'

'I've two things to tell you, Willie. Firstly, I've been checking up on the tourists who found uncle's car. You remember, the Downs, Jane and Alan. Would you believe that both the addresses which David Cochrane had for them are not real? There is no such address as 8 Birch Grove in Bracknell, Berks., and as for 8 Church Way, Aldgrove - well, there is no such place as Aldgrove anywhere in the UK.'

Morton fiddled with the blond strands at his left temple. 'Remind me how there come to be two addresses.'

Elizabeth smiled. 'Well…the Aldgrove address was jotted on a postcard and handed to David at Loch Dubh, but the Bracknell address was given to him verbally by one of the detectives who accompanied the Procurator Fiscal at his home, two days after the incident. You did say Alan Downs was an Australian pilot?'

'That's right. A pilot on holiday.'

'Then there's a further mystery. Although there's no such place as Aldgrove, there is an Aldergrove - and it's an airport - just outside Belfast.'

'An airport? That's a little coincidental?'

'Yes. But there the trail ends, I'm afraid. I checked with the British Airline Pilots Association and the Australian equivalent and spoke to pilots based at Aldergrove. It's a very small airport but no-one there has heard of a pilot called Alan Downs. They must have given the police - and David Cochrane - false information.'

'Seems so. Now why would they have done that? And the second thing?' he asked after a moment's reflection.

'The second thing? David Cochrane phoned me. He's living with his girlfriend now at Dalmeny, because he's worried about police harassment. Anyway, he's got photographs that were sent to him and wants you to see them. I said we'd drive down this evening. Was that alright?'

'Sure. You will have to drive. I had some wine at lunch…'

The 60 pound leather punch bag spun dizzily from its chain under a torrent of solid punches from right and left, each accompanied by a gasp of effort as the muscular man leaned in, his shoulders and arms co-ordinating the beating. Then the man, whose tanned and gleaming body wore only a white singlet and black nylon shorts began to experiment, weaving and ducking soundlessly on rubber soles, flinging a series of right hooks and left uppercuts at the bag. He stepped back and launched a spectacular flying kick, spun round and fisted the punch bag with a battery of rapid pummelling blows. Then he stopped, turned away from the bag and sat on the seat of the rowing machine, feeling the ache of his sinews. He sat back and momentarily closed his eyes, blinking in sweat from his forehead. The natural daylight from the small glazed apertures just below the low ceiling gleamed on the wooden walls of the small basement fitness suite and on the benches around the walls. McGinley came here every day that he was at home in a effort to counter the effects of advancing middle-age and dull days of desk work, reading files, inputting data - his *bete noire*. McGinley hated technology and longed for the Internet to disappear up its own arse.

His wrist-watch alarm began to ping. He looked at it resentfully and wiped the sweat off his forehead. He couldn't linger. He had set the alarm to give him barely time to shower and change before the video-conference departmental meeting.

Seven minutes later, still damp from the shower, he sat in black polo shirt and slacks in front of the computer screen and watched the matronly features of his immediate superior officer, Jo Haines, materialise on the screen. Crisp and efficient, and sitting beside her in the Operations HQ at Saltisburn, were two other members of the Scottish Nuclear Installations Protection team, Ron Ramsay and Ron Hemphill. McGinley greeted them coolly, hating the necessity of speaking into a microphone in a computer screen. Behind him he heard the sounds of his assistant, Kevin Gray, coming into the room.

'You're late,' he hissed out of the side of his mouth.

Gray glared at him, the light reflecting off his stubbly scalp, divested himself of his leather jacket and sat on the swivel chair next to him. 'Something came up, I'll tell you later,' he said in a low voice.

The meeting began with a progress report from each of the sectors, given by Ramsay and Hemphill for the North and, on behalf of Brian Kemsley of the Southern sector, by Haines herself. Then there was the usual service information from Risley.

Item 5 was the follow-up to Unicorn.

'Daniel?' Haines queried. 'Progress? Please tell me the loose ends have been tidied off.'

McGinley leaned towards the microphone. 'Most of the press are keeping well clear but we're still having problems with one journalist, who is being tiresomely persistent, but we have the matter in hand.'

Haines interceded. 'That'll be the *Scottish Standard*? Set up when the *Herald* folded, and now neo-nationalist? We have contacts at a high-level there and I'm sure pressure can be brought to bear in the right quarters. I'll put things in motion. Anything else?'

'We have still not actually retrieved the missing documents,' McGinley said, wearily rubbing a hand across his chin and under his neck, looking sideways at Gray, then back at the screen. 'I don't believe this journalist has any idea ...'

Gray interrupted him, loudly. 'Wrong!' He leaned forward into the webcam, his bony white face simultaneously filling the monitor in the corner of their own screen. 'Kevin Gray here, ma'am. I suggest that the journalist has got hold of it and has it now in his possession.'

Haines responded: 'Right, Kevin -- if that's correct, Daniel, then we have a serious problem on our hands. Daniel, you said you had spoken to this journalist.'

'I did,' McGinley said, starting to get angry. 'I warned him off, but there's a limit to what we can do. He has involved a friend who's a solicitor.'

'A solicitor?' Ramsay murmured sarcastically, 'dear me, that's that then. We'd better give up now. Pardon me for asking, but wasn't the target a solicitor and... eh, is he a big problem for us now?'

Jo Haines' flushed face returned to the screen. The resolution was so good McGinley could see specks of powder sitting on top of large pores on the end of her nose.

'Kevin, has your surveillance of this journalist suggested what he's going to do with this information?' she inquired.

'Yes, ma'am. He's collaborating with a staff journalist on a story about McBain's anti-nuclear role and he's going to question Dr Matthews to get quotes on the subject.'

'And Matthews agreed to an interview?' McGinley asked.

Gray nodded. 'Tomorrow at 1pm.' He beamed triumphantly, revealing a missing front tooth. 'He accepted my advice to have the interview at his home.'

'At his home?' Haines repeated. 'Where's that?'

'Near Inverness. In the Highlands. And no doubt the targets will have the memo with them...'

193

There was a blank few seconds as this information was digested by the members of the team at the two terminals. Haines was first to respond.

'Well done, Kevin. You and Daniel track them north. Ron's squad will prepare the reception. I want this Unicorn file tidied-up tomorrow, finally. We will have enough to do when the convoys start arriving. Which brings me to item 6.'

The instant that the meeting concluded and the computer was safely switched off, McGinley swung at his colleague.

'You arrogant wee bastard!' he snarled. 'You made me look like an amateur there. You should have up-dated me before the meeting. Why were you late?'

'Give us a break, Dan!' Gray responded, donning his jacket. 'I've been up all night like a fucking owl. Watching and listening. I had to babysit the tech division, to get the bugs into Morton's flat, which wasn't easy because he was in'. Gray's lower lip slid sideways and his eyelids flickered. 'Well, he was in but there was no-one at home, if you know what I mean. Tricky though. Then I had to see what Stark was up to.'

'And what the fuck *was* he up to?'

'He started off down the pub then he did a bit of shagging in his flat with this dame he's been seeing.' His lips twisted sideways in a knowing grin. 'She's on the list but she's got no connection. Then I had to get a report from the team watching the McBain girl. Nothing doing there. Long night of nothing.'

'You get paid.'

'Yeah, but never enough. Not as much as you.'

McGinley let that pass. He'd get his revenge in due course. The little shit! 'Did you hear anything about Cochrane? He hasn't been seen at his flat for two days. Has anyone thought of checking his friends' addresses?'

194

'It's in hand,' Gray said, 'but I need to get some sleep now. Early start tomorrow.'

Willie Morton felt odd being a passenger in his own car, even odder to be travelling in the car in a somewhat inebriated state. When Morton had taken drink he didn't have the car, travelling on foot, on the bus or by taxi and when he had the car he had no drink. It was one of his strictest principles, in fact, probably his only principle, apart from his self-discipline about smiling frequently to break up the doughy mass of his lower chin.

He smiled now, watching Elizabeth from the side, driving.

'*What?*' she asked. 'What is it?'

'Nothing, just feels odd, somehow, being driven in my own car.'

'Funny old car. Easy to drive though.'

The Volkswagen purred comfortably down the A90 towards the Forth Road Bridge in the gathering dark among a ceaseless serrated line of oncoming headlamps and lines of red tail-lights.

Elizabeth drove carefully, her slender fingers efficient with the thick, leather-wrapped steering wheel and stubby gearstick. 'We're beginning to get somewhere,' she said. 'Now we know why my uncle was murdered. Makes my blood boil that they think they can get away with it. And thinking about that radioactive equipment trundling along, unmarked, on our public roads. They are arrogant aren't they? They think we're all stupid.'

'Pigshite,' Morton murmured, dozing in the comfort of the passenger seat.

'I beg your pardon?' Elizabeth said.

'Oh, just something your uncle used to say. I heard him speaking at a conference once. He said, quote: "you dinna keep pigs until ye ken whaur tae keep the pigshite" meaning

195

the nuclear waste. He had very trenchant views about nuclear power. But what did he plan to do about the… that's the question?'

'About the… pigshite?'

Morton laughed. 'No! About the documents.'

'Oh. Of course.'

Elizabeth manoeuvred off the A90 onto a tiny B road and headed down to Dalmeny. The lights of the Forth Bridge could be seen and the wide silver expanse of the estuary through the increasingly thick screen of trees.

The road came out at the shore close to the high arches of the railway bridge and they continued along a narrow track. High trees on both sides threatened in places to engulf the car. The red lights of the bridge behind them danced in the side mirrors and Morton breathed deeply the fresh smell of salt water.

Ahead, the road emerged from the trees and diverged onto a long narrow pier jutting into the river. He saw some buildings. Lights.

'This must be it,' Elizabeth said, parking the car on the verge.

Two figures appeared in the bright yellow glow of the doorway, a man and a woman, and Morton recognised Cochrane. The tall, dark-haired girl was introduced simply as Wendy. She wasn't quite what Morton had expected Cochrane's girlfriend to look like and he told himself this was because she looked her age and Cochrane didn't. She had a sophistication which he lacked, her hair was neatly cut, looked smart, and she wore a black velvet dress and court shoes. Rather incongruous when you lived at the end of a jetty down a muddy farm track, Morton reflected.

'Thanks for coming, Willie,' Cochrane was saying. 'I know Elizabeth from school.'

'Yes, Falkirk High.'

196

'And look where you are now,' Cochrane said. 'The dreaming or is it the dizzy spires.'

'Something like that,' she said.

Morton enjoyed the view of the rising line of red lights high amongst the cantilevered iron of the bridge as the evening faded over the magnesium brilliance of the Rosyth naval base.

The interior of the cottage was bright and comfortable.

'I've been sent some photographs by Hamish McLennan,' Cochrane explained. 'He's the Councillor for the area that covers Loch Dubh. An Independent by the way, not SNP. He knew Angus quite well. Anyway, it's quite a tale...' He held up a small manila envelope. 'He got these from the garage mechanic at the McRae & Dick garage in Fort William where McBain's car was taken by the recovery vehicle. Are you with me?'

'We're with you.'

'Right. Now *he* got the pictures from someone who just happened to take pictures of McBain's car... I'm sorry... your uncle's car... as it was towed into the garage forecourt and who just happened to send the prints to him. They sat in that envelope in the garage office for... well, till two days ago... can you believe that? I mean, they were only discovered when the secretary was clearing out the office and that, by the final coincidence was on the day that Hamish's own car was in for its MOT. She knew him and so the photos ended up with him instead of being binned.'

Morton nodded. 'Some tale. So who was the photographer?

'Nobody knows. Certainly not a professional - as you'll see. Well, Hamish sent them to the local plod who returned them to him saying they weren't relevant and that the McBain case was closed.'

'Then he sent them to you?'

Cochrane nodded. 'He was annoyed to be told that the case was closed, as if no further evidence would be allowed.'

Morton sifted through the photos, or more accurately, the snaps. He felt disappointed. The car on the garage forecourt, but pictured from at least twenty feet away and some of the pictures were not properly in focus.

'Don't look much. That what you're thinking?' Cochrane said, coming across the room to kneel at Morton's feet. 'But take a closer look. Here. Forget the smashed windscreen. Look at the rear tyres. Wendy...' he turned to speak to the girl... 'have you got that magnifying glass?'

'The rear tyres?' Morton queried, staring through the glass.

'That nearside tyre is split new. Can you see that? There's almost no grime on the side walls. Compare it to the other... I'll bet that tyre has barely done ten miles. It's brand new!'

Morton looked up slowly, from the magnifying glass. 'Proving?'

'Proving of course that it was put on the wheel only a few miles before Loch Dubh. Elizabeth's uncle must have had a puncture that night somewhere along the road. '

Cochrane collected the pictures from Morton's lap and abstracted one. He held it up in triumph. 'This one... see here, this patch above the driver's door, on the roof.' He got to his feet and thrust it at Morton. 'Blood stains!' he declared.

Morton used the magnifying glass again. 'Hard to tell,' he said grudgingly. 'Could be rust.'

Cochrane was getting animated. 'Yeah, but why rust there and nowhere else? To me it looks like bloody fingerprints just above the door.'

'Calm down,' Morton said. 'This can be easily verified. Whoever took these pictures will be forced to testify when and where he took them, at the Fatal Accident Inquiry.'

Cochrane laughed jeeringly. 'Inquiry? They're not going to let us have an Inquiry. They're not going to risk that. But you're missing the point, Willie. If Angus had to change a tyre on that night… well, what does it say about his state of mind, eh? I mean, you don't calmly change a wheel then a couple of miles later drive off the road and shoot yourself because you've suddenly become suicidal!'

24

The detached house six miles south of Inverness, at the extreme northern tip of Loch Ness, was situated off the busy A82 trunk road, that narrow, often tortuous road which carries heavy tourist traffic around the shores of the lochs of the Great Glen. But go only a yard or two off the road and you might as well be in a jungle anywhere in the world, a jungle of dense, soaking vegetation and monstrously overgrown rhododendron which strangle and destroy even the largest trees. In some places, even the army called in by desperate landowners, have been unable to subdue such a fecund wilderness.

The tarmac of the narrow track was pitted and potholed. The lane was heavily overgrown, dark as if the light was slowly being suffocated out of it.

'Worth a few bob, I'd expect,' Stark said enviously as a large white house and fenced tennis courts and a formal walled garden finally appeared around a bend. He turned the white Honda Legend – hired on expenses - in front of the large bay-window, noting a number of gardeners working around the lawns.

'Check your voice recorder,' Morton advised, taking out his own and putting in fresh batteries.

Stark climbed out of the car. 'Doubt if he'll agree to it,' he said, patting his hair and inspecting his appearance in the side-window. 'But don't worry, I've sharpened my pencil.'

A fit-looking middle-aged man had appeared on the wide stone steps to greet them although his smile was decidely wan. Casually dressed in slacks and blue Pringle cardigan, his greying goatee was his most prominent feature. That and a certain hawkish cast to his eyes and nose. This was Dr Reginald Matthews, the CEO of AtomTech Ltd., and Chair of NuRMA. Morton knew that an interview with him was a rare event indeed.

'Two of you?' he queried. 'No, I can't agree to this. That wasn't our arrangement. Which of you is Mr. Stark?'

'This is my colleague, Mr. Morton,' Stark said, indicating Willie with his thumb. 'I hoped that it might be possible to bring him into the discussion.'

'Most decidedly not,' Matthews insisted. 'I am not interested in being...' he frowned... 'being outnumbered, so to speak.'

Stark looked meaningfully at Morton. 'In that case, it's no problem.'

Matthews turned on his heel with a muttered 'good,' then spun round to face them. 'One other thing, Mr. Stark. The interview is on the basis that your questions relate *only* to the subject of our French contract success. That is agreed? Follow me, please, Mr. Stark.'

Stark winked at Morton and shrugged. 'Sorry Willie, but I have to get something out of this. I'll just have to play it by ear.'

'I'll wait for you in the car.'

But Morton didn't immediately return to the car. Instead, he sauntered down the drive and once out of sight, waded into the overgrown jungle. The giant rhododendrons had mercilessly starved out the weaker weeds and the ground was soft and bare once he had fought his way in. He became a little disorientated in the lush green dampness, into which light filtered in tiny points between the overhanging foliage.

Struggling through the dim shade, he eventually found himself close to the back wall of the house, peering out upon a private tarmacked rear lane. Several cars were parked behind sheds at the back of the house. He immediately noticed the black Range Rover Discovery with the radio antennae. Morton closed his eyes until the nausea subsided in his guts. He inched nearer and watched and waited.

In the opulent lounge, by the bay-window at the front of the house, Danny Stark was making heavy weather of his interview with Dr Matthews, who paced around him, obviously ill-at-ease. Despite his earlier assurances, he had raised the subject of the INEA Conference on the accident at Bohunice.

'I know nothing about any of this, Mr. Stark. It sounds like pure fiction.'

'So you are not actually denying that an incident took place in the Czech Republic?'

'Not denying! Or confirming! I know nothing about it. Nothing took place. If it had I would have known about it. Can you really believe that something of… that scale… where people actually died… could be concealed from the world's media in this day and age? Of course not!'

'And has the INEA held any recent conferences? In February – in Vienna?'

'I can't help you there. I wouldn't know. AtomTech has delegate status but I would need to check with… the delegate…. And, frankly, I see no need to do so. These matters are confidential and, in fact, subject to media embargo.'

Stark was stymied. As a veteran, albeit still youthful reporter, he knew successful interviews could be obtained by sitting out the anger of the subject until they felt embarrassed at themselves and started to respond more co-operatively. The interview itself had reached a lull, as a housemaid poured out coffee. Stark stared vacantly out of the window, waiting for the interview to resume. From his low seat on the chaise longue, he could see a gardener standing under a large oak tree on the far side of the lawns. He wondered idly why the man appeared to be resting his face on the palm of his hand...

In the room directly above the lounge, Daniel McGinley also stared intently out of the window, behind the net curtains, and the object of his attention was the white Honda Legend directly beneath him. Behind him, keeping well back from the window, Kevin Gray was speaking to the 'gardener' on his mobile.

'Somewhere near the back of the house?' Gray repeated. 'He didn't pass you?'

'Ramsay,' McGinley said, without looking round. 'He's at the back. We don't want him to get out onto the main road.'

'Sure, boss,' Gray grinned narrowly. 'That'd be untidy.'

Morton crept out of the bushes and was moving quietly up the lane. He couldn't see anyone. He kept the Range Rover between himself and the windows of the house as he knelt down to examine the number plate. Taking out his notebook, he jotted it down and raised himself cautiously to the passenger's window.

On the black quilted vinyl of the Range Rover's passenger seat, in full view, was a black automatic weapon, some kind of machine gun. Morton stared at it for several seconds. It looked like a kid's toy but he knew instinctively it was no toy. Then he panicked. He fled up the lane. Blundering into the dense foliage, he fell onto his knees and immediately began to retch but nothing came up.

When his stomach subsided, he gulped mouthfuls of air and got to his feet and began warily circling through the dense bushes to the front of the house, taking care of each footstep on the leaf mould. The man in the shiny black leather jacket was beside their hired Honda. Morton observed him open the driver's door and take something from the dashboard. *The keys?*

But a second man suddenly appeared. Ten feet from Morton. Close enough to see his pockmarked face, shock of dark hair, his tight grim smile - and the dull lustre of something metallic in his hand.

Morton dropped behind a thick patch of nettles. He lay dead still. Except for the unbearable bubbling of his blood in both ears. His senses were crystal-sharp, magnifying the sinister silence. He smelled the clean wet earth and thought only of getting as far as possible from McGinley and his murderous spooks.

25

He burst out of the bushes gasping for breath and almost stepped off into mid-air. Traffic raced past nose-to-tail on the road a sheer drop of three metres below the toe of his shoes. How had he managed to be so high up? He grabbed a sturdy branch and held on. Then retraced his steps and came out of the undergrowth at a lower level. Waiting for a lull in the traffic, he raced across the narrow, tree-lined road into the undergrowth on the other side which sloped steeply to the water's edge. Fish were jumping in the green shallows under the leafy branches of overhanging trees and Morton could see shimmering millions of midges dancing over the surface of the water. This strip of water was an overspill of Loch Ness, separated by a narrow shank of bog. On its far side, the River Ness and the Caledonian Canal joined forces beside the white tree-shrouded boxes of a large caravan park.

Morton knew he had to keep off the main road. He began to work his way along the shoreline to the caravan park. It was raining, just to compound his miseries. A billion points of wetness interceded between him and this hostile landscape. Running in his head was the recognition that, unlike childish games of hide-and-seek, this one had no motive. He had forgotten exactly why he was running but kept on running nevertheless. Fear of McGinley and what he could do, was his only motive. It wasn't legal, it was criminal in fact, but then his solicitor was a hundred and eighty miles away in Edinburgh. A momentary vision of the kindly and tired features of his school pal passed in front of Morton's eyes. He'd give a lot to be in some woody pub in the Grassmarket reviving old rugger triumphs!

It took him almost an hour to get to the caravan park at Dochgarroch. Finally, he had to scramble up a grass bank, through a wire fence and between drifts of brambles and nettles, to come out at a gap in a thick hedge between the lines of static caravans. A dog immediately began to bark somewhere nearby. Morton saw signs to the Showers & WC and hurried over to the pre-fab block at the edge of the site. The Gents was empty but he was momentarily startled by the reflection of himself in the mirror above the wash hand basins. No wonder the dog had barked. Staring back at him was a bedraggled and far from respectable figure whose soaked jacket, shirt and trousers clung to his frame. His shoes were a pulpy brown shape and he saw the muddy trail they had left on the tiled floor. He noticed the coin-operated shower and laundry in the area adjacent to the toilet. Someone had even left a towel hanging on a rail. Gratefully, he stripped off his clothes and thrust them into a spin dryer. He looked at the shoes. They were past saving. If he tried to dry them in the dryer, they'd fall to bits. He could buy a pair of sandshoes if there was a campsite shop. He hurried into the shower.

The warm water, two fifty pences' worth, gushed over him and brought him back to life. Its warmth rejuvenated his body. Eagerly he gulped steam into his lungs. He wrapped the towel around him and sat down to wait for his clothes. A few minutes later, he heard someone moving about in the women's section, water running, toilet flushing, then it stopped. No-one came into the Gents.

Dressed in warm, dry but crumpled clothes half an hour later, he stood in the doorway, looking out at the slanting rain. There was no-one about. An elderly couple coming along the lines of caravans were heading in his direction, huddling under an umbrella. He waited for them to pass.

'Miserable day,' the old man said, out of the corner of his mouth.

'Great for the midgies,' Morton rejoined. Reluctantly, he put the sodden shoes back on. They felt horrible, mushy and sticky. He had no alternative.

The campsite shop, at the front gates, was closed but Morton could see, in the window behind yellow perspex, several pairs of sandshoes, walking boots and even yacht shoes and brown brogues. It sold almost nothing but footwear! He looked over at the main road, where the traffic was light. Only an occasional car or lorry came past the caravan site entrance.

Watching from under the shop's striped canopy, he saw a white camper van slowly approach the site gates and come to a halt. A map was being consulted inside.

Morton sprinted over, observing, as he approached, the stickers and small Stars & Stripes on the side window. He tapped on the window and smiled. 'Lost? Can I help at all?'

Two faces peered out through the condensation and the window came down. The white-haired, check-shirted man said: 'We're trying to get to the Loch Ness Monster Centre. I guess it's a little further on, right?

'Straight down the road, about... ten, fifteen miles,' Morton told them. 'Hey - any chance of a lift? My car's broken down.'

It was the white-haired woman who answered. 'Why, sure, young man.'

'Hop in, buddy,' the man said, leaning behind him to open the side door.

Gratefully, Morton stepped into the camper van and pulled the door shut behind him.

'Welcome aboard,' the woman said, folding the map. 'I'm Jean and this is my husband, Duddy, we're from Kansas?'

Morton was mildly amused by the interrogative tone the woman added to absolute facts. Americans seemed to end every sentence with a question mark. He knew they were waiting for him to say his name.

'Pleased to know you,' he said, thinking of a name. 'I'm… Ed Ainslie,' he said. 'Thanks for the lift.'

The man started to ask questions about the car, what kind it was, what had gone wrong, a professional interest. Morton struggled to stay awake. He had been up since 7am – when Stark had come by to collect him for the long drive north.

'Jean - that's a Scottish name,' Morton said, in an attempt to cause a diversion.

'You betcha, yeah. My forebears were Scaddish? McKinnons? You know the McKinnons?'

'Not all of them,' Morton muttered to himself, coughed and said: 'Well-known clan.'

'Them's my clan,' she said with obvious pride. 'Granmar was a McKinnon? Came over to Virginia at the time of the Clearances, after the big battle?'

Morton let them chatter away on this and that, putting in the occasional word. Meanwhile he was watching the road. Soon they were passing the entrance to Matthew's house but there was no sign of activity. What was happening to Danny? There was nothing on his mobile but he had "no service" anyway.

The conversation fizzled out as they covered the miles around the shores of the loch, with vistas of the water at every turn. Traffic was clogged and slow on the narrow road and the Americans drove timidly in the heavy, comfortable van.

'I guess we're here, Ed?' Duddy said as they entered Drumnadrochit. 'We have to park up. Sorry we can't take you where you're going?'

After thanking the couple, Morton sauntered across the road, glad to be in a place where people were numerous and he could be less conspicuous. The bend of Urquhart Bay with its panoramic views of the loch and spectacular castle was a major tourist attraction and coaches were parked in rows off the road. Morton's hunger sparked at the sight of a burger van. He bought a burger and coffee and looked for somewhere to eat. He moved to an area of picnic tables, too intent on his first bite of hot food since breakfast, to notice the two men watching him from the wooden bench. He raised his polystyrene cup to take a first sip of coffee and that was when he saw McGinley sitting there.

'Hi, William!' McGinley called mockingly, getting to his feet.

Morton let go the coffee and limped fast back the way he had come. His mind was squirming, trying to think of what to do. He ran into the road and made the corner. They weren't far behind. He cut off into some bushes, slithered up the hill in his busted shoes. Came out on the road at a higher bend. Saw a vehicle labouring in low gear ahead. It was the camper van and Jean and Duddy!

With a supreme effort, he caught up with it at the top of the rise and ran alongside, waving his arms. Jean was in the passenger seat. She saw him and said something to Duddy. The van stopped quite abruptly and the window wound down.

'Well….howdy…' Duddy started.

Morton wasted no time being polite. He yanked open the sliding door at the side and jumped in, pulled the door to behind him.

They stared at him in amazement and alarm. 'I guess we kinda changed our plans,' Jean said, after a few moments. 'Sneaky, huh?'

'I changed my plans too,' Morton muttered, lying flat.

'That joint was a mite crowded for us. We're now heading to the island of Skye,' Duddy said.

Morton said nothing, praying for him to get the van going. After what seemed like an age, the camper van began to move and gathered speed as it began to run downhill. Morton kept a vigil at the window but didn't see McGinley. It would have been better if he had, he reasoned, because that would mean they had not gone back for their vehicle.

As the camper van turned around a sharp bend, he did catch a glimpse of McGinley and the skin-headed man on the rim of a bluff further back, about a hundred yards behind. He hoped they hadn't seen the camper van stop.

The next dozen miles were uneventful. Morton's tension grew as the Americans dawdled along the road. He expected a road block, or an obstruction placed to cause the vehicles to stop which would allow McGinley to search for him. Also, the quiet normality of the Americans and their cheery good humour, far from reassuring him, was making him ever more anxious.

'Here's the junction,' said Jean. 'Coming right up. Better slow up, old boy.'

'Kyle of Lochalsh, yeah this is it, hold on back there, we're turning off.'

Duddy pulled the van off the A82 onto the narrower road to Kyle, and Morton saw a sign: The Invergarry Hotel.

'Hey, how about letting me off here?' I can book in to this hotel.'

'Sure thing, friend.'

As the van headed west it was quiet and peaceful, no cars, nobody in sight. He watched the white van ascend up into the trees above Loch Garry and turned to the hotel. It had been a Victorian shooting lodge and although he knew how nice it would be to book a room and lie down on clean white sheets and forget the McBain business, he knew it was impossible. He found the public telephone in the wood-beamed hall, next to the door of the public bar from which he heard the reassuring sounds of normal bar-room conversations. He couldn't use the Blackberry, too risky, even if there was WiFi.

He rang Elizabeth at the flat of a friend of hers, and she answered after only a few rings. Since she'd only moved to the flat yesterday evening, he thought it unlikely that the phone was tapped. He filled her in with the details, cutting out some of the hairiest moments and trying his best to make it seem like a hilarious exploit. He found that he was reluctant to put down the phone but when he did, felt much better for having spoken to a friend. Someone else who knew what he was going through. He made another call. Stark's mobile phone.

Danny answered immediately. 'Willie! Where the hell are you?'

'Never mind that. Where are *you*? Are you okay?'

'I came out and you'd buggered off. I'm at the Caley Hotel at Inverness. Where you're supposed to be…is anything wrong?'

'Why do you say that? Is anyone with you?'

'I'm alone. What took you so long to phone me?'

'So you're safe, then? They let you go?'

Stark's voice sounded amused. 'Willie? What's going on? You sound paranoid, man.'

'I'm not! Look - McGinley and guys with guns were all around the place. But if you're okay it must be me they are looking for. I saw a guy take the keys from the car and… well, I thought they might be after you, too.'

'No, as far as I know, everything's okay. The car keys were still in the car when I came out. Anyway, I did get a comment out of Matthews - though he might deny it. So where will I see you?'

Morton felt a shiver of apprehension. 'Right at the moment, I can't say. I'm taking it one step at a time. Stick to our plan. Write up the story and I'll contact you as soon as I can.'

Morton put down the phone and heard it click on its cradle. It was the sound of his last contact with the safe world of journalism being cut. He looked out of the open door to the road and the thick inscrutable forest beyond. It was mid afternoon, less than three hours since he'd fled from Matthews' house.

26

The early evening lights of Oban's main street were a welcome sight to Willie Morton, as the Fort William coach pulled smoothly to a stop beside the railway station. He dismounted from the overheated coach and saw the solid red sandstone mass of the Columba Hotel on the other pier, a patchwork of lights, and the lights of the MacBraynes steamer at the ferry terminal to his left. In the main street, the shops were brightly-lit and intensely inviting. He craved the normality of shopping. In a late-opening chemists' he bought a toothbrush, toothpaste, soap, a small towel, disposable razors and a small toilet bag. The assistant gave him a plastic bag to hold the lot and suddenly he was a bona fide tourist.

He ate at the Columba, in an almost empty dining room at a bay window table overlooking the silvered bay and Mull's silhouette beyond, hiding his scuffed and misshapen shoes under the table. Later, he booked into a small B&B halfway up the hill beside a bowling green. He locked his room as soon as he was inside, lay down on the bed and let sleep take him, which it did - almost instantly.

In the morning he felt a lot calmer. Looking out over the Sound of Kerrera, and a fine sunny day, while eating a hearty fried breakfast in a sun-dappled dining room, helped. He had given up trying to rationalise his situation. Why were they after him? They just were.

The brogues had almost dried-out. Morton strolled down to the town and bought a decent pair of walking shoes, dumping his brogues in a skip. He bought a copy of the *Scottish Standard*. He sat down on a bench and riffled through the news pages. Nothing. *Nothing?* Then he looked again and finally he found, on page 8, practically buried, a small article by Danny Stark; 'Dounreay French Deal Success'. So much for the promised joint-by-line! Morton read the article closely and then was glad it was only in Stark's name. It was an uncritical report of AtomTech's success - aided by the DTI - in winning a deal with French Nuclear to reprocess spent fuel. No mention of the Bohunice incident or the INEA memo. The government, it noted, had allowed AtomTech a temporary licence to reprocess foreign material, despite the SEPA ban. Morton was puzzled. Stark had said that he had got comment from Matthews, so why this pathetic non-story? It was possible that he had been leaned on. Was Stark right that the French deal was the reason Dounreay's workforce was expanding? Morton detected the hand of Alan Bailey in putting out such an insipid story. Not for the first time, he wondered about Bailey's malign influence on Stark. Danny was too ambitious to stick his neck out for long. Maybe he'd have done better taking the memo direct to Hugh and letting him stand up to Bailey? He trusted Hugh when it came to news value and Hugh wouldn't let anyone, even Bailey, put him off a good story unless there was a very good reason. Also, Leadbetter had a definite interest in McBain's death. Hugh would know immediately that it was the story of the year and back him all the way. So why hadn't he? It was baffling. Morton had to be absolutely sure that it came out right. His own safety might depend on it. It was all very disappointing. But at least he was free and safe and maybe there was another way?

He returned to John Menzies Newsagents and bought a lined exercise book and found himself a vacant corner table in the Pancake Place along the street with a big mug of strong coffee. He began to write the complete version of the story, putting in the finding of the INEA memo in McBain's briefcase, their full contents as translated by McBain himself, the radioactive convoys, and the harassment he had suffered from McGinley, which had caused him to use the services of

214

his solicitor. It came to twelve full pages. He redrafted it over a second cup of coffee, ignoring the chatter of middle-aged ladies in the now-busy lunch hour. The final version, 'Nuclear Police Implicated in Death of McBain - Was He Killed for Secret Document?' ran to 1,500 words. He reread the story, feeling that mixture of pride and calm assurance he always felt when he knew a story was tight and defensible from all angles. Then he composed a brief cover-note and posted it to Davie Begg at the *Daily Record* with the photocopied memo. They'd get it on Tuesday morning. Begg was nobody's poodle. He'd use it. He phoned Elizabeth at her friend's flat, but she wasn't there. There was nothing more he could do. He felt strangely calm and relieved. But he needed human company. Then he remembered Malcolm Farquharson lived across in Kerrera.

He bought sandwiches and started to walk out of Oban down towards Gallanachmore heading for the Kerrera ferry. It was a walk of just over half an hour in his new shoes and for most of it, once he'd passed the last house, he had the seemingly empty, low-lying north of the island to his right as the winding road hugged the shoreline. On his left, steep cliffs and trees growing at odd angles towered above him. There was little traffic. He felt certain that he had given McGinley the slip. His Blackberry was switched off.

There were no cars parked or pedestrians waiting at the Kerrera ferry as he tilted the white pole on the board and sat down to wait. He watched the boat emerge into the Sound from the island. The boat bobbed up and down in the mid-channel, then settled low-down in the water, the ferryman a dark dot on the heavy surge.

A car appeared on the road and came on, slowly. Some instinct made Morton drop down behind the dyke. He heard the car slow to take the bend, but it didn't stop. Heading for Gallanachmore no doubt. Better not to take any chances. He didn't want to be seen taking the ferry. Then he'd be trapped on the island.

The boat began to swerve in to the shore, creaming the black angry water. All at once, Morton felt some misgivings. What if Farquharson was not there? The open, honest face of the ferryman reassured him.

'Hello,' Morton said, happy to have someone to talk to. 'Nice job you have.'

'I like it fine,' the boatman said. 'Aye.'

'High swell?' he asked. 'It's high tide, presumably?'

The boatman nodded but didn't speak. He looked down the Sound to the firth, a rolling backbone of black water. 'She's runnin',' he said, mysteriously, poling the frail boat off the jetty. It lurched and ploughed into the swell.

Morton gripped the seat underneath him. They wouldn't make it! They were going to go under. He closed his eyes. And opened them. The engine hammered regularly, white wash smoothing out from the stern. He had a momentary sensation that he was actually sitting in the water. But the ferryman was impassive, his only concession to the conditions being that he gripped the smooth wood of the tiller with his hand instead of steering with the touch of his forearm.

'Pretty difficult passage,' Morton said stiffly, switching his grip to the gunwhales.

'High tide,' the man explained, 'you'll be alright.'

The full significance of the pronoun wasn't lost on Morton and he determined to keep quiet. It was all a matter of self-discipline.

The makeshift pier was already in sight and soon the ferryman was tying the boat up and Morton was stepping onto dry land. He looked back at the firth. It didn't look much. Somewhere in the distance, he heard the irritating and intermittent buzz of a helicopter which he could not see.

216

The jetty was a risky structure of concrete pillars and wooden duckboards up the steep incline of the shore. Morton stamped up the clinker path. A red telephone box stood like a discarded film prop, out of place in the blanched moistness. He set off at a rapid pace. There was only one track anyway; rutted by tractor tyres into long, jagged puddles which reflected the scudding fog. It ran most of the way down the eastern edge of the island, winding closely around the shore. Flocks of hostile, black-faced island sheep, braying aggressively, moved ungraciously to let him pass. This brisk walking in the rich, fresh air was good exercise, Morton thought to himself and strode even more briskly, muddying his shoes. He felt good.

About a mile further there was a small bay where an iron-hulled fishing boat was stuck in mud so deep that only a fin-shaped portion of the rusting hull could be seen. Three cottages picturesque in a row with ivy, sweet pea and clinging wild roses decorating their white window frames. A bleary-eyed, dreaming old collie watched Morton's progress up and beyond the cottages and round the bend of a hill. The track ended at the clinker driveway to a farmhouse and steadings which could be seen on the side of a further hill - one of only three farms on the island - and branched off into an overgrown and even less obvious track which disappeared around the bracken-covered hillside, heading south.

Morton took the narrower track. Thick, leathery bracken and bristling thistles dislodged dew onto his legs and shoes for a further quarter of a mile. The track opened out as it neared a small swampy pond within sight of a cluster of low stone buildings and a two-storey house sheltered on the steep slope of a substantial hill. A large satellite dish was positioned on the slate roof at the gable end.

A black goat startled Morton, its angry feral eyes glaring directly into his. It stalked off up the hillside into the mist, large head horning the air.

Rusted corrugated-iron roofs creaked loose on rotting wooden beams of mouldering and roofless ruins. Ancient farm implements stuck out of clumps of nettles and thistles. Deflated cowpats had, he observed, little green lochs in them. Nearby, waves dashed onto a shingle shore. Glimpses of a high cliff, the ruined ivied battlements of a castle and somewhere close by, in the middle distance, amongst the sea mist, phantasmic iron-age warriors shouting alien battle-cries that turned out to be crows and seagulls.

As he came in sight of Gylen farmhouse, Morton detoured up the hillside to sit in the sweet-smelling bracken and keep watch. From above, there was little obvious signs of life; dim light in a window, smudge of smoke from a chimney. It looked okay. He approached the house, and alerted by the dog's barking, the Old Testament figure appeared in heavy gumboots, with a snow-white beard and flowing hair, surmounted by his blue glengarry bonnet with a single sprightly feather. Farquharson wore a thick white sweater and baggy dungarees.

'Oho, visitors. Welcome – who-ever you are. A thousand welcomes!' he called, pronouncing the words precisely in a whimsical accent.

'Malcolm… hello.'

'Is it just yourself?'

'Willie Morton. The journalist.'

'Of course you are! Good to see you again. Welcome to Kerrera!' Farquharson shook his hand. He called the dogs to heel and with a 'come away in,' led Morton into the house. 'Mr Morton, I wasn't expecting you but you are very welcome to my humble abode.' Morton felt a huge relief and allowed the crofter to show him into the dusty sitting room. A dark, swarthy young man, very tall and thin, reclining untidily in a deep floral armchair, grinned amiably and uncrossed his long, denim-clad legs.

'Euan Drysdale,' he said. He sprang eagerly to his feet. 'Haven't met you before. Elizabeth mentioned you when she came to visit me. You're helping with her investigation?'

'That's right,' Morton admitted reluctantly, retrieving his hand. 'I'm surprised to see you. Elizabeth told me… I thought you were on remand at Shotts?'

'Out on bail now. Can you imagine?' Drysdale continued garrulously. 'I mean, one minute they're throwing the book at me for all sorts of letter-bombs and terrorist conspiracies and the next, I'm having a pint in the pub. I fancied a wee holiday, so here I am.' He strode around the room excitedly, arms jutting out stiffly at his sides.

Morton frowned. 'When is your trial date?'

'Don't know. Not fixed yet. I'm not even sure how many charges there'll be.' He laughed as if it is was a big joke.

They became aware of an engine fracturing the island's quietness.

'Yeah, what *is* that?' Morton asked. 'I've been hearing helicopters all day.'

'Perhaps there is an exercise nearby,' Farquharson surmised. 'Over on Mull. Or it could be a search and rescue. Shall we go outside and take a look?'

Farquharson equipped himself with powerful binoculars and the three men walked out a hundred yards to the cliffs where the crofter scanned the watery horizon. 'No, I can't see anything at all,' he told them, at last.

The engine noise was intermittent as if it was traversing among the distant mountains.

'Maybe somebody is in trouble down the coast, on one of the small islands off Seil,' Drysdale suggested.

Farquharson looked at him oddly from under his eyebrows. 'We would not be hearing it if it was as far away as Seil,' he said.

Drysdale impetuously jumped up onto a boulder and began climbing the rock. The other two watched his progress with mild amusement. At the top he began gazing out over the firth under his hand.

Morton borrowed the binoculars and studied the powerful launch which was lying a quarter of a mile offshore. 'What do you make of that?' he asked.

Farquharson was dismissive. 'Ach, tourists. They have been there for a day or two. They are diving on a Cromwellian wreck nearby. It is nothing to concern us.'

Drysdale's peculiarly excited voice shouted down to them. 'I can see somebody on it!'

'Careful up there, boy!' Farquharson shouted. 'By the way, Mr. Morton,' he added confidentially, 'how did you get on in your search for Angus's briefcase? Was it just another of my hare-brained hunches?'

The sun was declining over Mull, bleeding profusely into watery clouds. It was Elizabeth who had discovered the coincidence that Malcolm Farquharson had served in British Military Intelligence at the end of the war just like her uncle.

'I'll tell you later,' Morton said quietly, nodding significantly in Drysdale's direction. 'Now, I'm sorry I've sort of landed myself on you like this. I know this sounds silly but I'm sort-of on the run. That chap McGinley I mentioned to you, and some friends of his, are after me. I don't know why or what he's up to but I don't intend to ask him. I wanted to find somewhere safe I could hide out for a couple of days.'

'My goodness me,' Farquharson exclaimed, pulling thoughtfully at his long fleecy beard. 'I am thoroughly disgusted to hear of it. Does it not just convince you, Morton, that these gentlemen have something to hide? Undoubtedly they have been involved somehow in…'

Drysdale suddenly slithered and jumped in among them. 'So what have you found out about Angus's death?' he asked brightly. 'Anything new?'

Morton found his flippant attitude irritating and suspected Farquharson shared his distrust. He shrugged. 'I'm still interviewing people,' he said vaguely. 'How well did you know him?'

'Quite well,' Drysdale said warmly. 'Oh yeah, we used to meet in his office in Bath Street every week to plan Vanguard strategy. We liked to think of ourselves as an intelligence unit.' He began a sequence of bobbing and weaving, confronting an imaginary foe.

'For goodness sake, Euan, will you please stop jumping around,' Farquharson reproved, scowling at him.

Drysdale was chastened. 'Sorry, Malc. Anyway, Angus began to get really excited about something but didn't give us more than tiny clues. He said he had got hold of something pretty important. He was like a father to me, you know,' he interjected. 'You see - I lost my own dad when I was very young and my mother abandoned me. Anyway, Angus seemed to be onto something big.'

'But you've no idea what it was?' Morton asked. 'And when was this, by the way?'

Drysdale's hands flailed the air in front of him. 'The weeks before his death. He said the nuclear industry was up to something devious and we - Vanguard - could catch them out. As far as I know that meant a press conference. But we were to tell no-one, not even other members, until it was all arranged.'

'And have you?' Morton inquired thoughtfully. 'Told anyone, I mean?'

Drysdale grinned. 'No. Well, it's a bit too far-fetched.' He aimed and threw an air-grenade at the sea, making an explosive noise, glimpsed the reproving looks of the others and leaned apologetically against a rock. 'I mean - who'd believe me - even if I did tell? It was all up-in-the-air stuff. Some kind of stunt was planned - civil disobedience – and selected journalists were to get an hour's warning so that it would be the main news event of the next day. But I don't have a clue what the actual stunt was to be about.'

'I see,' Morton said uneasily, an idea forming in his mind. 'Any idea,' he asked casually, 'where this stunt was going to take place?'

'Don't know that either. He never said, but somehow, you know, I got the mad idea that it would be at the Pass of Drumtochter, you know, up on the A9, about midway between Perth and Inverness? Miles from anywhere. A funny place for a press conference, but see, I noticed that he had large-scale maps of the area on his desk and there seemed to be a cross marked on the road just there. He was always full of mad ideas though. Most never came to anything.'

Drysdale began jumping about doing karate kicks and going "pow!" and "wham!" while the other two stood and frowned at him.

'That's all you know?' Morton asked after a moment or two but Drysdale didn't hear him.

They heard again the noise of helicopter engines, nearer this time, apparently heading their way, then it died down and silence resumed, the sea on the rocks, seabirds, distant sheep, the slow drip of time passing.

'It would seem to have landed,' Farquharson said, voicing the suspicions of the others, 'somewhere on the island. I wonder why?' Morton noticed his raised eyebrows. 'Euan – is there something you're not telling us?'

Morton was noticing that Drysdale's face had gone pale. He began to babble.

'Okay. Look - I've not been honest with you guys. Sorry, Malcolm - but I escaped from the remand centre four days ago. You'll have to hide me…'

'Goodness! You mean that I am harbouring a *fugitive*?' Farquharson expostulated. 'That I am breaking the law? That I may at any moment be liable to criminal charges? This is really most unfortunate, Euan! Damn it all! You must telephone at once to give yourself up.'

'I don't want to do that,' Drysdale whined. 'I need your help. They're going to throw the book at me. They're going to do me for all kinds of crimes I had nothing to do with.'

'Hiding from it will do you no good at all,' the crofter sternly rebuked him. 'No, no, Euan, you must argue your case in open court. There is no other way.'

'I agree,' Morton said, sitting down on the low wall. 'It was a stupid thing to do.'

'I'm not *stupid*!' Drysdale shouted. 'You're stupid!' And he turned and rushed off ahead.

'Aw, come back here! What a silly young man!'

They watched him picking his way across the rocks.

'You found the briefcase then?' Farquharson said quietly. 'Where?'

Morton nodded. 'It was in the railway tunnel at Lochailort.'

The crofter's eyes gleamed. 'Angus did use our hiding place! That shows that he trusted me to the end. Mr. Morton… I…' he faltered… 'I am very pleased to have been able to help you,' he said, flushing, and produced a large white handkerchief. He blew his nose and after a few moments, asked: 'and was there anything interesting inside it?'

'There certainly was.'

They contemplated each other in silence for a few moments.

223

'Well,' Farquharson said, 'at my age, I could die of curiosity.'

'Drysdale's story isn't far out.'

'I see. Now, if Angus had something on the nuclear industry, perhaps your Mr. McGinley learned of it,' he suggested. 'And perhaps that was why our friend was eliminated?'

'Undoubtedly,' Morton said. He hesitated, then pulled the folded pages from his pocket. 'This document will leave you in no doubt.' He carefully smoothed them and held them out for the crofter to read.

'Ah, me…' Farquharson grunted. He produced a pair of delicate steel half-moon spectacles and held the three pages up to the fading evening light and studied them in grave silence.

'Of course,' Morton continued, 'I have no absolute way of knowing whether McBain's stunt - which I suspect involved intercepting the nuclear convoy in some way - was just a vague possibility or an agreed certainty. Most likely it was abandoned. Certainly, if McGinley had become aware that Angus had this…'

Farquharson interrupted him with an admonitory hand on his shoulder. 'Morton. Have you considered… considered at all the possibility that Angus might have been staying his hand until the convoy was underway?'

'Well, of course…'

'In which case, Morton, the convoy might not have travelled yet, or might already, even as we speak, be on its way.'

'Yes…' Morton faltered. That could be true.

They both heard the noise; a clatter of falling rock. Two heads had appeared above the ridge several hundred yards away.

'Look!' the crofter pointed. A third man appeared. 'Three men. They're heading for the house. I don't think they have seen us yet. You'd do well to hide for the moment, I think.'

'You're right,' Morton replied, sitting down in the bracken.

'You'd do best to keep out of it, I think.'

'Good, I will,' and Morton added urgently 'what about Drysdale?'

The crofter's face was stern. 'That silly wee lad can make shift for himself. They won't have any trouble from him - if it's the police - I'll try and get him to give himself up. And then we can talk. Let's just hope he has the sense not to tell them about you being here.'

Farquharson rejoined the sheep track and walked back to the house.

Morton burrowed deeper into the bracken and found himself a good vantage point with a massive black rock at his back and an easy escape route down to the caves and the beach.

27

The three officers standing at the window of the Customs & Excise block at Dover had their backs to the burly man in the wax jacket who sat at the table, leaning on his elbows, sipping from a polystyrene cup. Since the man arrived, conversation had become desultory. None of the men had anything to say in the presence of the newcomer. They were embarrassed to talk among themselves because they weren't sure who he was, or what rank he held. It was a slack time and below, in the Customs hall beneath the one-way mirrored window, the bays were almost empty, although several large container ships lay at anchor in the dock.

Nor had the newcomer made any effort to initiate conversation. There was something edgy and hostile about his manner and his grim features advertised disinterest in the social niceties of the situation. McGinley didn't care. He had been in perpetual motion for the last twelve hours. Flown to a military airport just outside Folkestone, transported by helicopter to Connaught Barracks and by army jeep to the Customs Shed. He had not had enough time to pack a toothbrush but plenty of time and thought had been devoted by others to equipping him with considerable firepower. He had not been briefed, other than by the contents of a flimsy manila envelope which he had read on the flight. He was, of course, more than aware of the background, the convoy of radioactive materials and their source and destination. He had, for some weeks, expected that he might be involved in its transportation through the UK. He had expected some advance warning. In the event, he got less than half an hour. So he was to ride shotgun on the convoy, accompanying it as inconspicuously as possible. To deal with unexpected problems, delays, protests or full-scale terrorist attacks; and without adequate mental preparation. He had not been given any indication of how far his powers extended. It was being left to his own discretion. He had to presume that he had normal 'shoot to kill' clearance to deal with any determined opposition because the convoy was a 'nuclear installation' as defined in the Special Constables Act, 1976. Even though it would be traversing an urban environment. McGinley was uneasy about the lack of official backing he had received. Strategically, he was in charge of the convoy of six vehicles that would thunder northwards from Dover to Dounreay, in charge of the six armed men already on board the convoy, who, for all he knew, might not understand a word of English. Who might not even have been informed that he was in charge. And what if he had to explore the limits of his jurisdiction? Who would back him up? He could not be certain of anything. The authorities were holding their breath that all would be well - refusing to contemplate anything going wrong - and so he was expendable. It was a convoy that did not officially exist.

He stood up abruptly, thrusting back his plastic chair which grated on the floor tiles.

The uniformed men at the window looked at their boots as he approached and made a space for him. They knew he was armed of course.

'Arriving now,' one of the men murmured, looking up through the one-way glass.

'1800 hours,' McGinley said, checking his watch.

'Tough job?' one of the Customs men ventured. 'I mean, long night?'

McGinley looked at him, a young man in his mid-twenties, shirt collar unbuttoned, chewing gum. They were shit scared of him, he knew. 'Piece of piss,' he said and grinned. 'One of you lads come down with me. That way it'll look official. And we're going out by the Folkestone Road, the A20.'

He turned at the door. 'Well come on, laddie, I haven't got all night!'

He could just make out the faces of the men standing in front of the pale walls of Farquharson's house. The short man was familiar, either a skin-head or bald, and he seemed to be doing much of the talking. The other two were new, a heavily-built man in a bulky leather jacket and cap and a younger, taller man in a pale windcheater. Their conversation became more animated as Farquharson began pointing vaguely to the north, towards the ferry. They didn't look like police or military, Morton thought. McGinley's thugs.

The bracken was rapidly taking on the sinister qualities of a dark sea and its fragrance, powerfully sweet, almost sickly, reminding him of Carnation-milk, tickled his nostrils. The figures at the house blurred to dark shapes barely moving and showing no intention of moving on as the minutes went by. He wondered what the crofter was telling them, but found himself losing interest in all but his immediate cramped situation, his eyes straining to see what was going on. He trusted Farquharson. He had to. After about an hour, he decided to seek a more comfortable location.

He heard furtive sounds and tensed, lowering his head to the earth. Someone was walking on the shingle beach. He searched for the moving silhouette against the patches of fading light in the surface of the sea. Euan Drysdale. He told himself that the best thing would be for Drysdale to be caught. Then after they took him away, he could go inside and have a drink and relax and discuss with Farquharson what to do. Maybe the old man was right? Maybe the convoy had not yet rumbled north to Dounreay? If he could get back to Edinburgh he could update Stark and get him to help find out. If he could get back...? Just then, Edinburgh seemed a very long way indeed to Willie Morton. What was he doing, crouching here in the dark on a windy, cold island in Argyll? He should be at home in his comfortable flat with his feet up, watching TV.

As Morton waited, the moon appeared and lightened the dark. It was almost full, low over the mainland, striping the Firth of Lorn. To the north, stars appeared in vast shoals to increase his feelings of isolation. The sky was heaving, immense, all-encompassing. He thought about a glass of whisky, making it a double, then a treble, then the first of several trebles. He could almost taste it.

The moonlight was helpful when he decided he had to move again, to regain the circulation in his legs. He withdrew to a small gulley nearer the house among an outcrop of reeds at the edge of a patch of marshy ground. He studied the warm lighted windows of the house and knew that the men were inside waiting. Was it Drysdale they were after, he wondered, or did they now know that he was here? He heard the rustling of bracken and crouched low so that the windows disappeared.

'Morton? Is that you?'

Morton froze. He had been quite sure he couldn't be seen. Drysdale's voice sounded scared.

'I'm here. To your left.'

'Give yourself up, man!' Morton whispered hoarsely. He heard scuffling noises and Drysdale appeared nearby, crawling on his belly, his face illuminated by the moon. 'I can't understand why you're out here too, Morton. Why?'

Morton had no intention of discussing the matter with Drysdale, certainly not in their present circumstances, but he needed to give himself a plausible excuse. 'I simply don't want them to know I'm meeting Malcolm,' he said. 'That's all. But you've ruined my plans. Best thing would be if you walked over there and gave yourself up. I'm sure that would help you when it came to court. And anyway, Euan, where can you go to here? Those guys will just sit in there all night till you give yourself up.'

'I can't do that,' Drysdale said plaintively. 'I'll be framed for all the letter-bombs and all the hoax devices which I had nothing to do with. You've got to believe me, there's no way I can get a fair trial.'

'You haven't helped your case by escaping from remand. That's like an admission of guilt.'

'You don't understand…' Drysdale complained, 'the pressure I'm under… I'm in an impossible situation.'

'What do you mean; *pressure*?' Morton inquired sharply. He was beginning to suspect the younger man might prove to be a danger to him. His question remained unanswered.

The back door of the house was opening, flooding light over the rough ground, silhouetting tussocks and weeds in the no-man's-land between. Another man had arrived and the figures stood in the doorway, testing torches and in the light, Morton saw several of the men were armed. One of the men appeared to be putting on a metal helmet.

Beside him, Drysdale sucked his breath in sharply. 'Night-sights! They've got infra-red. I'm getting out of here.' He began to scramble away on his belly. Morton watched as the men came slowly away from the house. If they had night-sights he would have to keep solid objects between himself and them. They couldn't see through rock! He hoped they'd quickly catch Drysdale and go. When he next raised his head, he was astonished to see how close the men were. They'd started to move more quickly. He stood up and ran as quietly as he could to the beach, fell headlong and badly bruised his knee, got up and carried on. He could feel blood trickling down his shin.

The sea was breaking upon black rocks with silver panes of light dancing in the void. Morton heard shouts from above. The rocks slanted into the firth on a black, jagged promontory which Morton found himself climbing along. A sudden surge of water thrust itself over his feet. Its icy coldness made him gasp. He felt the salt stinging the open cut on his shin. The moon revealed a tidal cave, barely two feet wide, behind a large rock and he made for it. It was a mad scramble in the turmoil of the tide and his legs slipped deep – the coldness taking his breath away - and he was floating, grasping desperately for rock handholds. His scrabbling fingers found seaweed and barnacle handholds. His shoes delved into the shingle. He flattened himself into the rock recess. He tried to get control of his breathing, and empty his mouth of the salt water. He watched the torchlights swinging closer. Heard shouts above the sounds of the tide.

But the searchers were baffled. The torches stopped, swung round and jogged along and then came back. Gradually became more distant. Seawater ballooned the clothes around his numb body up to his armpits and thrashed him regularly with a swell almost strong enough to dislodge him. He had to get to a safer hiding place. He slowly worked his way around the face of the rock and climbed, sodden and heavy-limbed, onto the ledge and over the top. He saw that the torches were out at the base of the cliffs below the ruined castle and noticed that there were four, not three, torches. And they were coming back!

Morton hunched over the top of the rock and jumped down the far side onto dry land - scrubby grass - and ran up the slope to his previous position, keeping the large upright rock between him and his pursuers. He crouched low and listened intently as the voices and footsteps drifted nearer.

'Over there, I'd say,' someone said very close to him. 'That rock slide. He must be in the bloody water.'

Morton couldn't make out the reply. They were moving away. He heard other voices and one of them was Drysdale's! They'd got him, so why were they still looking? Someone was speaking close to the rock. Morton heard a cigarette lighter click. He clasped a wet hand over his own mouth and nose and held tight.

'Thanks.'

'Don't mention it. So what brought you into this game?'

'Not by choice.'

Only a couple of feet away, Morton understood that he was overhearing a conversation between one of the men and Drysdale.

'No? You surprise me, mate.'

'Part of a deal I made. Plea-bargain. I had no other choice.'

The other man chuckled. 'Who has, chum?' There was a longish pause. 'So you believe all that Scottish Republic socialism stuff and that?'

'It's just that they're going to charge me with loads of stuff. If I help them, I'll get off. I'm not the only one anyway.'

'The usual story. Yeah. You married, chum?'

'Me? No.'

'Here - we'd best get on. Thought you said he was round here?'

'He was.'

'Well, watch your bloody feet.'

Morton dared to breathe as he heard them move down to the shingle. He heard their feet crunching the shingle. He peered around the edge of the rock and saw the torches in a line patiently probing the rocky shore where he had been only twenty minutes earlier. He didn't waste any further time and ran as fast as he could manage up the grassy bank and headed inland, wet clothes chafing him at the thighs, knees and ankles, his shoes heavy with mud. His head was crowded with questions and confusions. Drysdale an informer. *And he wasn't the only one.* They weren't on the island to arrest Drysdale. Drysdale was their tool. He would have no time to speak to Farquharson and anyway maybe Farquharson was…

He had to get off the island. He had to get to a phone. The callbox was at the pier. That was several miles away. Could he get there in the dark without being caught? Well, he had a head start on them.

28

For any motorist who pulled out to overtake the black juggernaut which thundered northwards up the motorway, there was a nasty shock. Expecting to pass one, or even a second vehicle, a driver would suddenly realise that there were no less than six, extending in an apparently unending line, nose-to-tail, with barely any gap between vehicles. It seemed to be some kind of military convoy. Several other vehicles accompanied it; an armed personnel carrier, just behind the final heavy vehicle, followed by what appeared to be an ordinary breakdown truck and a fire engine.

The appearance of the gigantic vehicles was intimidating. Each vehicle was more than forty-five feet in length. Painted matt black, they had no identifying marks, no licence plates, no chromium - even no door handles. There is something intrinsically sinister about vehicles which have no windows except for a narrow rectangle of black tinted glass at the front, meshed with black-painted steel. No visible signs of a driver. The convoy maintained a steady speed which rarely dipped below sixty miles an hour and often reached eighty and rapidly closed up any spaces which might occasionally appear between the vehicles. It was a solid, rapidly moving phalanx of steel, nearly 300 feet long, like an invasion force from a science fiction film.

Each juggernaut had four sets of wheels on the transporter and two sets of wheels for the armoured cab, a total of thirty-two heavy tyres. Almost twice the size of the familiar Mammoth Majors used by the military until the early 1990s to transport nuclear warheads - well beyond the maximum vehicle size permitted by the UK road regulations – and yet they handled roundabouts and junctions with ease. Ordinary traffic scuttled around behind the convoy like chaff, and those who observed it from the roadside or from buildings, would rub their eyes and ask themselves if they were dreaming. But not too many people did see the convoy, for the route had been carefully selected to avoid as many of these prying eyes as possible. Most of the journey would be achieved in the hours of darkness between 6pm and 8am. The selected route was a continuous one, avoiding all known pinch-points, rolling northwards ceaselessly from the M20, onto the M25, onto the M40, onto the M6. The journey to Dounreay was expected to take 20 hours and by daylight, they would be well into the central Lowlands of Scotland and past the main danger areas. Once past Glasgow, they could virtually disappear into the sparsely populated Highlands. The only problems they would face then would be the roads themselves, and their narrowness, the possibility of slow-moving rural traffic. But if there were to be any major protests or attacks, then these were expected to occur in the conurbations, or near the major cities, particularly Liverpool or Glasgow.

Because of the careful selection of route and the lack of advance warning - the element of surprise - the risks of a serious incident were officially calculated as 'minimal'. Sporadic protests were regarded as more probable but the main risk element was the factor of photographs of the convoy getting into the press. If this did not happen, the convoy itself would be denied, and all would be well. If it did, then there were a variety of PR strategies in place which would be deployed by AtomTech, Euratom, the INEA and the UK government's DTI - and which the security services would follow up on.

There were two drivers in each of the cabs who would swap seats at locations agreed at short notice over the short-wave radio during the journey. And in each cab there was a Special Escort Group security officer armed to prevent insurgents at these changeovers. These officers were linked by short-wave radio to the armed men in the armoured personnel carrier at the rear, and to the civil/military authorities co-ordinating the convoy.

Daniel McGinley sat in the passenger seat of the leading transporter, cradling his Heckler & Koch MP5 submachine gun, idly flicking the three-way switch that enabled single-shot, three-round burst or fully automatic fire. It was loaded with thirty rounds, capable of killing at 200m. It was a weapon McGinley was familiar with. He liked the fact that it fired from a closed bolt so there was no shift in the gun's balance to pull the bullet off target, even when firing on automatic. In his jacket breast-pocket though was his favourite toy, a Swiss-made SIG-Sauer P228, one of the most reliable, compact - and expensive - handguns ever made. The gun of standard issue to the FBI and US Presidential bodyguards, it had, more recently become the weapon of choice of the SAS and McGinley had obtained, through his services connections, one of the very first imported into the UK.

But he was already bored. He spent most of his time studying the road radar system which was tracking one mile ahead of the convoy. Any conversation that he had shared with the two drivers had come to an end some miles out from Folkestone and the relief driver was sleeping, stretched out on the bunk at the rear of the cab. Neither spoke good English and the effort of trying to comprehend was too great to make the effort worthwhile. So there was almost silence in the cab as the tarmac miles submitted to the rumbling thunder of the thirty-two tyres. The engine noise, so loud at first, was now barely registering in McGinley's consciousness, neither was he much aware of the names on the road signs they passed as he peered ahead intently and toyed with the retractable metal strut stock of the MP5, and tried to defeat the growing tiredness that had begun to fray the edges of his eyeballs.

He'd kept off the track as much as possible, running and tumbling into deep bracken, endlessly tripping over tussocks. He kept the moon-striped Sound always in sight except when he had to ascend the hill above the sparsely-lit cottages of Little Horseshoe Bay. He'd lost his way for a time there and had been further alarmed by a dog barking. His clothes had dried on him like clay and his shoes were a claggy, pulpy mess. His fear of being trapped was keeping exhaustion at bay.

When he found his way back to the track, at a place close to the edge of the water, he saw various mysterious moving lights over on the mainland. Each light pointed its long reflection in the water at him. The night was remarkably quiet, the slightest of noises carrying clear over the water. A car door slammed at the caravan park, several miles away. A sheep nearby in the bracken cleared its throat. Morton guessed the tide was out, the Sound silent, motionless, striped with moonbeams. Looking back, in the direction he had come, he saw a number of distant moving lights. His pursuers were on foot. He wondered where the helicopter was.

He made it to the jetty. The telephone box with its homely light afforded Morton another momentary surge of self-pity. He observed it for a few minutes, surprised that it was unguarded. They'd obviously expected to pick him up without any trouble at Farquharson's place.

Morton fumbled with the old-style dialling wheel, inserted his coins and waited impatiently while the ringing tone repeated. He could imagine it ringing out in the flat of Elizabeth's friend in Marchmont.

His despair increased as the ringing went on and on, getting louder in his head. Just as he was about to put the phone down…

237

'Hello?'

It wasn't Elizabeth. It was her friend, Samantha. 'Elizabeth's out,' she said, warmly. 'She said you might call.'

'Is there a message for me?'

'She said something about the Internet. Friends of the Earth - their website. Does that make any sense to you?'

'Was that all? She said nothing else?'

'It was something to do with some Lorries. A convoy. On the website, it says something like there's a convoy on the road, or something…'

'A convoy? On the road,' Morton queried excitedly. 'I think I get it. She saw this on the FoE website? Where was the convoy?'

'It had started from Dover, I think. She said it was something… something that she… that you… had been expecting. Sorry, I can't really explain any more of it. Best thing would be if you could ring back a little later this evening… hello… hello?'

Even though it had been small and had been passed in a flash of a second, McGinley hadn't missed it. What looked like a sheet, white, with the logo of CND and some words in red paint. It had been sagging in the rain so the words weren't clear but it looked like something…probably 'ban' and then 'foreign nuclear waste'. The slip-road near Junction 16, the turn-off to Northampton. He'd called it in. He could imagine armed AEA Police speeding to the scene to arrest the perpetrators. They'd be locked up overnight to prevent them communicating to others. He smiled grimly. It meant that someone had spotted them, though. Probably while they had had to slow down along the M25 through Surrey. Word was out. Not everyone was asleep then but Nuke Watch UK, the much-vaunted anti-nuclear intelligence system wasn't much cop. One hundred and fifty miles out of Dover and this was the first sign of public interest. No doubt there'd be more little protests but in another fifteen miles they'd be on the M6 and what could the anti's do then? They couldn't block the motorway. In the last ten minutes, since spotting the banner, McGinley had been assured over the short-wave radio that he had the full co-operation of the military and civil authorities on the remainder of his route. He had also been informed of the various decoy tactics that were to be set-up to counter tracking of his route, now that the convoy was public. In a way, the worst was over, he had cleared London. He was well on the way home. All too easy, really. Another victory over the ragbag army of the great unwashed.

The torches of his pursuers were closer now, just rounding the bend before the phone box and the jetty. To the north, Morton could see the twinkling lights of Oban only a mile away over shiny smooth black water. The birthday-cake candles of MacCaig's Folly had never looked more inviting. He remembered his warm room in the quiet guesthouse and his stomach lurched, reminding him of his hunger.

Two boats were tethered at the jetty but their engines, it seemed to him in the dim light, had been disabled in some way. He didn't have the time to properly investigate. The torch lights were now at the phone box, fifty yards away. He climbed the track and crouched behind the stone wall of the disused school building. The lights moved about on the jetty and he could see the men as shadowy shapes. He could almost hear their conversation. Keeping low, Morton backed out of the schoolyard and set off in the lee of the hill heading for the brilliant lights of the town and Oban Bay over on the mainland. The machair grass seemed shorter and less obstructed by boulders. It was easier to make progress but sometimes he stepped into marshes. He had no clear plan other than to keep out of the clutches of his pursuers. The

239

downward slope was gently returning him to the shoreline some distance north of the jetty. He'd put a hill between himself and the men. On this part of the island, he was closer to the mainland too. It was flatter ground. The island was petering out into marsh and he caught a glimpse of a white obelisk with a flashing light north of him just as he felt his feet tread into deeper water. He stepped back in alarm. He was standing in the Firth of Lorn! Dim shapes in the void gradually revealed themselves to be yachts or boats tethered by cables, some swaying gently and others lying apparently on their sides. He fell several times over the thick furry ropes that anchored them. Most of the boats seemed too far out to reach, even though the tide was at its lowest ebb.

He stumbled into a rigid inflatable dingy, which moved under him. It was completely black and almost invisible. He explored it and it felt reassuringly sturdy. There were wooden paddles in it. He clambered heavily inside the dingy and felt it wallow in the shallows.

The evening sky was torn by the shriek of an engine. Morton covered his ears in fright. The helicopter was taking off from the old school yard. From where he had just come, about half a mile away. He must have walked right past it in the dark! It rose slowly, dazzling him as it began to flood the hillside with search beams. The rotor blades made a whooping, scissoring noise above the broken ground.

Morton's fears multiplied to the point of nausea. He thought of the water beneath him, of the half-mile of the Sound, its unknown depth, treacherous tides. In the moonlight, it didn't look so frightening though. Low tide. There was nothing to be scared of, he told himself. He jumped out into ankle-deep water and pulled the dingy behind him, working along the rope that anchored it, then freed it from an iron weight and began to wade back out, pushing the dingy ahead of him. When he felt the water swelling up to his knees, he felt himself involuntarily urinate, took a few steps more, clambered with difficulty back onto the dingy, feeling it bobbing under him. It began to wobble and he reached for an oar. Frighteningly quickly he was out on the black water, adrift, in the grip of the open sea, alone with his fears and his disgusting anxiety. The dingy began to tug and buck under him and he gave up the pretence of paddling. The helicopter had turned inland then and the sky went suddenly dark.

After the first few minutes of fear of the vast emptiness of the water and his lack of control, he realised that the dingy was riding high. The regular slap of the small waves under the rubber hull began to reassure him. He wasn't reassured enough to dare to shift his position.

A few black, empty, wet, miserable minutes passed before Morton became aware of lights and voices. He saw he was drifting back inshore. Spiralling gently towards the jetty in fact. The armed men would be sure to spot him! Morton could make out the light bulb in the telephone box.

Leaning cautiously to one side he fumbled and found the paddles and fitted them into the rowlocks and, facing the telephone box, began to row gently away.

At first, his movements were erratic. The boat checked, twisted and continued to drift but shortly he developed more skill and began to pull more strongly. The phone box light gradually dropped to a pinpoint, disappeared. The water swelled gently underneath him and he was lifted up and down but there was a regularity to it that he became accustomed to. Nothing to fear. He was floating. He crossed wide lanes of moonlit water and wondered if he was midway across the Sound. He dared not turn to look, kept rowing steadily, minute by minute. He had no idea how far he was from shore, or whether he was making any kind of a straight course. The water slapping from his paddles sounded just as deep and black as ever but he was making progress. He must be getting somewhere. He was leaving behind the island and the helicopter and McGinley's men. That was all that mattered.

Weariness began to affect him in the shoulders and wrists and after a while he dared to steal a quick glance over his right shoulder. A powerful light was shining straight at him. He held his breath. But he saw that it was a car headlight. So near that it was almost on top of him! But just for a second. Then everything was black again. His oars struck something and the dingy jarred. And again. Rocks. The shore. Despite his ridiculous fear of deep water, he had actually crossed the Firth of Lorn and reached the shingle beach of the Scottish mainland!

29

Sometimes it seemed to Daniel McGinley that he was awake and watching the endless dark motorway rushing to meet him, then he would jerk and open his eyes and find that he had been dozing. He was angry that he had been given such an important assignment without any consideration for the length of shift and his need of sleep. He had been on duty for almost twenty-four hours and craved sleep but each passing hour brought greater demands on his concentration. There had been several more incidents and one had been potentially serious.

McGinley had seen the police cars on the outskirts of Birmingham, sirens, flashing lights. He heard over the radio that there had been thirteen arrests, at around 1am, and that many of those arrested had cameras with long-lenses. Some had been press photographers. It was going to be difficult to keep the story under wraps, even if they issued a D-Notice. Which would take time to go out anyway and the press would try to beat it.

The most serious incident had happened an hour and a half further on, just before Newcastle under Lyme, when a crowd of protesters, more than forty strong, suddenly ran onto the motorway and attempted to set up a roadblock. With only half a mile's warning, McGinley directed the convoy to a grinding unscheduled halt on the hard shoulder, to keep their engines running, while a furious battle was fought out on a slip-road a hundred yards further on and just out of sight. Motorists whose route had been blocked began to join in. It was a complete mess. It took almost half an hour for a detachment of soldiers to arrive from Uttoxeter Barracks and get the protestors and aggressive motorists hauled off the road. McGinley could be assured that any photographs which had been taken would be confiscated as the convoy continued northwards. A brief report over the short-wave indicated that the BBC had picked up some fragments of the story and were running a brief news item but had been unable to obtain a comment from the AEA, the DTI or AtomTech. By the time McGinley's convoy was bypassing Manchester, the 4am news bulletins were on. The BBC had dropped the story. They did not have enough to go on - no hard evidence - merely the word of anti-nuclear spokesmen and had come under pressure from government to drop it, which they did.

Morton heard the scrape of stones underneath the inflatable and clambered unsteadily onto the wet shingle, hauling the boat after him up into the gorse thickets below the stone parapet of the road. He found an easier part of the wall and pulled himself up onto the tarmac. He could see lights on Kerrera but they looked impossibly distant. He had made it! He had made it - and could hardly believe what he had done. The luminous green digits on his watch showed that it was 12.30. His stomach growled and he felt nauseous, but he set off as fast as he could manage in the moonlight along the cliff road towards the town's deserted streets. He wasn't finished yet, not by a long way!

Years before, when Morton was a student he had worked a summer vacation as a night porter in a hotel in Rothesay. It was an experience he preferred to forget but it had left him with the certainty that all hotels were alike behind the scenes. He studied the formidable edifice of the Ninian Hotel near the railway station. A quick glance revealed that a night porter was busy hoovering the main lounge on the ground floor. Morton entered the backdoor to the basement kitchen, which, as he had suspected, was unlocked. He located the stillroom and helped himself from the walk-in fridge. He took a long pull of cold milk, drinking straight from the churn by means of the ladle, unconcerned that half of it was cascading down his chin and onto the tattered remnants of his shirt. He stuffed the pockets of his jacket with slices of ham-and-egg pie, *vol au vents* and handfuls of chicken breast. Then he was outside sitting in the shadows on the edge of the pier in the lurid reflections of the Ferry Terminal enjoying his plunder. He could see the dark bulk of the island over which the moon was slowly drifting in cloud. It was almost 2am.

The insistent ping of the radio woke McGinley and he rubbed his eyes. He couldn't keep awake. It was his boss, Jo Haines, patched through from Saltisburn.

'Keeping you up, are we,' he said, attempting humour.

'Don't be flippant.' Haines was abrupt. 'I've had a message through from Kevin Gray. Your journalist…'

'Morton?' McGinley said.

'The journalist you were supposed to have dealt with weeks ago… well, it appears that he's given Gray's team the slip.'

'I'm surprised,' McGinley muttered. 'The whole team is out. Should have had him under lock and key yesterday.'

'Exactly. Well, it hasn't happened. I only hope that he's as clueless about the operation as you seem to think.'

'Where was his last location?'

'The island of Kerrera, off Oban.'

'Farquharson,' McGinley said. 'He must have been heading there…'

'We know that. We've taken him in, and we've also detained three in Edinburgh; Stark and the niece of McBain and another girl for questioning.'

'So even though Morton is loose, the fire is out. Unless he's managed to contact anyone else.'

'We don't think so. He made a phone call from a coin box on the island, clocked at 10.45pm, to an address in Edinburgh, which is why we moved in on the McBain woman. But, just to be sure, we're checking all mail sent from post boxes in Oban. I'll keep you informed. How are you holding up?'

McGinley frowned. 'Well, I am, just.'

'I'm hoping to have Ramsay take over from you at about lunchtime. Probably in the vicinity of Tyndrum. So you only need to keep awake for another six hours. Over and out.'

'That's easy for you to say, old girl,' McGinley moaned, and made a face at the non-comprehending expression on the driver's face. Another six hours.

He hadn't been able to get any sleep on a bench behind the Corran Halls and his telephone call to the flat in Marchmont was not answered, so, at dawn, Morton began to walk up the hill and away from the town. He couldn't wait for a bus or train. The road was deserted and peaceful and he could smell the freshness of the vegetation. He felt he could walk all the way to Edinburgh, and wondered if he was going mad. Certainly, he was a little lightheaded, numb, completely devoid of emotion. The experiences of the last few days, which he had not been able to share in any detail with anyone, had shocked him. He couldn't think straight. He had no plan of action. He believed that the Bohunice convoy was probably on its way north, but what was their route? And what could he, as an individual, a ragged and exhausted pedestrian, do about it? He wondered if he really cared about any of it, anyway. Mostly, his thoughts were about escape, about his own flat, the normal comfortable routines of his weekly life as a freelance journalist.

He heard the car coming a long way off. It didn't even occur to him that it might be McGinley until he heard it slowing down to take the bend. On instinct, he stuck out his thumb and it slowed and stopped. Let it not be them! Morton prayed. A battered Ford Escort van.

Morton peered in. Not McGinley! The driver was a stony-faced, middle-aged man in a blue Rangers sweatshirt.

'Christ. D'ye want a bloody lift or no?' he growled.

'Yes. Aye, I do,' Morton said, his cold fingers scrabbling for the door handle.

Then he was inside in the warm, on the soft tartan upholstery, hearing Country 'n' Western music. The man glanced at him as he let in the gears.

'Well, where are ye going, then?'

'Edinburgh,' Morton said without thinking.

'Och, I canna take ye further than the Power Station,' the driver said. 'Loch Awe. Ah work there ye ken. Early shift.'

'Loch Awe Power Station?' Morton repeated.

'I canna take ye any further.'

'No bother. That'll do fine. Patsy Cline this, eh?'

'Aye, wan o her best.'

This time it was Kevin Gray giving him a sit-rep. 'Morton's got off the island and is in the vicinity of Oban. He made a call from there, an hour ago. There's no way he can evade us now. He has no transport.'

'I'm surprised you let him get off the island, Kevin. How did he manage it?'

There was a long pause before Gray came back on, coughed apologetically and admitted he didn't know.

McGinley permitted himself a wry smile. The failure was Gray's, not his. If he could get the shipment safely to Dounreay, no-one could criticise him in any way. It'd be Gray's arrogance that'd come in for criticism. He glanced at the computer screen. It was 8am and the convoy was still close together as it rumbled round the curves of the A74 beneath the grey-green Galloway hills. The morning was slow to start, the sun seemingly reluctant to rise over the little roads of Scotland, and there was not much traffic so that they were able to maintain a steady pace. In less than two hours, they'd be cruising past Glasgow and from there it would be a piece of cake.

Water was pouring out of the rock faces that towered over the road, in slabs of oily blue-grey and tumbling down through grooves in the boulders and disappearing beneath the road into the black fiord, the unknown depths of Loch Awe on the other side of the glen. Up there, above the buildings, he knew was the mighty Ben Cruachan, the hollow mountain, the source of a staggering quantity of hydro-electric power. When you came to think about it, Morton reflected, Scotland had a vast amount of energy from natural sources, who needed blasted nuclear anyway! The country had always exported surplus energy to England. *Cruachan*. Even the word had an element of majesty about it, Morton thought, as he idled in the car park of the Visitor Centre. It wasn't open. Nothing was open. The driver had gone to his work on the workers' shuttle bus which trundled deep into the mountain along with some other weary-faced men. There had been little greetings, some forced cheeriness, and another knot of men had emerged from the mountain, had got into their cars and driven off. All of them back to Oban. Morton had asked for a lift but no-one was going the other way. He walked down to the outlet and peered gingerly over the wall at Loch Awe. The driver had told him to keep clear of the edge and warned him of the power and sudden noise of the tidal surge from the dam when it was shedding water into the loch. He remembered that in the depths of Loch Awe, primeval ancient fish called Arctic Char lurked. A long way down, in the depths. He shivered. He hated deep water and yet, yet – he had managed to row across the Firth of Lorn. He laughed aloud. Imagine? It was hilarious!

He walked along the road in the shadow of the rock face and began thumbing the few cars travelling eastwards. It was too early to try Stark at the *Standard*.

McGinley's good humour greatly increased when news came in of the large roadside protest at Glasgow. The anti's had been very busy, and everybody and their grannies were there apparently, the whole ragbag army, hundreds of them. And banners and megaphones. The police were holding them back, with difficulty. That was the joke of it. The protest was at the side of Junction 12, north of Riddrie, on the M8, and McGinley's convoy was fifteen miles further west on a completely different road! He just couldn't stop smiling. They'd detoured off the M74 at Junction 8 and taken the A71 as far as Strathaven and then cut up onto the tiny A726 to East Kilbride, through Giffnock and the Rouken Glen to Nitshill and onwards to Paisley. It was a daring and risky route on narrow and congested arterial roads but every single anti had clearly expected them to continue north on the motorway to join the M8 and then the M9 north. That would have been the obvious route. The detour had been McGinley's own idea and it had worked beautifully. By the time they reached the outskirts of Paisley, the message came through that the anti's had realised their mistake and had begun to disperse in confusion. He had every reason to feel pleased as he led the convoy without stopping up and over the high arc of the Erskine Bridge. It wasn't just a personal triumph for him and a victory for AtomTech, it was a massive publicity disaster for the anti's. And that made it all the sweeter. The sun had emerged from the clouds to herald his success and McGinley could almost sniff the fresh Highland air blowing down from Loch Lomond.

Being in the conducive company of friendly German tourists, Imogen and Mikke had made Morton unexpectedly garrulous. The anti-nuclear sticker on the rear windscreen of their battered VW Camper had put him in a truculent mood. '*Nein Danke*!' Yes, by God, he wished he could have said 'nein danke' when he'd been offered the McBain story by Leadbetter.

'See, when nuclear power started in the 1950s…' he began, 'we had promises of cheap power, endless cheap power, cheaper than water. Domestic fuel bills would be cut to less than one penny a week…'

Mikke grinned encouragingly over Imogen's shoulder, teeth white against his stubbly blond beard. 'Ja. So too in Germany. What is "penny"?'

'Very small unit of currency,' Morton told him.

'Like "pence" one hundred to one pound?'

'No, much smaller, pre-decimal. Well, as I was saying… forty years later, after many incidents and accidents and safety infringements and near-disasters and lies and clusters of childhood leukaemia, we now have the bloody truth. Nuclear power has cost us billions and hasn't reduced a single bill. And it will cost us billions more to clean-up and close-down all the nuclear power stations.'

'It is a big crime against the peoples,' Imogen said, shaking her head so that her long straight blonde hair swayed below her sharp-pointed chin as she concentrated on the road through her tiny gold-rimmed spectacles.

'Ja. The crime of the century,' Mikke agreed.

'But where are the jail sentences for the liars and the fraudsters,' Morton exclaimed, 'who conned us the public, and governments into the whole damn crazy idea in the first place? Not one single "nuclear expert" or pro-nuclear politician has ever been charged. Yet the lies they've told…!'

Mikke swigged from the mineral water bottle and offered it to Morton. 'Is true, ja, in Germany alzo…'

Even the beautiful scenery of lonely Glen Lochy in the mid-morning sunshine could do little to molify the anger which had emerged to replace his fear and anxiety. It had never really bothered him before. He wasn't particularly anti-nuclear. Amazing what a bit of fear can do! But he would get out of this. He would return safely to Edinburgh and his quiet life. And he would expose the activities of McGinley and his nuclear thugs.

He just needed a little time.

30

The convoy swept rapidly onwards without delay or interruption along the shores of Loch Lomond through the shaded bends, the narrow road forested on both sides, with occasional glimpses of the wide water. McGinley thought idly of the convoy's long journey from the Czech Republic. From a country of mountains and great lakes. He knew that it had originated from a remote area tucked in behind the Moravian Heights. A pretty area which was now a living hell of radioactivity and martial law. Whose inhabitants were slowly and painfully dying. He shuddered. It was a long way away. He hadn't given much thought to the contents of the vast transporters. Heavily-leaded sides, reinforced with steel. As far as he knew, it was mainly used fuel rods and sliced-up bits of machinery which had become contaminated. He had been told the walls and doors of the cabs were specially insulated with thick lead panels to protect the driver. The cabs were fully protected from radioactivity. He suspected nevertheless that Geiger counters anywhere near the transporters would go off the scale. It was madness really but it wasn't his problem.

A last glimpse of the loch at Ardlui and then back into the trees to pass the Drovers' Inn at Inverarnan. A final sit-rep from Saltisburn informed him that the M8 protest was an item on the 11am news on Radio Scotland, the anti-nuclear spokesmen having been forced to admit that their information may have been inaccurate. He laughed aloud to hear it. The driver looked at him as if he was mad. They ran on, into the long winding slope down to Crianlarich and the tortuous bends of Glen Falloch. At the junction with the A85, police had been stationed to prevent Council road workers from resuming roadworks which had been inconveniencing traffic all week. But the roadmen were in the pub and the convoy was waved through unimpeded. It continued at speed along the valley floor of Strath Fillan towards Tyndrum, and McGinley, very tired, was now within sight of the end of his marathon shift on duty.

Mikke, restlessly probing the radio dials on the dashboard of the VW Camper, almost slipped past the newscaster's announcement on Radio Scotland.

'Could I hear the news please?' Morton asked, looking at his watch. Midday:

> *Confusion surrounds a mass protest held this morning in Glasgow. Several hundred protesters attempted to block the M8 in protest at what they claim was the alleged illegal transportation of radioactive material. The protesters dispersed peacefully after several hours when no convoy appeared and the police have reported that there were no arrests. AtomTech, the operators of Dounreay are presently prohibited from receiving waste for reprocessing. SCRAM, the Scottish Campaign to Resist the Atomic Menace, claim to have received reports from anti-nuclear groups in England, which include eye-witness sightings of large vehicles on the move....*

It was happening. They were on their way. Morton felt a shiver of excitement swiftly tempered by the sobering thought that the shipment might be so near. He must contact Stark. Danny would have the details. He felt relieved that he was no longer the only one who knew. He wondered if his envelope had arrived yet at the *Record*.

'We stop here,' Mikke said, pointing to the sign; Tyndrum. Imogen went down the gears and slowed for the junction.

'Thanks for taking me this far,' Morton said, as Imogen carefully parked the camper van in a busy car park in front of a café with a wooden verandah. Morton had already noted an automated cash machine, which he intended to use. Food was his first requirement, then he would make various phone calls.

He got out of the vehicle and stretched his legs. Imogen switched off the engine and they all heard a thundering noise from somewhere as if a large aircraft was landing nearby. He saw people on the main street looking down the road and he walked over to the pavement to join them.

'Look at the size of those!' a middle-aged man with a rucksack said, pointing.

Morton saw, a hundred yards away, the gigantic black vehicles. He began to tremble, involuntary spasms affected his legs and hands as he watched the transporters slowing down and turning, one by one, off the road. Two, but there were more. Three, four. How many? Where were they going?

'What's down there?' Morton demanded peremptorily of the man beside him.

The man unhooked his rucksack from his shoulders. 'You mean where they are going? Nothing. Used to be holiday chalets, just, but they were knocked down. It's an empty space, sometimes used as a lorry park.'

Two more of the giant vehicles were turning awkwardly. That seemed to be the lot. Six. Morton saw several cars follow the vehicles and turn off. He saw figures on the road. Looked like soldiers, seemed to be armed. He turned to Mikke who had joined him.

'Have you got a camera?' he demanded.

Mikke looked at him slowly and smiled. 'Camera? Ja.'

Morton was panicking. 'Well, where is it?' He flapped his hands impatiently. 'Can I borrow it? Your camera. Come on! Camera.'

Mikke looked at Imogen who looked at Morton. 'Ah...
Imogen... It is... '

Morton had no time to explain. He turned and ran across
the gravel car park to the shop, The Climbers' Post, which
sold everything from sweets to rifles and fishing rods. Two
petite girls in green tartan pinafores were chatting to each
other at the till. They barely glanced at Morton as he rushed
in and whirled around the shop. What he was looking for
turned out to be right at the counter, in a glass case. The girl
called Lucy glanced over at him and continued discussing
with Debbie a forthcoming disco in Crianlarich. A boy called
Pete, and another called...

Morton banged his fist on the counter. 'Service!' he
shouted. 'I'm in a hurry. I want a bloody camera. This one...
here.' He pointed at a small digital camera. 'That'll do. Here's
my credit card.'

But the transaction took several minutes and Morton was
jumping on the spot while the girl processed the sale - and
then she attempted to wrap the camera.

'No! I'll just take it like that,' Morton said, ripping it out of
its box and tossing the packaging on the floor. 'Thanks!' He
was at the door before he remembered batteries. That took a
further few minutes. While the assistant was ringing up the
sale, Morton was fitting the batteries and the chip card into
the camera. He strode to the door and took a picture. It was
working. Fine.

McGinley climbed down from the open door of the cab on
the iron stepladder and greeted Ramsay with a nod. He was
exhausted and didn't want to waste time on pleasantries.
Ramsay handed him the keys for the Range Rover sitting on
its own under the trees near a small wooden footbridge over
a stream. Several armed men stood around, in front of the
trees. The drivers of the vehicles had congregated in a small

group and were speaking in what McGinley assumed must be Czech even although there wasn't the faintest chance of hearing any of the words against the deafening roar of engines.

'There'll be a sit-rep on the radio in five minutes to confirm the changeover is completed,' McGinley said, through his cupped hands into Ramsay's ear. 'They're all yours,' he said, handing him the Heckler & Koch with reluctance. 'I'm off to the hotel for some sleep.'

Morton hurried around the side of The Climbers' Post and raced to the end of the village of Clifton. He saw signs for the West Highland Way, the famous walkers' trail which continued up a steep hill but went off to find a spot behind and above the shop which gave him a good clear vantage point. He could see a section of the road and would get uninterrupted shots of the convoy as it passed, without making himself too obvious. He heard a change in tone of the roaring engines further down the road, which he assumed was the sound of gears being let in from neutral. He couldn't see far down the road because of the intervening roof of the shop and restaurant. He stared intently at the road. As soon as he'd got the pictures, he'd contact the *Record* and Hugh at the *Standard* and arrange to have them collected. With a sigh, he realised he'd probably have to deliver them in person. That meant hiring a car and driving... a weary thought.

McGinley sat in the black vinyl upholstery, with his favourite toy lying on the passenger seat. His responsibilities were almost at an end. He'd wait till the vehicles were clear of Tyndrum. The first vehicle was already slowly nosing its way back onto the main road...

Morton shot more than twenty pictures of the convoy, getting them in a line, getting shots of two and three together in wide-view and getting close-ups with the 3x optical zoom and the village sign behind them. He sat for a moment after they had rumbled out of view, feeling the surge of excitement overcome the exhaustion he was feeling. He was finishing what poor old McBain had started. He stepped back onto the pavement...

McGinley braked sharply without looking in his mirror. Morton! With a camera! He brought the Range Rover to a burning, screeching halt and reached for the squat black handgun then realised he could not possibly use it in such a public place. And Morton wouldn't be armed anyway. He tossed some papers on top of it and leaped down onto the tarmac and ran into the car park where Morton was talking to a young couple.

Mikke sensed the violence of his approach and half turned, so that McGinley blundered into him, knocked him off balance and Morton turning, saw who it was, and was already running when the security policeman had pushed Mikke off and twisted to reach for Morton, but Mikke in sudden irritation retaliated so that he stumbled and missed and Morton was clear, running towards the Esso filling station across the street, while McGinley was delayed by the need to punch Mikke hard in the face so that he went down and could no longer impede him.

He shouted: 'Morton!' but had to step back to avoid being hit by an ancient Land Rover covered in orange canoes.

Morton ran into the filling station, camera swinging wildly from his wrist on its thin cord. A business-man was walking from his car to the cashier. Some kind of Honda, white, expensive-looking. With miraculous vision, Morton noted the key was in the ignition. He got in, switched on the ignition, gunned the engine and closed the door with McGinley flailing for the handle, and falling over, and Morton turned across the forecourt and was away, heading north. Escape was his only thought.

In the mirror he saw the Black Range Rover on the move so he put his foot down as hard as he dared. He had to think… how could he get away…. where could he hide?

31

The mountains and forests of the central Highlands flowed smoothly under Elizabeth's feet. The sparkling blue lochs of the Trossachs reflected the sky, shimmering brilliantly in the sunlight like puddles in a field. She was wearing cumbersome noise-cancelling headphones but she could still hear the noise of the helicopter's engines. The Gazelle was very stable and Elizabeth's earlier misgivings were easing as they sped north west.

Sitting in front of her, just behind the pilot, studying the landscape with powerful binoculars, was Peter Stoddard, who had been keeping up a constant conversation with her since they had taken off from Redford Camp aerodrome.

It had been a confusing twenty-four hours. Arrested in the middle of the night with Samantha and kept separately overnight in the police cells, interrogated by a succession of detectives about Morton and her uncle. Shown various photographs and finally left alone for hours with only a thin blanket. In the morning, given breakfast in her cell and taken for further questioning but this time, the seated man in the grey tweed suit and green silk tie who was waiting to speak to her in the lime green interview room was Stoddard.

'Have you seen this man before, Elizabeth?' he'd asked quietly in his strained voice, placing a photo in front of her on the table. She hadn't.

'We believe his name is McGinley. Perhaps Morton has mentioned him to you?'

Elizabeth had considered for almost a minute whether or not to tell him.

'McGinley *was* harassing him,' she said. 'But then so were you.'

Stoddard smiled wearily, his mouth a grim broken dark line under the heavy moustache. 'I was doing my job,' he said. 'Trying to find out how this man, McGinley fits into the picture, how Morton knew him.'

'And did you?' Elizabeth asked. 'We thought you were working together.'

The facial muscles above his cheekbones tightened. 'No. I work for the government's security services,' he coughed dryly, 'ahem - although I was seconded to the Highlands Division of Customs & Excise... until... your Mr Morton put my picture in the newspaper and blew my cover. This man,' he gestured at the picture, 'seemed to me at that time, to be heavily involved in serious drug-dealing, although it is now established that his... his activities are quite otherwise.'

Stoddard flexed the bony fingers of his hands together and looked obliquely at her. 'We now know that he was directly involved in the death of your uncle.'

Elizabeth started. 'You mean he... he...?'

Stoddard remained impassive, eyes hooded in their fleshy sockets, giving nothing away. 'Miss McBain, you must not jump to conclusions. We cannot be certain precisely what form that involvement took... suffice it to say that we are interested in talking to him about it. Now, when did you say you had your last contact with Morton?'

'Late evening when he phoned. I missed the call by a few minutes. It was just before Samantha and I were arrested.'

'Yes. We're sorry about that. Though it was probably to your advantage.'

'Advantage!' Elizabeth snorted, tossing her head so that her hair swung solidly following the curve of her neck. 'How do you reach that conclusion? We haven't been charged. We've missed a night's sleep. I fully intend to raise an official complaint, you know.'

'Quite so,' Stoddard said. 'Nevertheless, I think we will be able to convince you that your arrest, although initially a blunder - comes under the terms of protective custody.'

'Protect from whom? You?'

'You misunderstand. This chap here, McGinley, is part of an organisation which is operating under a certain remit. Your friend Morton has come very close to upsetting their operations and has put his life in danger - just as your uncle also risked his life…'

'Drug dealers? Willie is in danger from drug-dealers?'

'Not exactly.'

'I don't understand. Why don't you explain exactly what is going on?'

'Sadly, at the moment I'm not at liberty to reveal the whole story and anyway, much of what I would tell you would be pure speculation. I have only told you this much in order to secure your co-operation. We need your help, you see, to try to extricate Morton from the dangerous situation into which he has maneuvered himself. We know that he is in the Highlands, in the Oban area. He telephoned you from there. At that time he was being pursued. Had been pursued for several days. We would be unlikely to get him out, assuming we could locate him, because he would assume - like you did - that we are working with McGinley. Now, he trusts you, Elizabeth. If you were with us we might be able to save him. If we can't, McGinley's men may kill him. Of course, we have no way of knowing for certain that that has not already happened.'

'Oh!' Elizabeth started. 'That's awful! But why do you want him? What has he done?'

'Frankly, we don't want him, my dear. We want to remove Morton safely from the scene so that we can get hold of McGinley without further trouble and put some questions to him about your uncle's death, and other matters, of course.'

'I could help. If you think I would be of use. But how?'

And that was how Elizabeth came to be in the red and white helicopter, flitting across the sky at 160mph, on a mission to find and rescue Morton.

Morton's foot pressed firmly down on the accelerator pedal until he came to the corner then he swapped it onto the brake. Accelerator, brake. Squealing around the corner, building up speed on the long straight. The road cut along the edge of forest plantations on his left, and on his right, the bare slopes of a steep and craggy mountain. But Morton had no time to admire scenery. The bull-bars of the Range Rover behind had bumped him several times and each time, Morton felt the force of the collision, felt the car shudder, each time he momentarily lost control as McGinley accelerated, attempting to ram him off the road. He could see McGinley's impassive face in the mirror, his staring eyes. Morton had one thought. To keep his car clear of the Range Rover's bull-bars.

They came at him again and he saved himself by jerking the wheel and careering wildly across the road. An oncoming driver flashed his headlights and Morton seized his chance. He stayed in the wrong lane, daring McGinley to follow him.

The Range Rover came on his inside, hoping to block Morton's way out, to force him to collide with the oncoming car. They were neck and neck. Morton realised McGinley meant to kill him, him and the other driver both. He would kill anyone who got in his way. He was insane. Even as this was occurring to Morton, he was seeing a way out. He suddenly swerved off the south-bound carriageway over into a passing place, letting the oncoming south-bound car shoot past, angrily blaring. As expected, McGinley overshot and Morton nosed in behind him back in the north-bound lane.

So the Range Rover slowed down and began blocking him from the front. But Morton slowed even more and pulled back. McGinley swerved across the road and stopped. Morton stopped. A lorry was bearing down on McGinley, flashing and blaring. McGinley would have to move.

Morton spotted a small road off to the left a little further back. He reversed rapidly and turned off down it. McGinley was foxed, his Range Rover was half turned, unable to reverse, yet unable to turn.

But Morton's glee was short-lived. He saw that the little road petered out into a single track road winding down into a lonely glen. Morton knew instinctively he could not go there. The main road ended at the Glen Orchy Distillery entrance almost hidden in the trees. Morton drove down a long, tree lined lane, into the deserted car park in front of office buildings and around the large whitewashed Distillery until he came to a high wall and could go no further. He stopped the car and got out. Had McGinley seen him enter the Distillery? Was he in a trap of his own making?

32

Stoddard's thin hand pressing on her shoulder shook Elizabeth out of a daydream as she gazed in rapture at the golden Trossachs below and Loch Katrine, on which sunlight was slanting.

'Miss McBain - Elizabeth…' his voice rustled through her headphones and she looked round, reluctantly abandoning the beautiful vista. She could see the mountains and scenery through the glass-front of the cockpit between the pilot and the two other men sitting up front.

'We now have a definite sighting… at Tyndrum. He was there only twenty minutes ago. We should be able to pick him up. It's not far.'

'How far?'

'About five minutes to Tyndrum. He has a headstart on us, so he could be ten miles north by now, but he'll still be on the road.'

'You hope! So how is he travelling?'

'Car.' Stoddard grinned, and his cheekbones stretched tight across his bony face. 'I'm afraid our journalist has stolen a car. And not just any car either. A car belonging to one of my officers.'

'That's not like him,' Elizabeth suggested. 'He must have felt that he had to do it. Perhaps he's in greater danger than we know?'

'We'll know soon enough. I've men watching the roads south, west and north of Tyndrum. They'll spot him if he's on the move. It's a white car, a Honda estate. So keep an eye out for him when we get nearer. We've a spare pair of binoculars.'

'Will we see him from up here?' Elizabeth asked dubiously.

'We'll go lower, to about 200 feet. This is a light-weight helicopter, specially made for air observation. But don't worry, these chaps here have got special equipment, it's not entirely down to you.'

'I hope Willie's alright.'

Morton abandoned the car and made off across the tarmac delivery road to the whitewashed warehouses. Somewhere to hide. But the massive black doors were padlocked. He ran to the rear corner of the block. Still no sign of McGinley. Had he shaken him off? There was a set of concrete steps at the rear and he saw an open door. He went in. In the meagre light he could see hundreds of oak casks, hogsheads or butts, on wooden rails in tiers of four and five, pegged with wooden blocks. McGinley couldn't find him here! He set about finding himself a hiding place in the cool dark silence.

The noise of the gunshot was terrifically loud. It resounded and echoed angrily at least four times. Morton was petrified with terror. This was it! But McGinley had fired at random. Must have, for he didn't fire again. Morton kept this face pressed to the oak, suspending his breathing.

'Morton! You can't get out.' McGinley's jeering voice seemed muffled and far away. 'This is the only door. It's only a matter of time, Morton, old chap. This time, it's for real.'

Morton heard him moving about, slapping the sides of barrels. He couldn't think what was best; move or hide… but could he move even if he wanted to?

'This is the end, Morton. Nothing personal.' McGinley's voice sounded sombre, an impression intensified by the sardonic laugh that followed it.

Two hundred feet above Tyndrum, the RAF helicopter swung northwards and headed down low over the dense forests. In the cockpit, the pilot, navigator, Elizabeth and

Stoddard combed the road ahead. A loch appeared and then Elizabeth could see out of the side window, the Buchaille, foursquare and steep, its jagged rock edges tearing at the sky. The helicopter swung around its cruel ridge into Glencoe.

'Maybe we've missed him,' Elizabeth heard in her headphones. 'Surely he couldn't be up this far?' She could see tiny parked cars lining the bends beneath the Three Sisters.

The silent minutes of semi-darkness must have been getting to McGinley too, Morton thought. He'd fired a burst of shots that seemed to go on for ever bouncing and whining around the room, digging holes in wood somewhere nearby. Random shots, though, Morton thought. There was a smell of whisky. He could see an arc of whisky peeing out of a cask onto the concrete floor. It looked white in the dim light.

'Aw, look what you made me do, Morton. A good malt wasted. You're not worth it.'

The voice seemed to be further away but McGinley was suddenly *there*. Right there, ten feet away, in silhouette, at the end of the line of casks.

His voice was sibilant. 'Ah, there you are, old chap!' he said.

Morton was behind the barrel and moving to the next line.

'You can't get away.'

He kept ahead.

There was a door, ajar. He ran through it, into another room, smaller, whitewashed, warmer. Huge copper stills and yards of pipes leading to the high ceiling. He dodged behind the stills.

'*Wharranggggg!*' a bullet dented the copper, shrieking around the room. McGinley fired another burst. The SIG-Sauer P228 had a double-action trigger for speed of firing. Morton was close enough to smell the cordite. He nearly tripped over a cat which screeched and bounded onto a long glass case, which McGinley's next bullets shattered. Water or whisky mash poured out of a glass bracket and McGinley slipped as he ran around it.

Morton heard curses behind him as he rushed into the next room and leaped up some metal stairs onto a mezzanine floor. He hid behind a large boiler, praying McGinley hadn't heard him come up the stairs. He could see in the room beneath, huge circular iron vats full of bubbling and steaming whisky mash.

'We've further information, sir,' the pilot said on the intercom, 'coming through.'

Stoddard heard the short message and issued instructions to the pilot, then he turned to Elizabeth.

'New information. He's at Bridge of Orchy. The car's been spotted at the Glen Orchy Distillery.' He grimaced. 'But he's not alone. I only hope we can get there in time.'

McGinley came slowly up the iron steps, the black chunky pistol held out in his right hand, watching the shadows on the iron floor at his eye level. He knew Morton was there somewhere, behind one of the three boilers. Which one?

He reached the iron railings and moved stealthily to the right, circling the first boiler, his back gliding along the rail, gun pointing. He began to grin. Morton must be feeling the tension. And he had no weapon. He had to kill him now. Get the camera. End it here. Like McBain, Morton knew too much.

Morton was trapped. There was no way out. McGinley saw his face and body as he fired twice to make sure. He was near enough to hear the terrible gasp of life exiting the body through the holes torn in the chest and he found himself tensely grinning.

The helicopter created turmoil on the gravel and dust car park, whirling everything into the air as the pilot set it gently down, a hundred feet from the Distillery office block.

'Stay here!' Stoddard ordered, as he removed his headphones. Elizabeth had no intention of going anywhere.

Stoddard jumped down the six feet to the skis and joined the three other men, all, armed, she saw, with pistols. She hoped Morton was okay. They had spotted the black Range Rover on the way down, its doors open, and several distillery workers waving their arms in panic.

McGinley's jeering grin was still on his face but it had developed a disbelieving quality. Morton had charged from behind the boiler and rammed him over the railings into the mash tun below. He fell in slow-motion, headfirst and didn't come up for several seconds. When he did, he flailed upwards, hands grasping for and failing to catch the sides... he went down into the white froth. The tun was twelve feet deep, kept at a constant 95°F, and the next time he came up, he was purple, his eyes pink.

Morton stood over the distillery worker whom McGinley had shot. He was out of it. Blood oozed, shiny black, from his chest onto his clean ironed blue boiler suit. An oldish man, white-haired. Some-one's father, grandfather.

When Morton next saw McGinley he was dead. Morton felt nothing for him. He looked down at the purple, bloated face as it swirled by. Froth was bubbling out of his open mouth.

He heard rushing sounds of people in the room beneath and looked over to see several guns trained on him. He felt sick as he slowly raised his hands. He'd thought it was over.

'Morton? You alright?' someone shouted. A familiar voice. He saw Stoddard.

'Put down your gun and come out. You've nothing more to fear.'

'Is this a Customs & Excise raid?' Morton queried peevishly. He stepped down the ladder, hands held high and two men rushed up to him.

'He's not armed,' one of the men said, checking him all over.

'Right.'

The men ran past him - and went onto the landing. One looked down.

'Christ! It's him.'

'Is he dead?' Stoddard asked Morton, at the bottom of the steps.

'Very. He's been... malted.'

'Oh dear. You can put your hands down, Morton,' Stoddard said in his strained voice. 'Elizabeth's in the helicopter outside.'

'Am I under arrest?' Morton asked wearily.

'We can talk about that, Morton,' Stoddard said. 'Nasty business.'

33

Rain clouds scudded low over the white VW Beetle as it timorously climbed the rutted track. On all sides, heather moors cowered in the shifting shapes of the mountains. Lightning signalled through the mist and thunder rumbled over the Atlantic but there was no rain, merely a moistness on windscreen glass, not enough to switch on the wipers. He reached the low stone dyke and saw the iron gate, hanging at a broken angle. Morton recalled that few of the relatives had attended McBain's funeral, here, in the middle of nowhere. The will had stipulated it be held as cheaply and inconspicuously as possible, the last self-denigratory act of a desperate romantic.

The heavy gate rudely grated on flaking flagstones, and rust flaked off, into the roots of robust thistles and nettles that guarded the entrance. Gravestones, bleached and pitted, leaned sideways among overgrown grass like teeth in a broken mouth. McBain's was marked only with a small stump of marble, blank, unlettered, at its head. Six feet down, inside a cheap coffin of unpainted, orange plywood, McBain's sightless eyes would be staring at the Saltire placed on his face at the graveside by Elizabeth, now back at her studies at Cambridge. Morton regretted that. He might never see her again. He had a momentary image of her dark glossy hair swinging over her cheek as she turned to look at him.

Thick sea-mist was rolling relentlessly in from Loch Nan Ceall, the inlet where the mighty Atlantic tests the Arisaig coastline. A breathlessly vacant moment was illuminated by the transience of lightning.

Even the roadside cairn at Loch Dubh had mysteriously disappeared during the last four weeks. There was little really to mark McBain's passing. His intended ambush at the Pass of Drumtochter would have failed - even if he had been able to carry it out. It was the wrong road.

He wondered about McGinley's funeral. Elderly parents, probably in some small Scottish town, parents proud of their son at school, pleased that he was good at sports, expressing misgivings about his joining the army early, postcards from his years of service abroad then an unexpected official letter; 'killed in the line of duty on active service', a few former colleagues and friends of his parents' around a marble stone in a cemetery, marking a life of duty. Morton felt sorry for the man. He had done what he thought he had to do, like generations of Scottish soldiers, Union Jocks, dutiful servants of the British state, generations all the way back to Culloden.

The room was of the kind used for committee meetings or briefings, functional, plainly decorated, flipcharts and an overhead projector. There was no natural light in the room, banks of fluorescent tubes hung from steel chains performed that task. The room smelled dusty. A large oval oak table around which forty could be seated with ease, filled most of the space, though only three seats were occupied when Morton and Elizabeth were ushered into the room.

The two plain-clothes officers who had brought them from Redford Barracks in the black Jaguar, stood on either side of the entrance as Morton and Elizabeth were seated side by side across the table from Peter Stoddard and two other men.

The older man, middle-aged and balding was tall and well-built, distinguished, in his dark double-breasted suit. There were traces of grey at his temples. 'My name is Roger Sandwells,' he had said equably, 'I am a senior official from the SIS/Home Office Committee. You already know Peter Stoddard, operational officer with MI5, Scottish Region, and this...' he turned to the thin young man in the tweed jacket who sat hunched over a notebook, 'is Edwins, an official clerk, who will take notes.'

Sandwells looked peremptorily at the contents of several buff folders, flicking open the covers with his fingertips, as if to remind himself what he had to say.

'Now that we know who we are,' he said at last, 'we'll kick off. This is a highly unusual situation, I'm sure you'll agree?' He appealed to both of them for confirmation before proceeding. 'Indeed. The death of Mr. McBain and the part played in that by Mr. McGinley, and of course, the harassment which he caused you, Morton to suffer...'

'And the small matter of the... radioactive shipment from Bohunice to Dounreay,' Morton said, finding his throat dry from lack of use.

Sandwells and Stoddard exchanged glances, and it was Stoddard who responded, in a quiet, hesitant voice.

'Ah, no, Morton, I'm afraid that matter is... is not on the agenda here.'

'The convoy is directly related to my uncle's death,' Elizabeth complained. 'It was the cause of it. The INEA memo which he had obtained... undoubtedly was McGinley's motive.'

'No, Miss McBain,' Sandwells asserted smoothly. 'That is not, and cannot be, the case. There is no so-called secret memorandum. The document you claim to have obtained...' he hesitated, choosing his words with care... 'which is now missing...'

'....which you *stole* from my solicitor's office...' Morton interpolated.

'....which is missing,' Sandwells continued firmly, ignoring the interruption, 'is most certainly not genuine. Nor is Her Majesty's government aware of any nuclear incident in the Czech Republic such as - you claim - it purported to describe.'

Sandwells smiled affably at Elizabeth, 'my dear, the tragic death of your uncle has no wider context. Daniel McGinley was operating on his own initiative, and well outwith his official remit and authority.'

'And what *was* McGinley's official remit precisely,' Morton inquired. 'If I'm allowed to ask, of course?'

'Certainly,' Sandwells assured him. 'We now know he was Scottish field supervisor for the Nuclear Installations Protection Squad.'

'Oh ho!' Morton said. 'Now we're getting somewhere.'

Sandwells sniffed. 'We have established that, although it would be true to say, he was employed in a freelance, self-employed capacity. I can also tell you the Chief Officer of the Squad has already tendered her resignation over the matter - in advance of a full internal inquiry.

'Oh, goody,' Morton said sarcastically.

Sandwells pursed his lips. 'I can understand your irritation, Morton, but we are - all of us in this room - unable to determine precisely what took place at Loch Dubh or why. We have had access to McGinley's incident report and notes - but they are not particularly informative.'

'And can we have access to them?' Elizabeth asked.

'I'm afraid not, my dear. As I understand it, Mr. Morton is working on some kind of a book on the case?'

Morton's anger was beginning to surface after the numbing anti-climax of his ordeal. 'So basically,' he snapped, 'you're giving us nothing? Nothing official to prove McGinley's involvement, except your word here in this room?'

Sandwells nodded. 'I'm afraid that is the way we work, Morton. Secrecy is the basis for maintaining our – yours too - national security. And as a journalist, you will be well aware of the dangers of unsupported speculation in such a sensitive

273

area, bearing in mind that two…' he winced… 'three men have died.'

'Oh, it will all come out at the FAI. You must see that,' Morton said.

Sandwells opened a buff folder and extracted a letter, which he handed over the table to Elizabeth. 'There will be no FAI,' he said. 'This is a copy of a letter to your father from the Lord Advocate's office. You may keep it.'

Morton read the letter over Elizabeth's shoulder. It was short and specific. Mortimer expressed regret that in the "over-riding interests of national security and state protocol" he could not grant the request.

'We'll see what the public makes of that!' Morton declared. 'These are matters of public interest.'

Sandwells picked rapidly at the side of his neck above the tight white collar with the tip of his forefinger. 'A D-Notice has been issued to all editors covering matters pertaining to Mr McBain's death. I think you know what that is, Morton? Yes, and - although this is confidential - all parties have readily agreed to respect its authority,' he said.

'What about the Scottish Government?' Morton asked. 'They will be sure to take an interest in what's been going on.'

Sandwells smiled faintly. 'There will be liaison at a discreet level of course, as is proper, but there is nothing here to concern Holyrood. Nuclear matters as you well know, Morton, are reserved to Westminster. Oh yes, Scottish politicians might wish to interfere, but then again, they always do – and it gets them nowhere.' He chuckled drily. 'As you might have noticed, they may make noises from the sidelines but there is nothing they can actually do, much as they might wish it otherwise.

'Outrageous!' Morton spluttered. 'But my book will print the full story. You can't suppress the truth.'

There was silence for several moments in the room. Sandwells began putting his papers into his briefcase.

Stoddard attempted, in his throaty way, to be amiable. 'Of course there is your book, Morton, yes, and you are at perfect liberty to write whatever you wish - within the normal laws of libel of course. And I wish you luck in finding a publisher. But you should remember that you yourself... have not been entirely blameless... there has been the death of McGinley, a serving security officer, for which you alone are responsible, the tragic death of the distillery storeman, Robertson, in which you were involved, and the theft of a police vehicle. You could be facing charges on all these matters.' He smiled and the thick hairs elongated around the area where his lips must be. 'We have been very understanding. You should give us credit for helping you.'

'Well - what about my camera?' Morton said. 'I want it back.'

'No camera was found.'

'Come on! It was in the car.'

'*Your* car?' Stoddard inquired pointedly.

'You know what I mean. I can prove I bought it...'

'No camera was found. Perhaps it fell out on your hazardous journey to Bridge of Orchy, who can tell.'

'This is outrageous!' Morton fumed.

Stoddard remained calm. 'Look at it this way, Morton, you have your liberty, your health, you have no injuries of any kind. You're not being charged. You're both free to go. You have our apologies for the harassment you have suffered and you can be satisfied that HM Government will be acting firmly to investigate the remit of the Nuclear Installations Protection Squad to weed out any other potentially bad apples like McGinley. What more can we say?'

'I think the meeting is now at an end,' Sandwells said, rising, and offering his hand to Morton, who declined to take it, and Elizabeth who limply complied.

The plain-clothes officers moved forward to assist Morton and Elizabeth and escort them safely to their respective homes in the city.

The rusted iron gates closed immutably behind him. The dilapidated silence of the cemetery resumed, water dripping insistently onto stone which continued to flake and break up, the process of time, a name here, a carved date there, requiescats gradually becoming indecipherable, the history of an invisible nation. Morton walked slowly away, leaving Angus McBain alone and completely anonymous in the earth. Who really cared? What had McBain's efforts achieved? It seemed such a waste. He inhaled deeply, filling his lungs with moist sea air. Perhaps Stoddard was right. He had his health, his liberty - perhaps that was enough? Certainly, Stark had thought so. A man of straw after all, already on his way, it transpired, to the *Guardian* newsroom. 'It's only a story, Willie, only a story. You can always find another one.' Behind him the sea mist, advancing like Jacobite ghosts among the crumbling stones of the dyke, sifted through the whins and impaled itself in tiny crystals of ice upon the spikes of thistles.

COMING SOON

From Twa Corbies Publishing

The second Willie Morton conspiracy thriller

Scotched Nation
Andrew Scott

Five months after Scotland's Independence Referendum, freelance journalist Willie Morton discovers he has a look-alike who works for a shadowy pro-Union group, GB13.

They are working to prevent Scotland ever leaving the Union by using 'all means possible.' It's a game of high stakes and soon Morton is hanging from the swinging door of a train, and fleeing sinister thugs through the dusty dereliction of the roof spaces of the Palace of Westminster as he tries to investigate the group.

He wants to confront the reclusive leader of GB13, whisky magnate Lord Craile, in his remote mansion on Mull and ask him one question – Why? But things are never going to be as simple as that…

ISBN 978-0-9933840-6-6 Publication: October 2019

Lightning Source UK Ltd.
Milton Keynes UK
UKHW022005140419
341001UK00001B/1/P